THE SIN TRILOGY, BOOK III

GEORGIA CATES

Published by Georgia Cates Books, LLC

Copyright © 2015 Georgia Cates

All rights reserved.

This is a work of fiction. Names, characters, places, brands, media and incidents are either the product of the author's imagination or are used fictitiously. The author acknowledges the trademarked status and trademark owners of various products referenced in this work of fiction, which have been used without permission. The publication/use of these trademarks is not authorized, associated with, or sponsored by the trademark owners.

Sign-up to join the monthly newsletter for Georgia Cates at www.georgiacates.com. You will get the latest news, first-look at teasers, and giveaways just for subscribers.

Editing Services provided by Jennifer Sommersby Young

Interior Design by Indie Formatting Services

ISBN-13: 978-1508518990

ISBN-10: 1508518998

To J, F, and M.
You are my dream come true.

CHAPTER ONE

BLEU BRECKENRIDGE

OH, STELLA BLEU. YOU ARE IN SOME DEEP SHIT THIS TIME.

I'm trapped in the back seat between two of my three kidnappers: Broden and The Order member poking a gun into my side. I'd like to see how tough he is without a pistol in his hand. I'm certain I could kick his ass. But I'm pregnant. I can't risk putting my babies in danger.

"You know, the gun does the same job if you simply point it at me."

He rams it into my ribs a little harder. "Shut up."

Despite the goon's obvious lack of experience, this situation couldn't be worse. My wrists are bound and I'm hooded. I'm concentrating on my breathing, talking myself down from a panic attack. In slow and deep. Out steady and gradual.

Broden and his thugs have made it impossible for me to do anything but sit, wait, and see what they have in store for me. None of which I'm good at doing.

Why couldn't they have put me in the trunk? At least there, I could've busted the latch and made a run for it.

Right. That's why.

My captors drive about twenty minutes before making a final stop. Broden grips my upper arm and plucks me roughly from the car. It pisses me off. I jerk my arm from his hold once I regain my balance. "I'm mobile. You don't have to yank me around like a rag doll."

"Damn, ye are a mouthy little bitch. I bet ye give Sinclair hell."

He removes my head covering. We're at an isolated warehouse. I don't recognize my surroundings so I study the details, the ones that speak without words. A shiny metal fence, unoxidized by the elements, around the building's perimeter. And the building's new, which means this premises is probably recently acquired. This might be a problem except Sin has hired Debra to watch all moves made by The Order, including any new property they obtain. That's reassuring.

The building's exterior is well covered by security cameras. Whatever's inside, they mean to keep it safe.

I'm ushered into the warehouse under Broden's firm guidance. I study the wooden crates I pass as I'm steered through the building. They're marked with a language other than English.

My final destination is a dark, tiny space in the corner of the warehouse. Probably originally a storage room. I don't fight going inside. It would be useless.

I'm walking through the doorway when Broden delivers a firm shove against my upper back. I twist my body as I go down to prevent landing belly first. A searing pain ignites in my shoulder and hip.

I keep my mouth shut, despite the pain. To yell out would give them too much satisfaction.

The man called Reuben uses his foot to nudge me over on to my back so he can zip tie my ankles together. It's terribly uncomfortable lying on bound hands but my complaints would only fall upon deaf ears.

"Can't have ye running off. Mr. Grieve wouldn't be at all happy about that."

Broden stands over us, monitoring Reuben's handiwork. "Tighter, ye fool."

I roll to my side when he's finished so I can regain sensation in my hands. "No attempts to escape, Mrs. Breckenridge. I can promise ye that we won't hesitate to kill ye now instead of later."

Kill me now instead of later?

My kidnapping is about more than a trade for bomb makings. They mean to kill me regardless of the exchange.

If I die, my babies die with me. That can't happen.

Zip-tie restraints are useless on the wrong people. Most don't understand that the tighter, the better for the one bound by them. Lucky for me, Reuben and Broden made mine exceptionally taut.

After they're gone, I roll to my stomach and wiggle until I'm kneeling. I position the tie lock clasp between my wrists so it's facing outward since it's the weakest spot. I lift my arms and bring them down hard against my butt, spreading my elbows on impact. Once. Twice. Again and again, six times before the tie clasp finally breaks.

I stand and bunny-hop to the door. I lie down and lift my legs, slamming the ties against the frame until I break the restraints around my ankles.

I check the door. The knob turns but it's barricaded from the other side. No surprise there.

I have no way out. There's nothing for me to do but wait.

I sit on the cold concrete floor for hours before my kidnappers return with a fourth man I've yet to meet. But we need no introduction. Intuition tells me who he is. Torrence Grieve.

Tall and lanky, slightly humped with a dropped shoulder. His head is slick as an onion but he sports a black and gray goatee. It's in need of a grooming.

He sneers. "My, my. Aren't you the clever one?"

I don't reply.

"Mrs. Breckenridge. I'm sure you're aware that ten o'clock has come and gone." I'm not wearing a watch but I suspected as much.

The bloody message on the wall stated I might survive the night if Sin returned the bomb makings to their warehouse by 2200. "Have you come to take me to my husband for the exchange?"

He shakes his head. "Your husband didn't show."

He's lying. Sin would not leave me in the hands of The Order. "I don't believe you."

"Thane came in his son's place. He tells us Sinclair encountered a bit of a mess on the drive over. Seems he ran into Detective Buchanan and got himself arrested for murder."

"Whose?"

"One of your own. Malcolm something, I believe."

No. No. No. Sin can't be charged with Malcolm Irvine's murder. It was me. I'm the one who killed him.

"Your father-in-law made a hard barter for you. He was willing to trade everything The Fellowship has in exchange for his son's wife. That has me wondering what makes you so special. So valuable."

"And I have to wonder why you'd refuse his generous offer."

"Thane isn't the one I want to deal with."

I was right. This is about Sin, how Grieve plans to make Sin suffer for killing his son, Jason. Torrence needs to understand what happened. "Jason stabbed Sin from behind. He fired on him before he realized his attacker was so young. He didn't intentionally kill your son."

Torrence appears unmoved. "Intent doesn't change the fact that my only son is still six feet under. That's unfortunate for you since your husband loves you. His affection gives me leverage. A lot of it. So you have the honor of dying for his mistake while he watches. And he gets to spend the rest of his life thinking about your death and how he caused it."

I am the smartest person in the room with the biggest reason to live. My babies. That means I have to turn this around.

I've approached Torrence from the wrong angle. I see my mistake now. I hope he hasn't. "You're wrong. Sinclair Breckenridge despises me. Our marriage was arranged to unite our families. There's little he would love more than to see me die. You'd be doing him a favor. Thane is the one who wants me back."

"Because you're valuable to The Fellowship?"

"So my father doesn't come after him."

"Who is your family?"

I was an FBI agent. As part of my career, I became fluent in US criminal organizations. I studied them intently so I could familiarize myself with common practices. That knowledge is about to serve me well.

I choose one of the most notorious Irish-American gangs in the US. One with a daughter my age. "I'm Cassidy Abban. Carrick Abban's daughter. Everyone calls him Little Abbot. I'm sure you've heard of him."

Derry Abban was the founder of The Four Families gang. Today, his son, Carrick Abban, is the leader. I'm certain someone in Torrence's position would be very familiar with Abban.

"Your name is Bleu."

"It is. Cassidy Bleu Abban. I prefer to be called by my middle name."

It's a good cover. One he can't verify without doing quite a bit of digging. Should he decide to investigate, I'll be long gone before he can figure out that I'm lying.

"If that's true, I'm sure Thane will send his son for you. He has no intention of starting a war with Little Abbot."

I hope that means Torrence believes me and doesn't plan to start one, either.

Grieve waves his hand in my direction. "Plans have changed. Looks like we'll be holding on to Mrs. Breckenridge for longer than expected since Sinclair isn't coming for her until he's released from jail. We can't leave her here since she's proven to be competent at removing restraints. We'll move her to the cottage with Lainie until her husband is free."

Torrence's plan has been thwarted by Sin's arrest. I think I may have just evaded death. For now.

The head covering is replaced and new zip ties are placed around my wrists. "Break these a second time and you'll lose your hands."

We drive about twenty minutes before the hood is yanked from my head a second time. I'm taken into an old stone cottage. Again, I'm shoved through the door. Same story, second verse. Except this time I maintain my balance.

The room we enter is vacant of furnishings. The walls are white and veined with cracks and chipping plaster. Aged planks of wood cover the floor, many rotten and buckling.

It's cold despite the burning fire. The air reeks. Reminds me of decomposition. I hope it's a dead varmint and not a body.

Broden comes toward me, pulling a knife from his pocket. Most people would be afraid. Maybe I should be but I'm inclined to think he would've killed me already if that was his goal. "Hands."

He pushes the sharp edge of the knife between my skin and the zip tie. In one fluid motion, he frees my wrists. "Mrs. Breckenridge. Meet your companion, Lainie Grieve."

Grieve. She must be Torrence's daughter. Except I was unaware he had one. I thought Jason was his only child.

None of the men say another word before leaving. The clicking sound from the other side of the door confirms I'm locked in.

They've left me unbound with this woman to guard me?

The woman's a small blond with childlike facial features. Round face. Big brown eyes. Thin and frail, maybe even sick. She doesn't appear to have the physical strength to fend off a mosquito. She has no weapon that I can see. I'm almost offended they think she's capable of wardening me.

Go ahead, Grieve. Keep underestimating me. Continue making mistakes like this and see where it gets you.

At the same time, it isn't wise for me to underestimate this woman. Just in case. She could be a chameleon.

One of the first rules of abduction: make your abductor see you as a person so it makes it more difficult for them to harm you. I need to develop a rapport with Lainie. "Hello. I'm Bleu Breckenridge. But I guess you already know that."

"Why would you assume I know who you are?" Lainie continues eating her sandwich without looking up. Her voice is monotonous and deadpan.

Something is off about this. "I assumed Broden or one of the others told you ahead of time that I was coming."

"You're Mrs. Breckenridge. I know because that's what Broden called you and you just told me the same. With a name like that, I would assume you're Fellowship. Beyond that, I'm clueless."

This woman doesn't appear to be on alert at all. I could attack and kill her with my bare hands right now.

"They didn't tell you anything about me?"

"Why would they?"

"Aren't you here to act as my guard?"

She bursts into laughter. "No. I'm their prisoner, same as you."

She's related to Torrence because they share the same last name. I would expect her to be the top of the hierarchy instead of the bottom. "But you're a Grieve."

Her laughter disappears. "Don't remind me."

This woman clearly isn't pleased to call Torrence family. That could work in my favor if I play it right. "What turn of events made you a prisoner here?"

She shrinks into herself and looks away, saying nothing. Within two minutes of knowing her, I can read her body language and plainly see that she's been abused. "What have they done to you?"

"I'm sure you're aware Torrence's only son was killed."

"Yes." Very aware.

"Torrence's wife, Cordelia, had difficulties carrying babies. She lost many pregnancies before she gave birth to Jason. She almost died having him and was told by doctors to never become pregnant again. Because she had done her duty and provided Torrence with a son, it wasn't a problem … until Jason was killed. Torrence was left without an heir and with a wife who couldn't give him another. That became a huge problem fast. So he killed Cordelia and replaced her with a young, fertile wife. Me."

My God.

"My parents arranged our marriage knowing he murdered Cordelia for her inability to provide him with another son. I wonder what they think he'll do to me if I can't give him one either."

"I'm sorry." I really am. Doesn't matter if this woman is part of The Order. No one should be subjected to such treatment.

"I'm nothing more than a breeding machine for his next heir. Believe me when I say he reminds me on a regular basis."

"Are you pregnant?"

She shakes her head. "Unsuccessful two months in a row." I can't tell if it's relief or regret I hear in her voice.

"Two months can't be considered unsuccessful."

"Try telling him that. He's impatient and angry. Says he could get Cordelia pregnant any time he tried so it must be my fault it's not happening. I'm fearful of another failure. I don't know what he might do to me."

She probably should be fearful of what he might do to her if she doesn't conceive.

Torrence is aging so he must be desperate to produce a son as soon as possible. Even if this woman becomes pregnant now, the child would have to grow into an adult to take his place as leader of The Order. Doesn't make sense. He should choose someone else as his successor.

"I don't want his spawn inside me but I almost wish I would get pregnant. At least then he'd stop coming here and forcing himself on me."

Lainie is tiny. I'm sure he easily overpowers her. That's likely one of the factors to sway his decision in choosing her. A wife with strength would be more difficult to subdue.

I feel nauseated.

Torrence Grieve is a monster. I have very strong opinions about what I believe should happen to his kind. "Why are you a prisoner in this place? He took you as his wife. The very least he should do is care for you in his home."

"I knew him for the devil he is so I ran after my parents traded me to him. He was furious so this is my punishment. No contact with my friends or family. I'm stuck here."

What has happened to this woman is a tragedy. She's so sad, and it makes me want to save her. But I must concentrate on saving myself—and my babies—first.

"Would you run again if you had the chance?"

"Without a doubt. And I'd do a hell of a better job next time. But I won't get another chance. Torrence has made sure of that."

He's beaten her down. "There's always a way out."

"If there is, I haven't found it in the two months I've been here." She goes to the window and pulls back the dated floral drapery, revealing planks of wood covering the glass. "It's dark so you couldn't see this when they brought you in. They're boarded up from the outside. There's no getting out."

She goes to the front door, turns the knob and pulls. "Padlocked from the outside. Trust me, I've tried. There's no opening it from this side."

Lainie is an Order member but I can't see her as my enemy. If anything, this tortured soul is my ally. I'm neither afraid nor ashamed to use that to my advantage. "We have the same goal: to get out of here alive. Are you willing to put aside your loyalty to The Order if it means escaping?"

"I have no allegiance to The Order. None. Any obligation I felt was terminated the day my parents traded me to a man who would repeatedly rape me and consider killing me if I'm unsuccessful at conceiving his child. I want out of here and I'll do whatever it takes to make that happen."

She may be broken but she's angry. I can use that. "All right, then. Tell me about their routines."

"Broden or Reuben checks in every two days. Deacon brings food and supplies every four."

That's a new name. "Who's Deacon?"

"My brother's mate. He's kind. Not like the others at all. Has a soft place in his heart for me."

Ah. That has potential. "Is this soft spot big enough to free you?"

"No. He isn't willing to die so I can escape." Not the answer I was looking for.

"How often does Torrence visit?"

"Only when I'm ovulating."

He should burn for what he's doing to her. "When will that be?"

"I have four days left until he'll come for me five nights in a row. And just so you know, I don't fight him because that can get me killed, but that doesn't make it consensual." Her eyes become distant while staring at the white cracked plaster wall. "I can't go through it again. I'll kill myself before I let him touch me again. I even have a plan on how to do it."

Her threat isn't empty. If she's formulated a plan, she's a serious contender for suicide.

She needs reassurance, to know there is a way out. "My husband is coming. I don't think there's going to be a peaceful trade so we can probably expect guns blazing. Either way, I won't leave you behind."

She comes to attention, her head jerking in my direction. Her sunken eyes enlarge. She places praying hands against her lips and mutters something I can't decipher before dropping her hands to her lap again. "Swear to me."

"I swear I'll take you with me."

I fully expect an all-out war when Sin comes for me. We should be prepared.

"My father-in-law tried to barter for me but Torrence wouldn't agree to a trade. Thane offered him everything we had and still Torrence refused to hand me over."

"Something bigger is going on. Torrence loves money and power too much to refuse a bountiful offer," Lainie says.

"He wants revenge for Jason's death more than he wants those things."

Lainie lifts her brows and nods. "Aye. Now this makes sense."

I pray Sin suspects the same thing when his father tells him Torrence turned down the deal.

"Why didn't your husband come to negotiate for your return?" she asks.

"I was told he was taken into custody. After tonight's events, I suspect his arrest might have saved my life. I'm hoping Sin won't contact Torrence for a trade."

"What would he do instead?"

"I hope he and the brothers will rush this place as soon as he's released. We need to be ready to move in a hurry."

There's no time to waste. "Do you know how to fight?"

She snorts. "Do I look like a brawler?"

Appearances can be deceiving. She doesn't look like she could punch her way out of a wet paper sack but even the smallest person can be taught to deliver powerful blows. "I'm going to show you some defense and attack maneuvers." I get to my feet. "What's his signature move?"

She shrugs.

"Show me how he usually restrains you."

She comes forward and places her hands around my throat. At five six, I'm looking down on her several inches. "He chokes you?"

"Always."

I look at her neck and see the faded yellow remnants of his last attack. Fucking bully.

"Watch my motion." I lift my arms over my head and rotate my body. I bring my left arm down slowly over her wrists, forcing them from my neck. I use my right hand to grab her wrists and demonstrate how to hyperflex them.

"Show me again," she says.

I demonstrate several times before reversing roles with her. She gets a feel for it quickly.

"It takes twice as much energy to swing and miss as to swing and hit. Are you right-handed?"

"Aye."

I pat my right shoulder. "Reach across my body and put your hands here. Pull me down diagonally to your right." I bend at the waist to show her what I mean. "You'll bring your right knee up to kick his face. Do it fast and hard."

"When do I stop?"

"You don't."

CHAPTER TWO

SINCLAIR BRECKENRIDGE

THE BOOKING PROCESS IS LONG AND TEDIOUS. AS A SOLICITOR, I'M NEVER involved in this part. My clients have already been charged and booked by the time I arrive.

I'm escorted to an interrogation room and left to sit in an uncomfortable chair at a lone table. There's a video camera mounted on a tripod in the corner. I hope they don't think they're going to question me without my attorney present.

I don't sit long before Buchanan comes into the room. "I want to speed this process since it's late. I hope you don't mind that I took the liberty of calling Rodrick for you. He should be here any minute."

I don't reply.

"Might as well pass the time with a little friendly conversation. Is married life all you thought it would be?"

I give him nothing.

"I have to hand it to you, Breckenridge. That little wife of yours is one fit piece of arse. But I guess you already know that."

He's trying to provoke me but I won't fall for it.

"I bet it's killing you to know they have her. And I'm guessing I'm not the only one who thinks your wife is fit. The Order is probably putting their filthy hands all over her right now. And there's not a damn thing you can do about it."

Hold it together, Sin. Stay in control no matter what he says.

"I guess you should be grateful she's already pregnant so she doesn't come back to you knocked up by your nemesis. That would put a real damper on the honeymoon phase."

It's taking every ounce of self-control I have to not jump over this table and strangle the fuck out of him.

"I wonder if you'll ever be able to touch her again without thinking of all the nasty things they did to her."

He's enjoying this way too much; I refuse to contribute to his satisfaction.

"Oh wait. I don't know what I was thinking. You're going to jail for the rest of your life so you'll never get to fuck your wife again. Damn. That must be depressing as hell knowing you'll never get between those fine legs again. But don't worry. I'll check in on her from time to time to make sure she's doing all right. I can even come back and give you a report on how things are going."

I clasp my hands behind my head, lean back in my chair, and prop my feet on the desk. I want to appear as nonchalant as possible. He won't stop this game if he thinks he's getting to me.

Buchanan. Meet my poker face.

It works. The motherfucker gets up to leave. "I'll be back when Rodrick arrives."

I may appear calm on the outside but a shitstorm brews inside me. I'm a fucking mess.

Rodrick arrives but Buchanan gives us no time alone. I'm unable to get an update on what's happening with Bleu. Bastard. He's doing this on purpose.

"Do you understand your rights before we begin questioning?"

I was unaware Buchanan believed I had any.

"We understand," Rodrick answers.

"How did you know Malcolm Irvine?"

I'm questioned for the next two hours. The longer I sit here, the more I realize that Buchanan's grasping at straws. He doesn't have shite on me and we both know it. I'm going to walk on these charges but it's going to take time to be released. The evidence will have to go before a judge—he'll decide if there's a case against me. There clearly isn't.

This has to be a set-up. But by whom?

The questioning ends and I finally get a private word with Rodrick. "Tell me what you know about Bleu."

"Thane met with Torrence. Of course he made a very generous offer in exchange for your wife but Grieve refused. He's demanding to see you."

"That's not the report I was hoping to hear."

"Torrence wants to deal directly with you. He was adamant about it. That should be enough to keep Bleu alive."

"I know what he's up to. If I make a trade, he's going to kill her so he can avenge his son's death. That's the whole point of this game."

"Then don't make the trade."

"I'm not." I couldn't if I wanted to. The bomb makings have been confiscated by the authorities.

"We both know these charges are shite. You'll walk but it's going to take a couple of days. When you get out, you have to go after your wife immediately. The Order can't discover that you've been released and didn't reach out to them for an exchange as soon as your feet hit the pavement. They'll know something is up and the whole thing will fall apart at the seams."

Bleu and the babies will be the ones to pay. That can't happen.

PEOPLE LIKE ME DON'T NEED BARS. WE BUILD OUR OWN CELLS.

That's what I used to think. Until I met Bleu. She freed me from the prison I'd built around myself, around my heart.

I'm lying in my jail bed thinking of her and our babies when I hear movement rushing toward me in the dark. Instinct sends me hurtling forward. I tackle my assailant and feel a sudden sharp pain in my thigh.

"Prepare to die, Sinclair Breckenridge."

My attacker and I wrestle on the floor but I easily overtake him. The lights turn on and an alarm sounds. Three guards rush into our cell and yank me off my cellmate. I didn't pay attention to him when I was brought into the cell but now I take a closer look. Young. Skinny. Hair in need of a cut. I don't recognize him but he certainly knows who I am.

I notice a huge blood smear on the floor and then the bloody gash on my leg. Fuck. It's right above my amputation.

I can't afford for people to find out about this.

"Looks like he got a stab in on you, Breckenridge. You'll need to have that seen to."

This isn't good. I don't need anyone else knowing about my prosthesis. The guard who saw it when I changed my clothing is more than enough.

"It's just a scratch. I don't think that'll be necessary."

"You don't get a choice. Can't have you suing us over an improperly treated injury you sustained while in custody."

I'm taken to the infirmary and locked inside an exam room. I'm given a towel and told to hold pressure over the bleeding wound to my thigh until the doctor arrives. It isn't long until I see Jamie come in.

How the fuck did he pull this off?

"Mr. Breckenridge. I'm the on-call physician for the jail tonight. I'll be taking a look at your wound to see what kind of treatment you require."

"I'm happy to see you," I whisper.

Jamie cuts a slit in the upper leg of my pants so my prosthesis isn't exposed. "Doesn't look too bad. A few stitches and it'll be fine."

The guards are leaning against the wall talking, not paying any attention to Jamie and me. Perfect.

"Any word on Bleu?"

"Thane brought Debra in to assist with finding her."

That pleases me. I've come to trust Debra and have complete faith in her abilities to track my wife.

"Tell Dad I'm not negotiating. I want our most experienced men prepared to move as soon as I'm free. We're going after Bleu before The Order has a chance to realize I've been released."

Jamie cleanses my stab wound. "Damn."

"Sorry. My choice of antiseptic supplies are limited."

"No complaints. I'll take what I can get."

"I don't know how you made this happen but I'm glad you're here. I wasn't looking forward to anyone else finding out about my leg."

"I might have called a colleague and volunteered for the jail rotation when I found out you were here. Turns out people are generally pretty happy to give those up. Good thing since you can't stop getting yourself injured." Jamie uses stainless steel pliers to grasp the needle portion of a suture and pulls until it's freed from the packet. "Whoever supplies the infirmary is functioning under the belief that incarcerated people have no nerve endings. I can't believe this place isn't stocked with lidocaine. Ridiculous."

Jamie pushes the needle through my skin for the first suture. "Not your first experience with little to no anesthesia."

Doesn't matter. Still hurts like a son of a bitch.

I recall Bleu talking me through the pain when Jamie was fishing for the bullet in my shoulder. Breathe in slow and deep. Exhale gradually.

"Sometimes I feel like I went to medical school just so I could learn how to treat your arse. I was hoping that would change since you're married with a baby on the way."

Maybe I take chances but now isn't one of those times. "This cannot be considered my fault. My cellmate jumped me with a shank. The only reason he didn't get a better jab in was because I was awake —too worried about Bleu."

If I had been asleep, I'd be a dead man.

It's my guess that Buchanan put me in with someone from The Order. And while my cellmate was obviously privy to knowing I'm Fellowship, I wasn't given the same courtesy regarding his allegiance. Again, likely thanks to that bastard Buchanan.

"Your wife is going to be all right. You're going to get out of here soon and rescue her like a white knight should. You'll be her hero and she'll love it."

It's time to make good on my promise to protect her. And I'll do whatever it takes, even if it means wiping out every member of The Order.

CHAPTER THREE

BLEU BRECKENRIDGE

I OFFER TO PREPARE LUNCH SINCE LAINIE COOKED BREAKFAST THIS MORNING. There are two of us eating from the supplies for one. The man she calls Deacon hasn't come with groceries so the cupboard inventory is shrinking fast. "Pickings are slim. How do you feel about BLTs?"

"That's fine. I'm not accustomed to gourmet meals around here."

I'm nauseated. I don't really feel like eating but I'm fatigued more than usual today. I need iron from a food source since I don't have my vitamins or iron supplement. Pork is the best option I see from what's left in our scant food supply.

We're eating our sandwiches when Torrence arrives with Broden, Reuben, and the third man present during my kidnapping. I never heard them say his name so I call him the short one.

Terror spreads over Lainie's face. "Don't be afraid. He's here for me," I whisper.

"Mrs. Breckenridge. I trust your accommodations suit you."

Like he cares if I slept well. I won't whine. He'd enjoy that. "Can't complain."

"Did you become fast friends with my wife?"

He doesn't need to think Lainie and I are chummy. We can't afford for him to suspect we're partnering. "No. She's not terribly friendly."

He looks at her and snarls, "She certainly isn't. But the two of you will have time to become better acquainted. You're staying a while longer."

I don't care for the sound of that but I need to keep up my

charade. "Let me guess. Sinclair is refusing to come for me." I shake my head and purse my lips. "That son of a bitch will be sorry when my father finds out what he's done."

"Sinclair isn't coming because he's still sitting in jail. Which I don't mind, except it's putting a wrench in my plans for you."

Rodrick should've gotten him out first thing this morning. What's taking so long?

I should use this opportunity to convince Torrence that Sin and I aren't in love. He needs to believe killing me in front of Sin won't accomplish what he hopes. "Good. Maybe they'll keep his ass in jail until it rots so I don't have to look at him again."

"Your hatred for Sinclair Breckenridge seems passionate, yet you defended him. You said he didn't mean to kill my son. That sends mixed messages."

Shit. He's right. I shouldn't have defended Sin.

Now is the time to steer this in a different direction. "I was trying to save my own neck. I thought you might consider releasing me if you thought my husband didn't intentionally kill your son. But he did. The bastard even boasted about Jason's murder. The Fellowship celebrated his death."

"My son was so young. He had a promising future ahead of him. He was going to take my place as leader one day."

I hate speaking about the man I love this way but I have no choice. I must win Torrence over. "If you intend on making Sinclair suffer, I can assure you that killing me isn't the way. He loves another—a woman Thane wouldn't let him marry."

"That's interesting. If it's true."

"It is. And he's kept the whore as a lover after marrying me."

"You're jealous." He's laughing.

"Not jealous. Pissed off and determined to get even is more like it. I was forced to leave the man I loved in America and move to Scotland to become Sinclair's wife. I lost my beloved. He deserves to lose his as well. And I won't be happy until I make that happen."

"He deserves to lose much more than a woman."

I think I could be persuading Torrence in the right direction. "I absolutely agree."

"Who is this woman?"

I call off a bogus name. "Kenna McGregor. He brought her into our home as a housekeeper. As though I'm too stupid to know what they're doing behind my back."

"This is good information. Definitely something I can work with. Many thanks, Mrs. Breckenridge."

Torrence and his men are barely out the door when Lainie releases a heavy sigh. "Quite the tangled web you've spun. But I think he walked face first into it."

"It sounded good?"

"Hell yes. I know the truth and I almost fell for it. You're very convincing."

"Good." I have to be. I have a lot to lose.

TWO DAYS HAVE PASSED AND NOTHING. NO TORRENCE. NO MEN FROM THE Order checking in. Most importantly, no Sin. What is happening with my husband? He hasn't come for me yet. Something is wrong.

I've tried everything I know to find a way out of this place but Lainie is right. It's locked down. There's no way out until someone opens that door from the outside.

So I wait. I have no other choice. But sitting on my hands is killing me. I'm accustomed to a proactive course. This pussyfooting around doesn't cut it.

"We're running out of food. Do you expect your brother's friend to come today?"

"Aye."

I've been thinking about this. I believe it's time to make a move. "We should make a break for it when he comes."

"No. Torrence will kill Deacon if he allows us to escape."

Does she forget that the alternative is killing us? "Your brother's friend won't be allowing anything. We'll take him by force. Torrence won't kill him if he's overpowered."

"You're wrong. It isn't possible for Torrence to be rational about anything."

"That's exactly right. He is irrational. He killed his other wife because she couldn't give him an heir. If you don't become pregnant soon, he will do the same to you. You'd better wise up and think about that."

She says nothing.

"That monster will come for you tomorrow night. Would you prefer to be raped again or be gone when he arrives? Your choice."

She still doesn't answer. Maybe her priorities aren't in order but mine are. "I don't plan on being here tomorrow night."

"I can't put Deacon in that kind of danger. I love him."

"You love Deacon because he's your brother's friend, or you *love* love him?"

"I *love* love him."

Things are beginning to make a little more sense. "Is he in love with you?"

"I think he was before my parents traded me to Torrence." She covers her face with her hands and her voice cracks when she continues. "It's like he looks right through me when he comes."

I'd bet money Torrence knows Lainie loves Deacon. It's another cruel way to torture his wife for trying to run away. And the bonus is tempting poor Deacon with the accessibility of helping her escape. But every time he doesn't, he proves to Lainie how little he feels for her.

I need to be brutally honest with Lainie so there's no mistake. "It boils down to two options: stay to protect Deacon, or make a move to get out of here. Regardless of what you choose for yourself, this is happening when he comes."

"How do I condemn the man I love to death so I can go free?"

"You do it because staying could leave you with one choice. Death. He has the option to make a run with us if he's so inclined."

"But he won't."

"If he doesn't, that's his choice."

There's a sound at the door. Someone's coming in. "Stay out of the way if you aren't going to help."

Torrence and two of his men enter. Shit. He's either come early for Lainie or something has happened with Sin.

"Good afternoon, Mrs. Breckenridge."

He ignores Lainie sitting next to me. "Evening, Mr. Grieve. To what do we owe this pleasure?"

"I'm guessing you're hoping I'm here to say your husband has been released from jail and has come forward to trade for you. But that isn't the case."

"I thought I was clear about my feelings regarding Sinclair Breckenridge."

"You were. Except everything you told me was a lie."

I have fucked up.

I knew Torrence would eventually disprove my story but I thought I'd be out of here before that happened. Now it's come back to bite me in the ass.

I must remain convincing. "I don't know why you'd think that."

"It began when I learned Carrick Abban doesn't have a daughter. At least not one who still lives and breathes."

Cassidy is dead? That must have happened recently.

"I don't know who told you that but they're lying."

"I think we know who the liar is."

"I may have glossed over the truth a little. I'm his other daughter. The illegitimate one by his mistress. I'm sorry I lied but he's still very much my father and will be upset should anything happen to me."

"Lies. All of it. There's no chance of a falling out with Little Abbot. I can do whatever I like with you."

"That would be a huge mistake."

"I think not."

Torrence slithers to stand behind me where I sit at the kitchen table. He fists my hair and pulls me back so hard, I'm balancing on the two back legs of the chair. "You'll pay for the lies you fed me."

He drags me from my seat and down the hallway toward the bedroom. "Since she can't seem to give me an heir, maybe you can."

Broden and Reuben don't follow. He has done this to Lainie enough, they're probably confident he doesn't require their assistance. Wrong.

I wait until we're inside the bedroom to escape his grasp since I don't want to alert Broden or Reuben. I surprise Torrence with a punch to his throat—always unexpected, and temporarily debilitating.

He grabs for his throat because my assault causes him to feel like he can't breathe. It's the perfect time to strike a second time so I can wrestle him to the ground and put him in a chokehold, the same one I used on Malcolm when I killed him.

I loop my arms around Torrence's neck and lock them into a death grip. This is kill or be killed, and I have no intention of being the one to go down.

We scuffle for a moment before landing on the floor. We're a tangled mess when we crash into the rails of the bed, shoving it across the rotted wood planks beneath it. He struggles against me but his upper body strength is weak.

I count so I'll know how long he's been without oxygen. Sixty seconds. One hundred and twenty. I need a full three minutes to accomplish my goal.

This needs to sound like he's the one winning.

"No!" I yell at the top of my lungs. "Stop. Don't. Please don't!"

I'm at two and a half minutes when Broden taps on the door. "Everything all right in there?"

I scream at the top of my lungs to discourage him from investigating further. But the bastard opens the door. Dammit.

He rushes me, gun pulled and aimed at my forehead. "Release him or the wall will be newly decorated."

Thirty seconds more. That's all I need and Torrence Grieve will be no one's problem ever again. But my time is up.

I release his throat and show my hands. He sputters, gasping for air as Reuben grabs him beneath his arms and drags him away.

"Who are you?" Broden asks.

I shrug while continuing to hold my hands out.

Torrence lies on his side catching his breath. His cold eyes stare at me. He grabs Reuben by the shirt and pulls him down so they're face to face. His voice is scratchy and hoarse. "Beat her until she can no longer move."

Broden grins. "Gladly."

"Shoot her if she resists," Torrence adds.

My children and I are dead if I fight. No question about it. I have the responsibility of protecting the two tiny lives growing inside me so I do the only thing I can. I curl into a tight ball around my precious babies to protect them the only way I know how.

CHAPTER FOUR

SINCLAIR BRECKENRIDGE

My father offered The Order everything they could possibly want, plus some. Still, they refuse to return Bleu. That sends my red flag to high alert.

She's been in the hands of my enemy for three days. I have no idea if she and our little ones are safe. That's the sum total of what I know about my wife and children.

And I'm about to lose my fucking mind.

I'm finally freed, all charges dropped associated with Malcolm's death. The whole thing was a conspiracy and I've no clue about the instigator. But I will find out. And when I do, he'll be sorry.

I leave the jail and dash toward the dark sedan waiting curbside. I'm pleased to find Dad in the back seat. I've barely shut the car door when Sterling pulls on to the street.

We skip discussions concerning my legal battle and dive straight into planning my wife's rescue. "Everyone's at Duncan's awaiting instructions. We need to come to a decision before arriving so this can proceed as quickly as possible."

The pub is a ten-minute drive. That doesn't give us much time to discuss options.

"The Order doesn't know you've been released. That's an enormous advantage to have over them but it won't take long for word to spread. You must decide how to proceed."

If this were about property or possessions, Grieve would've gladly taken Dad's offer. "He's demanding I come make the trade for Bleu, even willing to wait until I'm freed from jail. I'm predicting he's planning to kill her in front of me."

"I agree. This has everything to do with avenging his son's death."

"Tell me you know where Bleu is."

"Debra has been tailing Grieve since Bleu's kidnapping. He and his men recently made a visit to an isolated cottage not far from here. It's boarded up. By all appearances, it looks abandoned. We believe it's very likely Bleu is there."

But no one knows for sure and maybe doesn't cut it in this situation. "I need my wife's location confirmed if I'm to make the best decision concerning her safety."

"I wasn't willing to send men into that cottage without your approval. If Bleu wasn't there and The Order discovered our rescue attempt, they might have killed her without a negotiation. I couldn't give that order because she isn't my wife. She's yours to protect so it must be your decision."

"My gut says Grieve isn't visiting a boarded-up cottage for no reason. He's holding her there. We'll gather our best men and storm the location."

Our meeting at Duncan's is brief. It only lasts long enough for me to choose ten of my most trusted and combat-experienced brothers along with two men to act as drivers. We load into the back of a transport truck. I don't waste time talking at the pub. We can use the drive to the cottage to nail down our final battle plan. "This is going to be a snatch and grab. The goal isn't to kill Order members. We're storming in without warning, taking my wife, and getting the fuck out of there. The battle will come later when they realize she's gone. The only goal now is to get her out safely."

"Four of us will go in through the front door. Dad, Alan, Derek, and myself." I give orders to the remaining eight to surround the cottage and cover from all sides. "Any questions?"

I've fought beside these men for years. I trust them with my life. And my wife's.

We're approaching the cottage when my father's phone vibrates in his pocket. "It's Debra."

"We're almost there," he tells her. "Thank you for calling."

He ends his call. "Torrence and two of his men just arrived at the cottage."

"Dammit." I was hoping we would find Bleu alone so she wouldn't be placed in danger during an extraction.

"Grieve doesn't know you've been released. He'd have more men guarding her, and protecting him, if that was the case."

Dad's right. Torrence would be nowhere near Bleu if he knew there was a chance I was on my way. He's a coward. He never joins his men in a fight. He sits behind the line of safety and watches.

"You want to stick to the same plan?"

My father is letting me make all the calls. First, Bleu is my wife so she's mine to protect. But two, this is his way of letting me gain decision-making experience. I'm certain he wouldn't hesitate to override my plan if he felt I was making the wrong moves.

"We should adjust the numbers since we know we'll have three Order members on the inside. Six will go in so we have twice their number. Neil and Ross. You'll join us."

"I agree. Six men are sufficient."

"Everyone needs to understand something. I'm out of that cottage with Bleu as soon as I find her. Sterling and Jamie will be waiting for us in the car. You'll have two getaway vehicles. If you're detained from returning to this one, I have a second in place. It will be waiting on the south side of the property."

"Protect the brother next to you so you'll have someone to cover for you," my father adds.

The truck stops. My chosen men and I file out through the back. We creep toward the cottage and find the door is unlocked. Perfect. That eliminates the need for a noisy break-in and betters our chances of being undetected while gaining access.

I listen a moment before entering. Nothing. It's the eerie kind of quiet before the storm. It makes me terrified of what I'm going to find. "Let's move."

I open the door. The six of us storm inside but find no one in the first room we enter.

This is all wrong.

Guns drawn, I lead my men through the cottage. I stop dead in my tracks when I see a young blond woman huddled in the corner of the next room. She's curled into a ball, her arms wrapped around her head as to deflect an assault. "Where is Bleu?" I whisper.

The woman lifts her tear-streaked face from her knees. She's been beaten to a bloody pulp.

She points to the hallway. "I tried to stop them from hurting her."

I'm too afraid to ask what she's referring to. My mind imagines the worst. "Someone get this girl out of here. Put her in the car with Sterling and Jamie."

Without thought for a quiet attack, I stalk down the hallway toward Bleu.

Torrence and two of his men are standing over my Bonny Bleu, looking at her battered body. One of the men uses his foot to nudge her shoulder but she doesn't respond. She appears completely lifeless.

They've broken my china doll. And now they stand over her laughing at what they've done.

I see red. My first instinct is to choke the life out of them. But that doesn't help Bonny.

My men enter the room, guns drawn. The surprise on Torrence's face when he sees me is perfection. But I can't enjoy it, not when my Bonny Bleu is lying in a puddle on the floor.

I rush to her. She has a pulse; I listen for breathing.

"Don't worry. The bitch is still alive," Torrence says.

She's so badly beaten I'm afraid to move her. She's almost indistinguishable, her face a mask of fresh blood. "Someone fetch Jamie. Quickly."

"Your timing was really unfortunate. Had you given us another five minutes, we could have ridded you of her altogether." Torrence's voice is the equivalent of nails on a chalkboard.

I had so many plans for how I would make my nemesis suffer. Take him to the black site. Torture him. Drag his death out for days. But none of that matters now—only Bleu and our babies matter.

I stroke the top of her hair. "I'm going to take you away from this place. Everything is going to be fine and I'm never going to allow anyone else the opportunity to steal you from me again."

I hold her hand and kiss her forehead. "I love you, Bonny Bleu," I whisper.

Torrence laughs. "This is the reason you never love a woman. It weakens you."

Jamie rushes in and kneels next to Bleu. "She'll need X-rays to confirm she has no fractures to her neck or spine. The safest thing to do is put her in a C-collar so we can get moving before other Order members arrive."

"Hold her neck like this." He places my hands in the correct position. "We're going to log roll her. I'll slip the collar on from behind."

We roll Bleu on to her side and I do as he instructs.

"Where is all that blood coming from?" my father asks.

I glance downward to see what he's talking about. My heart stutters when I see the dark pool collecting beneath Bonny. "Jamie. Why is she bleeding like that? Where is it coming from?"

He fastens the collar. "We need to get her to the hospital immediately."

"Sterling has the car at the front," my father says.

My men lift Bleu and carefully transport her down the hallway to the front door where the car awaits.

I stand and face Torrence and his men. I don't have time to say or do any of the things I'd like. "You'll never hurt my family again."

I shoot them one by one, leaving Torrence for last so he can see what's coming for him. A single shot between the eyes.

Blood and brains spatter the wall but it gives me no satisfaction. A bullet to the head is too merciful for Torrence and the men who beat my Bonny Bleu.

"Leave their bodies for The Order to find. Their property. Their problem."

Jamie says Bleu's neck and spine should remain straight so I crouch on the floor of the back seat so I'm sitting next to her head. He sits with her feet in his lap.

I grasp her hand, kissing it often. I can't stop touching her. These past three days have been brutal.

"I love you and our babies so much," I whisper in her ear, remembering how her voice seeped through the dark walls of consciousness while I was sick.

There was so much blood pooled beneath her. My mind knows it's evidence of a miscarriage but my heart holds out hope. "Do you think she's losing the babies?"

"Babies?"

"Aye. Twins. We found out the day she was taken."

"Obstetrics aren't my specialty, Sin," he says quietly. That's all he says but I can guess what he's thinking. No woman can bleed like that and not lose her pregnancy.

The young woman turns around in the front seat. "Bleu didn't mention she was expecting. But it's best she didn't. Torrence wouldn't have stopped until he was certain he had beaten those babies out of her along with any chance to conceive more in the future."

I look at this petite woman in the front seat of my car. The top of her blond head is barely visible over the seat from where I'm sitting in the floorboard.

"Who are you?" I demand.

"Lainie." She hesitates before saying the rest. "Grieve. Before you ask, yes. I'm Torrence's wife. But not by choice. He's a monster who held me prisoner in that place for the last two months."

Lainie bursts into tears. "Bleu said you would help me and you did. You'll never know how grateful I am. Thank you so much."

I'm not often shocked but Lainie Grieve has just managed to do so. And while I have many questions about what's happening within The Order, it's not my focus right now.

We arrive at the hospital's emergency services entrance. "I have to walk away at this point," Jamie says. "I can't risk being seen with you. Some of the people from my medical program like asking too many questions."

Jamie's right. My face was all over the news after my arrest. Being seen with me will bring up issues he might not be able to explain away. "Of course."

"Sterling. Go inside and fetch help."

Jamie opens the door to get out. "Call as soon as you know anything."

I remain next to my wife while we wait for help to arrive at the car.

I don't know what has happened to Lainie, but I suspect her face isn't the only thing damaged. "You need to be examined."

She nods, tears cascading down her crumpled, bruised face. "My head hurts. So much." Her whole body shakes, though from fear or pain, I don't know.

"They'll have to report your attack to the police. I don't care what kind of statement you give as long as it doesn't include me or The Fellowship."

"I was assaulted by an unknown attacker. I didn't see his face," she says. I suspect this isn't her first time to tell that story. "I'll enter the hospital separately so they don't make the connection."

"That's probably best."

"Thank you for rescuing me from that monster." Those are her last words before getting out and disappearing.

A swarm of medical personnel surround the car. They slide a board beneath Bleu's body and transfer her limp form to a waiting gurney. "Sir, is this your wife?"

"Yes. She's pregnant with twins. Six weeks."

I see the looks exchanged when they note the extensive blood on her clothing. "We're going to take good care of her. And your babies."

MY MUM STAYS WITH ME WHILE BLEU'S GONE FOR TESTS. FIRST, THEY MUST ensure she has not sustained damage to her head, neck, or spine. Thankfully, they rule out any neurological problems but I'm still concerned. It's been hours and she remains unconscious.

The doctor and nurses assure me they see no reason she won't wake on her own soon but it's unsettling to see her lying in what appears to be a comatose state.

The ultrasound is last and they won't allow me to be present when it's done. I have no idea if our babies survived. When I ask, the nurse tells me the doctor will be in to discuss the findings. I think they would've told me if everything was all right, so I assume he'll be delivering bad news.

I need my mother's advice. "The first thing Bleu's going to ask when she wakes is if the babies are okay. How the hell am I going to tell her they're not?"

Mum halts the crocheting project on her lap. "Bleeding isn't supposed to occur during pregnancy so when it does, expectant parents panic. The amount of blood seems like much more than it actually is. I know because it happened when I was pregnant with your brother. I was certain I was miscarrying. As you know, I didn't so you must believe that all is well with them until you know otherwise."

My mum returns to crocheting. I think she's doing it as a distraction. She's only half-finished with the piece but I can clearly make out what it's going to be—a baby blanket. Seeing it makes all of this surreal.

I've never lost children before. I only know one way to be ready for it. "I'm preparing myself for the worst."

"There are plenty of situations where that's an appropriate attitude but parenting isn't one of them. You prepare for the best by hoping for it."

Mum holds up her crocheting project. "I'm already done with the first blanket. This one should be finished by tomorrow. All I'll need to do is add the pink or blue ribbons after we find out what they are."

"I went back to the office right after we found out about the twins. I don't even know what Bleu wants. Boys? Girls? A combo?"

"She'll be happy with whatever you get."

I left her at home alone. "This was my fault, Mum. Torrence took her because of me. We could lose our babies because of what I did."

"You can't think like that, son."

"She has every right to blame me if they don't make it."

There's a knock at the door, and then it opens. "Hello, Mr. Breckenridge." Bleu's obstetrician.

I'm numb as the doctor introduces himself. All I can think of is the news he's about to give us. "There are concerns we need to discuss but I know your immediate question for me is the condition of the pregnancy. Let me start by saying that we detected two heartbeats on ultrasound."

Oh, thank you. Thank you. Thank you.

My mum releases a sigh of relief. "I knew our babies would be okay. I told you, didn't I?"

"As an OB/GYN, I'll only address your wife's health from an obstetrical and gynecological standpoint. I found significant bruising on her inner thighs. Because Mrs. Breckenridge remains unconscious and can't tell us what happened, I had to follow protocol, which means examining her for sexual assault. I'm happy to report that I found no evidence supporting that."

I didn't allow myself to wonder about it because to do so meant it was a possibility.

"Moving on to the pregnancy. The babies look stable. But as you know, your wife has had a very significant bleeding episode. The trauma to her abdomen caused a marginal tear in the edge of the placenta. That means it has a slight separation from the womb. But the bleeding has stopped. We'll keep her hydrated and on bed rest and see what happens."

I wonder if "see what happens" is an official medical prognosis. "Do you think our babies will be all right?"

"All we can do is watch and wait."

BLEU MOANS OFF AND ON BUT IT'S MORE THAN TWO HOURS AFTER THE obstetrician's visit before she finally stirs for the first time. "Bonny."

I squeeze her hand and her eyelids flutter. She struggles to open her eyes because they're so swollen. When she does, they're slits. "Ahh. There's my sweet Bonny's baby blues."

She blinks lazily. "Hi," I say.

Her eyes flicker several more times, I think trying to focus on my face.

"Hi," she whispers. Her simple one-word greeting is music to my ears.

"How do you feel?"

She closes her eyes. "Nauseated. I think I'm going to be sick."

My mum moves faster than lightning with the little bucket they left for such a thing. "It's all right if ye get sick."

Mum points to the drawer where the linens are kept. "Wet a washcloth with cold water for her face."

I scramble to the small sink in the tight washroom, wet the cloth, and hand it back to my mother, my own hands shaking. Mum places the wet cloth against Bleu's forehead. "There, love. This'll help ye feel better."

A few seconds later, Bleu rises in the bed and moans loudly while dry heaving into the basin my mum is holding. Once. Twice. Three times.

Very few areas of her body are free of bruising. She must be in terrible pain.

"Oh!" Bleu's eyes grow large when she wretches the last time. "I just felt something come out down there."

Mum pulls the covers back for a look. "It's just a little blood. That's all."

"Why am I bleeding?" Bleu's hand goes to her stomach. "Oh God. I lost the babies."

Worry can't be good for her or them. I need to reassure her everything is all right. "You had some bleeding but both babies are okay. They did an ultrasound and saw two heartbeats."

"I'm going to fetch the nurse. She needs to know Bleu is awake so she can assess her and call the doctor."

I bring Bleu's hand to my mouth for a kiss. "This is all my fault, Bonny. I'm so sorry I didn't protect you and our children."

She's sobbing, tears rolling from the corners of her eyes on to the pillow beneath her head. "I'm bleeding. Does that mean I'm going to lose them?"

"The doctor says they look stable."

She strains to sit up and winces. "Oh my God. It hurts."

"What hurts? Where?"

"Everywhere."

I feel helpless. I can't make this better for her.

"Mum went to get a nurse. We'll ask her to get you something for pain."

The nurse comes quickly but is taking forever to assess Bleu. "She's in agony. Can you give her something and then do this?"

"I'm sorry. I can't do that, Mr. Breckenridge, but I promise I'm hurrying."

I'm not at all pleased by how long it takes Bleu to get medication but I can tell when it begins to work. She's much more relaxed. "Feeling better?"

"A little, but this is going to hurt like hell for a while."

"I'm so sorry."

"At least the narcotics help."

"No. I mean I'm sorry this happened. It's all my fault."

"You didn't do this to us. Torrence Grieve is to blame."

"I left my pregnant wife at home without protection while I knew that my enemy was lying in wait. I was foolish and careless with the people I love most in this world. There's no excuse." I clasp her hand tightly. "Can you forgive me?"

"I thought I was fine and could protect myself. But I guess I'm not invincible. I think we both learned valuable lessons." That can't be the extent of how she feels. Maybe her mood is altered by what they gave her for pain.

She has sleepy eyes. "It's all right if you want to take a nap."

"I'm so tired." Her voice is slowed.

"Go to sleep. I'll be by your side. I'm not going anywhere."

"Maybe just a little snooze."

Bleu shuts her swollen eyes for less than a minute before they pop open. "Lainie! I promised we'd take her away from that place!"

"We brought her with us."

"Where is she?"

"She was in bad shape and needed to be examined."

"Is she all right?"

"I don't know."

"No one is with her?" Bleu is alarmed.

"I guess not."

"Someone from The Fellowship needs to be with her in case Torrence or one of his minions comes for her."

"I can assure you that Grieve won't be coming for her."

"You killed him. I'm glad."

I've never been more pleased by a person's death. "Aye. And the other two who beat you. Killing Torrence was the best move I could've made for us and our people."

"But the others could come for Lainie."

"Bonny. She's Order. Our enemy. It's not our job to protect Lainie from her own people. I wouldn't have taken her out of there if I'd known who she was."

"But they're horrible people."

"True, but members of The Order are part of that circle by choice."

"Not Lainie. Her parents traded her to Torrence for money and power. She tried to escape and he locked her in that cabin. She's been there for two months. He's been raping her so she'd become pregnant with his child."

At the very least I owe Lainie my help and support since Jason's death set off a firestorm that has severely impacted her life. And I mustn't forget she tried to help my wife and took a beating for it. "Mitch is in the waiting room. I'll send him to sit with her for now. We'll figure out the rest later."

"Thank you."

The door to Bleu's hospital room should be swapped out for one that will revolve. A parade of no fewer than a half-dozen doctors pass through it over the next couple of hours. Like clockwork, one leaves and another enters within fifteen minutes. It's much the same with our friends and family. The Fellowship wants to show their support for their leader and his wife.

But Bleu is exhausted. I see it in her heavy lids. It's time for all visitors to go. Even Lorna and Westlyn, although I know it won't be easy.

"Bleu's too nice to say it so I'm going to do it for her. You've done an excellent job of seeing to her every need. But she's really tired and needs her rest."

"Maybe we can step out for a while," Westlyn says.

Lorna nods in agreement. "We'll sit in the waiting room."

Stepping out to the waiting room means they'll be back in a little while. "I'm here to take care of her, so go home. You can come back tomorrow after she's rested."

I don't give them a choice. I can tell they don't like it much but they do as I tell them.

It's finally the two of us. "Thank you for doing that."

"All part of a husband's dirty job."

She lifts the covers. "I want to be close to you. Come lie next to me while I sleep."

I kick off my shoes and slide in beside my wife. I'm forced to leave my prosthesis on, something I never do when I get into bed.

We lie on our sides spooning. "It's all right for you to be angry with me about what happened. I promised to keep you safe and I didn't. I deserve every bit of your fury."

She sighs. "I never once thought I needed you to safeguard me. I fancied myself doing you a favor by agreeing to let you play the part of my protector. But I had it all wrong. I'm tough but I put myself in danger by not seeing my own weaknesses." She curls into me like a frightened child. "I can't believe I was so wrong."

She's trembling so I tighten my hold. "I'm so sorry. I swear that will never happen again. Things are going to be different when we go home. When I'm away, you and the babies will have a minimum of two bodyguards at all times."

"I can't believe I'm about to say this, but I think I need that to feel safe again."

My wife doesn't feel safe. That breaks my heart because it's a testament to the husband I've been. But I'm going to do everything in my power to gain her trust again.

"Debra called me right before The Order took me. She got the evidence we needed to prove Abram is innocent. At least of my mother's murder. I'm sure he's guilty of plenty of other offenses."

I know Abram is capable of a lot but I never believed he was guilty of Amanda Lawrence's murder. "How do you feel about that?"

"I should be happy your uncle didn't kill my mother. But I'm not. I hate him."

She should. He's done terrible things to her. "Abram is finished badgering you. I'll see to that personally."

There's a knock at the door. When it doesn't open right away, I know it's not a doctor or nurse. They don't wait for an invitation to enter.

I told my people no interruptions. I was very clear about it. And now someone is disrupting one of the most important conversations I've ever had with my wife.

"Hold on," I snap. "Fuck!" I toss back the covers and swing my legs around to replace my shoes.

Bleu touches my back. "Don't get up."

I twist to kiss her forehead. "I'll only be gone long enough to reprimand whoever this is disturbing us."

I open the door and find Kyle, one of two men I've assigned to guard Bleu's door. "I told you no disturbances. My wife needs rest," I growl. What part of that does he not fucking understand?

"We have a problem, Sin. A big one," he whispers.

CHAPTER FIVE

BLEU BRECKENRIDGE

"I NEED TO STEP OUT WITH KYLE. I'LL ONLY BE A MINUTE."

"No." I try to sit up but stop when the pain is too great. "Don't go."

"I'm not leaving you. I'll just be right outside the door for a moment. Promise."

Wrinkles crease Sin's forehead. The deep ones only make an appearance when he's worried. "Something's wrong."

"Fellowship business. Nothing for you to be concerned about. Rest and I'll be back before you can miss me."

He leaves, shutting the door behind him, not giving me the chance to argue further.

Rest? He has to be kidding. Like that's going to happen when I know there's a problem.

God, I hope nothing has happened to Lainie.

Sin returns and plants himself in the chair next to my bed. "I'm going to tell you what's going on but do not get upset. It isn't good for you or the babies."

"Telling me to not get upset makes me get upset."

"Ellison is in Edinburgh."

"What! Why? It's only been four days since we spoke. She doesn't know this happened, does she?"

"I don't think it has anything to do with your kidnapping. I'm inclined to think she's here as a surprise."

Shit. Talk about bad timing. "She's going to have a come-apart when she finds out I'm in the hospital and haven't called her."

"She's at Agnes's because I can't let her into our flat." Right. That damn bloody message on the wall. She'd flip the fuck out if she saw it, as would any normal person.

"I have a crew working to erase all evidence of what happened. New paint in the living room. New furniture. But they'll need at least a day to make it happen. What should we do with her in the meantime?"

There's nothing to consider. "I don't have a choice. I have to see her." Like this.

For a moment, I push away the worries of how I'll explain everything. I'm happy. I get to see my sister after being apart for months.

"She's going to want answers."

"Of course she will. And she'll get explanations."

But they won't be the truth.

SIN'S PHONE ALERTS HIM TO A NEW MESSAGE. "IT'S JAMIE—TEXTING TO LET ME know he and Ellison just arrived."

I may throw up. Really. "I'm more nervous than a fox at a hound convention."

"At least you still have your humor." Sin sits on the edge of my bed and places his hand on my leg. "Don't be so tense. The story's a good one. She has no reason to suspect it's a lie."

"Anyone still here?"

"My parents are in the waiting room. And Mitch, but he's still with Lainie."

"He's been with her for hours."

"I sent Kyle to relieve him but he said he was fine and wouldn't leave." That's a little strange.

"Will you tell Kyle and Blare to not allow anyone in my room while Ellison's here?" The less contact she has with The Fellowship, the better.

"I've already put out an order for everyone to stay away from the hospital. A large crowd draws attention. I'd prefer the staff didn't figure out it was my face all over the newspaper the past few days."

Agreed. I don't want my nurses to realize who Sin is, either, but right now I'm more concerned with my sister figuring it out.

There's a light tap on the door. Ellison doesn't wait for an invitation to come inside. I'm not sure if that's a nurse thing or a sister thing.

The smile she's wearing when she enters fades when she sees my face. "My God, Bleu!"

She looks at Sin and back to me before darting to my bedside. "No one told me you were in the hospital because you looked like this. What the hell happened to you?"

Lacerations decorate my forehead. Edema has almost forced both of my eyes closed. The discoloration of my face darkens by the hour. This must be a terrible shock for her.

I put my hand to my cheek and smile. Even that hurts. "I assure you it looks much worse than it really is."

"Who did this to you?"

"That's the question of the day. I was mugged while walking to the market."

"What kind of mugger stomps the hell out of a woman while stealing her purse? And how did you let anyone best you? You're able to kick anybody's ass."

She isn't buying what I'm selling. My sister knows I've been trained well to handle such situations. "The guy was huge and I was caught off guard."

"Bleu. You're never caught off guard."

She's right. "Even I get preoccupied sometimes."

"So this guy just walked up, kicked the shit out of you, and then ran off with your purse?"

I need to add something more to the story to make it seem real. "Yeah. He was acting like a raving lunatic. He had to be high or something."

"Are the police doing anything to find the asshole who did this to you?"

"They are. Two very nice detectives came to see me and assured us everything possible was being done." That part is true.

"Are you sure there isn't more to this? There are two men guarding your door."

"That's just Sin being overprotective."

"I don't think he's being a bit overprotective after what you just went through. What about the babies?"

I'm not going into details about the tear in the placenta. She'll freak out. I know I did when Sin finally told me about it. "I've had some bleeding so I'll be on bed rest for a while."

"Then it's a good thing I'm here. You're going to need me."

There's an impending war with The Order. I can't think of a time when I need her here less. "We spoke four days ago and you didn't mention a word about coming."

She looks away, avoiding my eyes. That's not a good sign. "I wanted it to be a surprise."

I don't believe her. "Liar. Something happened."

"You using your human lie detector skills on me again?"

"Maybe."

"Well, a little something might have happened."

My idea of a little something and Ellison's often differ greatly. "What kind of a little something are we talking about?"

She drops her face and pats the top of her head. She always did this when she was a kid and got into trouble. "Oh God. It's so stupid, Bleu."

She looks over at Sin and Jamie before whispering, "And embarrassing."

I look at my husband and nod toward the door. It's my cue for him and Jamie to give us some privacy.

He understands and comes to kiss the top of my head. "Need anything while I'm out?"

It's been hours and no one has told me anything about my new friend. "I'd love an update on how Lainie's doing."

"Of course. Want anything to eat?"

I still don't have an appetite. Getting your gut stomped doesn't do much for that. "I don't think so. But don't worry. I have the IV."

"Will you try to eat something for the babies?"

God, I'd kill for some Lipton's sweet tea with lemon. The good ol' syrupy kind. But it's a southern thing. People around here look at you like you're crazy if you ask for sweet tea.

I can't think of a thing that sounds good right now. "Surprise me."

"A double order of haggis it is, then." I wrinkle my nose and pretend to gag.

"Sorry, Bonny. Couldn't resist." Sin chuckles.

Ellison waits until they're gone. "I take it you don't love haggis?"

"Nope."

Ellison plops in the chair at my bedside. "You aren't going to believe the level of stupidity I've been able to achieve since you've been gone."

She's stalling. I hate that. "Come off it already."

"I had to leave my job at Southaven."

I don't have it in me to drag this out of her. Not today. "Because?"

"I was given a random drug screen … and I failed."

What? My sister doesn't take drugs. "There must've been an error."

She shakes her head. "No. It was no mistake."

"What did you test positive for?"

"Ecstasy."

"Since when do you take that?"

"Since never … except for this one time. I went out with some friends from work. We met these really cute guys on Beale Street … and they were musicians … and I guess we got a little carried away. It was supposed to be a fun night but now I'm totally fucked."

"You said you left your job. Does that mean you weren't fired?"

"The hospital told me I had to take a leave of absence and enter a voluntary rehabilitation program if I wanted to maintain employment with them."

"So do it."

"No way. It's ridiculous." She looks completely outraged. "I don't have a drug problem. I took ecstasy one time while I was partying with friends. Why would I commit to a drug rehabilitation program when I don't have an addiction?"

I know Ellison doesn't have a drug dependency. "You do it because you want to save your job."

"Do you have any idea how humiliating it is to have all my coworkers know I tested positive? I can't go back to work with those people."

"Then get a different job."

"I'm on probation with the Board of Nursing. I can't apply for a job without disclosing that. It's on my record. No one is going to hire a nurse with a drug offense."

I hope she has a backup plan. "Then what are you planning to do?"

"I have no idea. But it's a total clusterfuck of suck back home. People are calling to *help* when all they really want is to hear the lowdown on what happened with my head nurse. I couldn't take it anymore. I had to get away so I could think without being badgered."

I don't need Ellison here now, but I can't turn my back on her. I've done that too much already.

My doctor has ordered me to be on bed rest for a while. That's the perfect excuse to stay home and out of the line of fire of anything The Order might do. "You're welcome to stay with us as long as you like."

"Sinclair won't mind?" She chooses now to ask? That's just like Ellison.

"Of course not. You're my sister. You're always welcome in our home."

"Oh my God. You have no idea how relieved I am to hear you say that."

"Sin's going to know you didn't up and decide to come here for no reason. And I won't lie to him."

"I understand. I don't want to cause any problems between you but can you please make sure he knows I've always been a law-abiding citizen? I don't want him to think I'm some kind of criminal."

I barely contain the laughter threatening to escape. "I can promise you without a shadow of doubt that Sin will not think less of you because you broke the law one time while having a little fun with your friends."

"I know, but he doesn't really know me. I don't want him to have the wrong impression of me."

It's difficult to withhold the grin threatening to spread across my face. "No worries, Elli. He'll be cool about it. Promise."

Sin gives me an hour with Ellison before returning. "Okay to come back?"

"Sure. Were you able to find out how Lainie is?"

"She's fine. No concussion so they're getting ready to release her."

The Fellowship didn't take Lainie. She voluntarily walked—no, ran—from The Order. She's bound to them until death. "She won't have anywhere to go."

Sin lifts his brows. "And?"

"She can't go back to them." The Order could kill her. I don't dare say those words in front of Elli but surely Sin knows this.

I really need Ellison to go away for a few minutes so we can discuss this further.

I'm very afraid for Lainie's safety. I don't think it matters that Torrence is dead. "Her husband has friends in high places," I say.

"He does indeed."

"His reach is long and she's going to need help."

"I'm guessing you mean ours?"

"I'd like her to stay with us until she can make other arrangements."

He's quiet. I'm hoping that means he's thinking it over rather than coming up with a way to tell me no.

I haven't had the opportunity to tell Sin about the days I was held captive by The Order. "Lainie has been very kind to me. I consider her a good friend. Offering her safe haven is the least we can do for the kindness she showed me."

"All right. I'll have Mitch stay at our flat with her until we can figure out something else."

I'm certain my sister will wonder why Lainie can stay at our flat but she can't. I need to offer an explanation. "Thane and Isobel have a guest house. I'm not comfortable asking them if a complete stranger can stay there, so it's better for them to host you."

"I'm a complete stranger to Sin's parents," Ellison says.

"Not really. You've never met, but you're my family. Isobel is a hostess at heart so she'll be thrilled to have you. And their guest accommodations are luxurious. There's nothing to not love about it. You'll probably want to stay indefinitely."

"I don't want to put them out."

"I'm certain they won't mind a bit."

"My mum adores Bleu," Sin says. "She'll do anything for her."

Ellison needs convincing. "And she'll adore you as well."

"Okay, okay. Stop twisting my arm."

"How long do we have the pleasure of your company?" Sin asks.

Ellison adjusts in her seat and clears her voice. "There are circumstances surrounding my visit. I haven't worked all of that out just yet."

Taking ecstasy once will be a trivial offense in Sin's book but Ellison doesn't need to see how unconcerned he is about it. "There's no need to hash all of it out again. I can fill Sin in on the details later."

"Bleu tells me she'll be on bed rest. She's going to need someone with her around the clock so I'll stay as long as she needs a caregiver."

No. That's the last thing I need. "You're here to be my sister, not my nurse. We can hire someone to do that."

"I'm your sister and I'm a nurse. It's silly to hire someone you don't know when I can take care of you. Think it over before you immediately say no."

Who am I kidding? She isn't going to take no for an answer.

Sin interrupts. "All right, then. I'll have Jamie take you to Agnes's to gather your belongings and then he'll drive you to my parents' house."

"Ah, Jamie." She looks dreamy eyed. "Can't say I'll mind being stuck in a car with him again."

She need not go there. "Don't get any ideas. He's all wrong for you."

"He's hot. That's never wrong. What does he do?"

And here we go. "He's a doctor, last year of specialty training in emergency medicine." Jamie fits Ellison's type perfectly—handsome doctor—so I can predict this is going to be trouble. "Don't even think about it."

"Why not? Is he gay?"

"You know, I've often wondered the same thing," Sin says without the hint of a smile.

Ellison has no idea he's kidding.

"Fine, if that's his thing. I only asked because I never want to waste my time again on a guy who prefers the company of men." Her former boyfriend used her as a cover to hide his homosexuality—or bisexuality—from their coworkers. Either way, it's clear she's still harboring some pain about it.

"Sin is pulling your leg. Jamie isn't gay but his specialty

traineeship keeps him very busy. He doesn't date. Work comes first so you shouldn't waste your time pursuing him." The truth is I have no idea how Jamie feels about medicine.

"Loving what you do isn't a personality flaw."

I shouldn't have worded it that way. Ellison has a strong attraction for doctors who are passionate about medicine. It's always the common denominator with her and any man she dates.

I look to Sin for help with discouraging her.

"Jamie fucks around whenever he feels like it. He's not really into dating or relationships," Sin says.

Shit. That's not at all what I needed him to say about Jamie. Ellison loves a challenge.

My husband and I typically do well on our nonverbal communication but we must work on it where Ellison is concerned.

"I just texted Jamie. He's in the waiting room with Mum and Dad but says he's about to leave."

"Then I guess you should take Ellison out to meet Thane and Isobel and make the arrangements."

"I'm certain Mum and Dad will want to stay here but it won't be a problem. Their housekeeper should be there today. She can help Ellison get settled in."

Ellison comes to me with open arms. "God, I'm so relieved you're okay." She puts her hand on my abdomen and pats it. "And these two little peanuts."

"I'm happy you're here." Her presence causes huge problems I can't even begin to address but I'm still thrilled to have her here.

"Me too. We have months of catching up to do." She kisses my face. "I'll be back as soon as I'm able to get a ride. How should I handle that, by the way? A taxi?"

"Sin will give you his number. All you have to do is call when you're ready to come and he'll make the arrangements to get you here."

"Sounds like Sinclair knows how to make things happen."

She has no idea. And I hope she never does. "Sometimes."

"Should I expect jet lag?"

"Definitely, so don't feel like you have to get here early. Sleep in."

"I'll probably send my driver for you," Sin says. "His name is

Sterling."

Ellison spins around. "You have a driver?"

I haven't volunteered a bit of information about my life in Edinburgh, and Ellison hasn't asked. I'm sure she's been under the impression that my lifestyle with Sin is similar to the one we had growing up. It's not.

I have a strong feeling every assumption my sister has about my life as Mrs. Sinclair Breckenridge is about to change. And not for the better.

CHAPTER SIX

SINCLAIR BRECKENRIDGE

THE LIVING ROOM WALLS HAVE CHANGED FROM OFF-WHITE TO LIGHT STEEL GRAY since Bleu was home.

"Wow. Looks great in here. No one will ever be able to tell that there was once a bloody message smeared all over that wall."

"Mum picked it. She suggested we keep it neutral since we'll be putting the flat on the market as soon as we find our house."

The last conversation we had before The Order kidnapped Bleu was about buying a new house for our growing family. I go to her from behind and hug her gently. I lace our fingers and press my head to hers as I search for a way to put my thoughts into words. "You will never know how terrified I was for you." My palms migrate to her still-flat stomach, taking her hands with mine. "And our little ones."

She twists in my arms so we're face to face. "I need to tell you everything that happened."

She isn't aware that I already know what Torrence tried to do to her. "Your doctor told me about the findings of your exam."

"I need to tell you everything so I'm certain you understand exactly what happened."

This isn't necessary. "I don't need you to torture yourself about what he did by reliving it."

"Torrence tried to rape me. But I was able to stop him."

"You don't have to do this for me, Bonny. I don't need to hear it to be okay."

"I need to do it for me."

She tugs on my hands, leading me to our sofa. "We struggled for a minute. He was really weak so I easily got him into a chokehold. It was almost too easy. The man had no upper body strength. I was literally only seconds away from choking the life out of him when his men came into the room and stopped me. As you can imagine, he was pretty pissed off so he told them to beat me. The anemia from the pregnancy weakened me so I wasn't able to fight. All I could do was curl into a ball on the floor to try to protect our babies."

I hope she isn't feeling as though she didn't do enough or that I'm disappointed. "You survived and you kept them safe. You did what you could and they live because of the way you protected them."

"I know I had no other choice, but I needed you to know that as well."

"Bonny. I know you'd give your life for these babies, just as I would. Never underestimate my opinion of you again."

"I'm not a bit sorry you took his life."

Neither am I. And that is why we make the perfect couple. "I'm not the forgiving kind but that's even truer when it comes to someone hurting my family."

I get up. This time it's me tugging on her hands. "Come. The doctor released you to home with the stipulation that you'd remain on bed rest. And you agreed."

"He said modified bed rest. There's a difference."

"Brief showers and quick visits to the toilet is what he said. This is neither."

"I'm fine, Breck."

Like it or not, she can get ready for me to be on guard. She will do as the doctor advised as long as I'm around. "You are, but we're not taking any chances until the tear in the placenta is healed."

"I suppose I have no choice but to allow you to be overprotective after this week's events."

Damn right. "And I suppose I'll allow you to believe you have a choice."

"Ah. Mr. Breckenridge is a witty one today."

"As is Mrs. Breckenridge."

She comes to a stop at the office door and peeks in at her wall of suspects. "I'll need to solicit Debra's help with the investigation since

I'll be out of commission for a while."

"I think that's one of the better ideas you've had in a while."

"How do you feel about temporarily turning the office into a bedroom for Lainie? Just until she figures out what she wants to do."

My actions had a direct domino effect on Lainie's life. I killed Jason, which led Torrence to rid himself of his wife and take Lainie as a breeder for his next heir. Although he was the one who abused her, I harbor guilt about the things that happened to her. I can't turn her away. "I think that's a very good idea, Bonny. Honorable and generous."

We enter our bedroom and Bleu releases a long, drawn-out, "Aww."

She goes to the bed and picks up the two Scottish teddy bears I've left for her. Both are wearing kilts, one in red and black plaid, the other in green and navy. "You remembered."

"Only Scottish bears for our babies."

"These are their first gifts. I love both."

"I bought them while you were in the hospital but …" I don't want to finish the sentence. It makes it too real.

"It's okay. You can say it."

I put my arms around her. "The fear of losing them made me realize I wanted these little ones more than my next breath. I was wrecked when I thought you were losing them. And even though the imminent danger is over, I'm still scared."

"Dr. Kerr said the placenta will grow to cover the tear and clot. The problem will mend itself as long as I keep my activity to a minimum. So they're going to be fine."

"If the key is keeping your activities limited, I will see to it personally." I gesture to the bed. "Sit."

I go to her set of drawers and take out a cotton nightgown, her black yoga pants, and her favorite concert T-shirt. I hold each up on display. "Which do you want, milady?"

"The yoga pants since I probably won't get to wear them much longer."

"You think you'll outgrow them soon?"

"I have no idea what to expect with one baby, much less two. But I'd think twice the babies means growing twice as big."

"I need to replace the pregnancy book I bought for one about twin gestation."

"I turned seven weeks today, so we should read it tonight. Make a bedtime ritual out of it."

I like that idea. "It's a date."

I crouch before her. "Foot up."

"I'm not helpless. I can take my own shoes off."

She should get ready for some pampering. It's happening whether she likes it or not. "Hush, Bonny. I'm doing this. You're my wife and I want to take care of you."

"Yes sir, Mr. Bossy Pants." She obeys, lifting her feet.

"I've missed home." Me too. We haven't been here in a week.

I pull back the linens. "In you go, china doll."

She climbs in and I cover her. "I have a ton of work to do. Can I get you anything before I start?"

"Will you work in here with me?" She bats her lashes playfully and I turn to putty in her hands.

I'll get zilch work done in here with her. "I shouldn't. We both know you'll distract me."

"Not the way I'd like to." She shouldn't be making sexual innuendos. It's going to be a long time before that happens again.

"Not the way I'd like you to, either, but it'll wait." Modified bed rest includes pelvic rest. That's medical terminology for no sex. "Hello, abstinence. Nice to see you again. It's been a while."

Bleu is undeniably amused, the proof in her laughter. "Anticipation, Breck. It's the best kind of foreplay. Just think about how good it'll be when you finally get it again."

Those words sound very familiar. "I haven't forgotten how much you enjoy making me wait."

"I never enjoyed it. You just thought I did."

"I know. All part of your master plan to make me see you were worth the wait. And you were. And this time will be too." The end result will be babies. They'll be worth every minute.

"What are you hoping for? Boys, girls, or one of each?"

I'm afraid to say one way or the other. Once it's out there, I can't take it back. "I'll be thrilled with whatever we get."

"That's what everyone says. I want to know what you see when you envision our family."

There's no point in not being honest. "I see us with a combo package. A boy and girl."

"Me too. But like you said, I'll be thrilled with whatever we're blessed to have."

"You're going to be an excellent mother."

"I wish I had one of my moms here to help."

She won't be alone. My mum thinks of her as a daughter. I think she probably likes Bleu better than she likes me. "You'll have my mum. She'll be more than happy to help. And I strongly suspect you're going to have your sister around for a while."

Ellison is insisting she be Bleu's caregiver while she's recovering. I don't think she has the intentions of leaving anytime soon.

"I'm not sure what I'm going to do about that. I'm afraid my attack has given her a small taste of what losing her only remaining family member would look like. She's terrified of being alone, so much so that she's mentioned staying long-term."

Before Bleu and I married I was very decided. Ellison could never know about us. She could never visit. But now I see a side I didn't before. "What do you want?"

"I'd love nothing more than for my sister to stay, but we both know why that's not wise."

Bleu misses her sister terribly. If she wants her to be here, I can make that happen. "We can't keep our world a secret if she decides she wants to stay permanently."

"No. Ellison can never know about The Fellowship."

"Harry was very understanding. Ellison might be as well."

"My father understood your way of life because he had a career that demanded he be educated about all the ins and outs of the criminal world. My sister is clueless. In her head, this kind of life is fictional."

Bleu fails to see the possibilities. "You can be exceptionally close-minded at times."

"Like someone else I know."

I want Bleu to be happy and I know having her sister near will do that. "Think about it."

"I'm not. To tell Ellison about our life would be to make her part of our world. I'd be taking her choice away once I told her about it. I won't do that to her."

"You weren't expecting to but you fit perfectly into this world. She could as well. You might be surprised."

"Ellison is soft. She's not cut out for this life. It would eat her alive."

I think my wife is taking her role as big sister a little too seriously. "She was raised by Harry MacAllister. She can't be that delicate."

"I beg to differ. Besides, she couldn't become one of us without initiation. Someone would need to step forward and accept responsibility for her. No one is going to go through endurance so my sister can be part of my life."

"Maybe not, but she's attractive and her company is pleasant. It's possible there's a brother out there who would do it because he wants Ellison for himself. Perhaps you should be open-minded about bringing her into our circle."

"I'm the first initiate of my kind. We didn't get a lot of shit about it. But you're a leader. You think the brotherhood will accept this as a new means for bringing females into The Fellowship when it's not a leader involved?"

"They will if the leaders tell them it's an acceptable method."

Bleu looks hopeful for the first time. "If I tell Ellison, it must be a secret. No one can find out she knows in case she balks. Because that's a real possibility."

"Whatever you say, Bonny. Your game. Your rules."

I'M SITTING IN THE CORNER CHAIR OF OUR BEDROOM, MY FEET PROPPED ON THE ottoman with my laptop on my legs. I've gotten much more work accomplished than expected. That's probably because Bleu has been asleep for the last hour.

We aren't home three hours when our first visitors arrive. Miraculously, the bell doesn't wake my sleeping beauty. She must still be exhausted from the trauma her body has been through.

"Unfuckingbelievable," I mutter beneath my breath as I get up. Who the hell is showing up unannounced?

I discover Ellison standing on the other side of my front door with

Jamie holding what I assume are her bags. A lot of them. "Oh, good. You've already made it. I was afraid we might have beaten y'all home."

Ellison walks past me and into the living room. "I love this decor. Understated class."

She stands in the middle of the room, hands on her hips. "I know Bleu didn't do the decorating but it's totally her style. She doesn't do froufrou."

Jamie holds out two of Ellison's bags for me to take. "Sorry. She wouldn't let me call. She wanted her arrival to be a surprise."

"Since when do you let anyone tell you what you can and can't do?"

"Have you met her?"

Jamie already has her figured out. "Aye. Quite the princess."

"I'd go with queen."

"My apologies for putting her off on you these last few days."

"She really wasn't a problem. I enjoyed her company during our drives. She's ... interesting."

"I couldn't trust my wife's sister to anyone but you or Leith. And frankly, I didn't have a lot of confidence that Leith wouldn't try to get into her knickers."

"You're wise for that. She's a very fit lass." Seems Jamie is taken by her beauty.

Ellison comes back into the foyer. "The guards from the hospital are here. In your apartment."

"I extended their services to home. I don't want Bleu to be without protection when I'm away at work."

"But you're here now. And so are they."

"Their services are paid for, so I'm utilizing them."

"I'm beginning to think there's more to this mugging than anyone is telling me."

Another smart MacAllister woman. "The mugger took Bleu's purse so he knows where we live. This area of Edinburgh is known for being occupied by wealthy residents. He'll know we have money and could possibly get ideas about coming back for more. I'm not taking any chances where Bleu's safety is concerned."

"That makes perfect sense. Looks like you can afford it, so why not?"

Ellison reaches to take her bags from Jamie. "I can get them."

"It's all right. I don't mind taking them to the guest room for you."

"Thanks." Ellison grins and points at Jamie's back as she follows him. She fans herself and mouths, "Hot!"

Ellison spins around in the entrance to the hall. "Is Bleu in bed?"

"Aye. She's been asleep about an hour."

"Then I'll work on getting settled in while she's napping. You'll let me know when she wakes?"

"Sure."

Jamie returns from the guest room alone. "All right. She's all yours, mate."

"Again, I appreciate you taking care of her for us." I think he may have enjoyed it.

"Like I said, she was no problem."

I motion for Jamie to follow me into the living room so Ellison can't overhear our conversation. "Thank you for being sensitive to the fact that she knows nothing about the brotherhood."

"I gave no thought to you marrying Bleu, but now I see why a marriage outside of The Fellowship is discouraged. It can become a problem quickly. That's going to be a difficult charade to keep up."

"It'll be all right for a short time but Ellison has expressed interest in staying long-term."

"That poses a bigger problem. How do you plan to handle that?"

I sit and Jamie joins me. I'm hopeful it's a signal he has interest in Ellison staying. "We can't hide The Fellowship from her if she stays. Bleu is considering telling her about us."

"How would you pull off bringing a second American into The Fellowship?"

He's right in assuming it would need to be handled in a diplomatic manner. My wife's love for her sister won't cut it. "The same way I brought Bleu in. Initiation. If she stays, I'm confident the right man will step forward and volunteer."

Jamie's never been in love. He doesn't understand that it has no limits but I want the idea in his head so he can think about it. "A man will go to hell and back for the woman he loves. Trust me. I know what I'm talking about."

"I wouldn't know. I can't think of a single woman within The Fellowship I'd consider dating, much less claiming or marrying."

He should broaden his horizons. "There could be a new prospect soon."

"Why would I consider Ellison when I know upfront that being with her means getting the hell beat out of me?"

"You can't understand now because the feelings aren't there. But when they are, it changes everything." There would be no doubt in his mind.

"You forget I saw what Ferguson did to you. Some tingly feelings labeled 'love' aren't going to make me unsee that."

I hardly even remember the endurance now. "It wasn't so bad."

"Bullshit."

I have something interesting for him to consider. "Think about this. No other brother has ever had Ellison. Whoever gets her would be the first. And last."

He crosses his arms and sits back. Grinning. "I doubt any of us would be her first."

I'm about to blow his mind. "I wouldn't be so sure about that. Bleu was a virgin."

He shakes his head. "You're a fucking liar."

I hold up my palm. "Swear to God. I'm the first and only man to ever have my wife."

"A fucking virgin. I didn't think those existed anymore."

"Neither did I until she came along."

"Seeing you happy with Bleu gives me hope."

"It's all in finding the right one. Your Mrs. Breckenridge is out there. You just have to find her."

"IT FEELS GREAT TO BE HOME IN MY OWN BED WITH MY HUSBAND BY MY SIDE."

"Agreed. It's nice to not have your nurse standing over us bitching that I must get out of your bed."

Bleu lies beside me, her hands clasped over her tummy. "Read to me? I love listening to your accent."

"Like my Scottish brogue, aye?"

"It's hot."

I clear my voice and read the growth and progress for week seven from the pregnancy book I bought Bleu when we found out she was pregnant. I'm amazed by the changes our babies are experiencing this week. And also Bleu's body. Specifically her breasts.

I stop reading and look over at Bleu's chest. "I have not had the opportunity to properly inspect those."

She shimmies her gown up until both are bared and looks downward. "They're definitely bigger."

Yes, they are.

"They're magnificent." I reach out and palm one. But I'm not able to enjoy their new plumpness because my eyes are drawn to the purple bruises scattered over her body.

She's battered from the top of her head to the soles of her feet. It's nothing short of a miracle that our babies survived.

I look away because I can't stand seeing her body like that. It's evidence of how I didn't protect her.

I finish reading and place the book on my nightstand. "That's it until next time."

"Is the weekly read about our babies growth going to be the highlight of my week while I'm limited to bed rest?"

"I hope not because that sounds damn bleak."

"I might not be able to go and do but I can't be idle."

I have complete faith that Bleu can be productive from the bed. "Whatever you need, Bonny. I'm happy to get it for you."

"I have some things in mind. First, I'm going to have Debra come by every few days so we can brainstorm about the investigation. Two heads are always better than one. And I have a project I want to begin planning for the women of The Fellowship. Self-defense. They need to learn how to protect themselves."

She's expressed interest in that before. I'm happy to know she wants to execute a plan. "I think that's a wonderful idea."

My wife wasn't born Fellowship but you'd never know it by talking to her. I don't think she could embrace this world more if she were genetically one of us.

My phone vibrates next to the pregnancy book. There's typically only one reason someone phones me this late.

I look at the ID. Abram. Dammit. I have to take the call. "Aye?"

"Sorry to trouble you but the presence of a leader is required. Since I'm no longer in that role, I must drag you away from your injured wife."

He's enjoying this a little too much. "What has happened?"

"The Order killed a couple of our girls outside the casino. Sisters. Lewis Adamson's daughters. He's demanding swift justice."

Of course he is. "I'm on my way."

I end the call and lean over to kiss Bonny. "I have to go. The Order killed two of our women."

Her face is pained as she places her hand over her heart. "Oh no. Who?"

"Davina and Annis Adamson."

She narrows her eyes in concentration. "I can't recall them."

"Probably because they've been away at uni."

I dress and go back to Bonny when I'm ready to leave. I sit on the edge of the bed and take her hand. "Don't be afraid. Kyle and Blare will be here with you."

She brings my hand to her cheek. "That doesn't make me less frightened for you. You're going out to hunt down killers."

"I'll be fine."

I lean forward for a kiss and she catches my face in her hands. She holds me firmly in place so we're eye to eye. "Come back to me safely."

"Always."

CHAPTER SEVEN

BLEU BRECKENRIDGE

IT'S BEEN FOUR DAYS SINCE SIN RESCUED ME AND KILLED THE ORDER'S LEADER. Their organization may be in chaos but that won't stop them from avenging their leader's death. Killing these two women isn't it.

Every life within The Fellowship is of value but the deaths of two young women with no connection to the head of the brotherhood won't suffice as retaliation. They're going to want something bigger. Someone at the top.

Sin or me.

Only our deaths will satisfy them so I brainstorm why they'd attack two innocent women. I know they're cowards and prey upon the ones they consider weakest but it doesn't make sense. Their deaths cost us very little. Unless it's a trap to lure Sin into their clutches. Or away from me.

Kyle and Blare are here but I still take my Beretta from the drawer. I need to be armed in case The Order comes and manages to get through my bodyguards.

Lying in this bed makes me a sitting duck if they come through the door. I gather all the pillows from the bed and go into the closet. I make a pallet in the corner.

I have Ellison to think of as well so I go to her room. "Elli. I heard a noise. Come to my bedroom. Bring your pillow and bedspread."

We bed down in my closet to await Sin's return.

"Why isn't Sin here?" I hear the confusion in her voice.

"One of his clients was arrested so he was called away."

We have nowhere to run. I don't love that but it's better than being in the open without cover. At least here I'll be able to get the first shots on anyone opening the door.

I'm terrified for Sin. I pray he isn't walking into some kind of trap.

"Are your security guards here?" Ellison asks.

"Yes. Outside."

We're aren't in the closet for long when we hear gunshots. Several. My heart speeds like that of a galloping racehorse nearing the finish line.

I move to a sitting position and aim my gun for the door.

I hear voices in my bedroom. Maybe Kyle and Blare? I can't be sure so I remain still and firmly grip my Beretta.

I hear Sin call out my name. Bonny. Not Bleu.

"Sin."

He swings the closet door open and I rush into his arms. "My gut told me to come back to the flat to make sure you and Ellison were safe."

"I heard shots."

"There was an intruder. We presume it's the mugger." He doesn't have to explain further for me to understand. "Kyle and Blare are taking you and Ellison to my parents' house."

I look at Elli. "Pack a bag quickly."

I wait until she's gone to ask what happened.

"Kyle and Blare just killed three Order members."

My gut feeling was right. "They were coming for me."

"Aye. I think Annis's and Davina's murders were intended to draw me away from you."

I feel horrible. "Those poor women. They died as part of The Order's plot to take me again."

"That's why it's important for their father to know that I'm personally avenging their deaths. Now. Not later."

I don't like him leaving me again but I understand why he must go. It's his place to avenge the wrongs against our people.

That makes me proud.

DEBRA AND I HAVE HAD A PRODUCTIVE MEETING DESPITE IT TAKING PLACE IN MY bedroom. We've narrowed the suspects of my mother's murder to three. The mystery isn't solved but I feel us nearing the end of the tunnel. It's the same feeling I'd get when I was on the edge of closing a case.

Debra points to my violin on the dresser. "You play?"

"Yes. And more often since I'm confined to this bed." I have become well practiced the last few weeks. With Sin's help, I've mastered "Amanda."

"Sin plays as well."

She laughs. "I definitely wouldn't have pegged him for a violinist."

"Few do since it doesn't go along with the image he's created for himself."

Debra scoots to the edge of the chair as though she's preparing to leave. "Same time next week?"

"Yes. But before you go, I'd like to discuss an idea I'm kicking around."

She settles back into the corner chair of my bedroom, propping her long legs on the ottoman. "Sure."

Debra is tall and slim with shoulder-length brown hair. Not a bit of gray. She reminds me of Katey Sagal. Not in her Peg Bundy days but her badass Gemma role on *Sons of Anarchy*.

"Would you be interested in teaching self-defense classes with me for the women of The Fellowship?"

"You gonna teach from that bed?"

I probably would if I could. That's how strongly I feel about it. "I'll have another ultrasound in two weeks. I'm confident I'll be taken off bed rest if everything looks all right. I'd really like to get rolling with these classes as soon as possible. If I can prevent one woman from being harmed by an assault, then it's worth every bit of work and effort I invest. But I can't do it on my own. I'll need an able body to do the physical part. I'd pay you well."

Debra smiles for a moment before responding. "This life suits you. I wish Harry were here to see the person you're becoming."

Her words surprise me. "You think he would be proud?"

"Damn sure do. And I am too. I'd love to help you. Just tell me when and where and I'll be there."

I've already put a lot of thought into this. "We have a small warehouse currently not in use. I think Sin will let us turn it into a gym."

"You have it all planned out."

There are a lot of things churning in my head. "I have a lot of free time these days."

"It's serving the women of The Fellowship well."

I'm happy to know Debra thinks so. I hope the women I'm to lead will feel the same.

"You blew Harry's mind when you told him to train you so you could go after your mother's killer. What were you? Twelve? Thirteen?"

I wasn't aware Debra knew those kinds of details. "Barely twelve."

Debra laughs. "Harry didn't know what to make of you. And I didn't, either."

I'm not quite sure what to call this feeling I have in the pit of my stomach. Maybe shock mingled with a little dose of betrayal. I thought my secret with Harry was just that—a secret only we shared. "I didn't know Dad had told anyone."

"Your father thought you needed to see a psychiatrist but he was too afraid to take you. He feared you'd be taken away from him and placed in some kind of institution. He couldn't talk to Julia about it but he desperately needed advice. I was the only person he could trust. Don't be angry."

Anyone else would've taken me to a shrink. "Why didn't you try to convince Dad that I needed psychological help?"

"Someone murdered your mother and then left you for dead. I don't think anger and a drive for retaliation are irrational reactions. It's not as though you asked him to teach you how to kill an innocent person. I saw it as another form of justice."

Realization hits me. "You encouraged him to train me."

"Yes. Harry and I made a lot of decisions together about the proper way to train a young girl."

Debra has kept up with me all these years. It's all so clear now.

"I've watched you from afar for a long time. I was very happy when you reached out to me," Debra says

I don't know how I didn't see this before. "Harry asked me to watch over you while you were undercover within The Fellowship."

Then she saw everything. "You had to know that I was seducing Sin."

She laughs. "I saw that coming from a mile away."

"Thank you for not telling Dad." He would've completely flipped out. Probably would've gotten out of his hospital bed and come to Edinburgh to kill me and Sin.

"I've been there, Bleu. We all do what we have to in order to get the job done. Harry knew that, but it all went out the window when it came to you. You were his little girl."

"Always will be."

Debra leaves and first thing on my agenda is the quick daily shower my doctor granted me. For the first time in a while, I don't dress in yogas and a T-shirt. I have an engagement for the night.

The last three weeks of my life have been spent in one of two places: the bed or the sofa. Not fun. It's enough to nearly send anyone over the edge. That's why I'm so excited about hanging out and having girl time with my sister and friends.

But I'm sad. Lainie has made the decision to leave us. She fears The Order will discover her whereabouts, putting me and my babies in danger. Being in Edinburgh probably isn't the safest place for my new friend, but I will miss her terribly. At least Sin was able to negotiate a safe place for her in Dublin with The Guild. That means I'll still be able to see her.

Sin is such a sweetheart. So thoughtful. He has arranged a girls' night in with my friends during his Fellowship meeting this evening as a going-away party for Lainie. He bought four bottles of wine, plus a sparkling grape juice for me so I don't feel left out. He even arranged for Agnes to prepare hors d'oeuvres for us.

He's so good to me. And patient. I'll need to find a way to thank him for his thoughtfulness. I think I have just the thing in mind.

Of course I'm only allowed to move from lying in bed to lying on the sofa. But I'll take it without complaint. I've missed Westlyn and Lorna and our weekly girls' night out to the casino or to dinner. They're the ones I turn to when I need to giggle and have girlie conversation. Female friends. Something I've never had before. But I consider them my best friends aside from Ellison. I feel like I've missed a lot over the last few weeks, so I'm excited to catch up with what's happening in their lives.

Lorna is sitting on the couch, opposite me, my feet in her lap. She's painting my toenails. "Like?"

I let her pick the color. Bad decision. She went with flamingo pink. Yuck.

I hold my foot up, wiggling my toes. "It looks girlie. I probably would've chosen black. Or maybe a dark gray."

"I went with pink because I'm pulling for girls."

"Ellison wants girls so she can spoil them rotten. She says boys will be little mean asses."

"Oh, I'm spoiling them either way," Ellison says.

"They'll be precious if they're anything like their father. Sin was a sweet little boy. Always so kind to me," Westlyn says.

Lorna taps my ankle. "Pull your shirt up so we can see your belly."

I'm thankful the bruises covering my body are almost gone so I don't feel self-conscious showing them.

I pull it up but there's nothing impressive to see. I'm only ten weeks so my bump's maybe the size of a large orange. "Got a long way to go."

"I hope you have two girls because I don't want to see Sin take a boy from you. My mum told me how heartbreaking it was for Aunt Isobel to lose him and Mitch."

Oh my God. Tell me Westlyn didn't just say that in front of my sister who knows nothing about The Fellowship or what she's talking about.

I suspected having Ellison here long-term without telling her about The Fellowship would become a problem at some point, but it was a risk I was willing to take. I'm still not ready to make Ellison a part of this.

Ellison instantly perks up. "Sin would never take their son from Bleu. He adores my sister. Plus he knows she'd kick his ass before letting that happen."

Think fast, Bleu.

"Westlyn didn't mean that literally. Just that she hoped I had a girl so we'd have a mother-daughter bond. Isn't that right?" I lift my brows and bug my eyes at her.

"Exactly." Westlyn nods. "Of course I wasn't suggesting Sin would do something so vile."

Ellison seems satisfied with our explanations since she says nothing more about it. Disaster averted. For now.

Lainie chooses one of the opened bottles of white wine and refills her glass. "It's too bad you can't have some of this, Bleu. It's really good."

"It's okay. I'm not much of a wine drinker. I prefer Johnnie Walker."

"You and Sin both," Lorna says.

Lainie holds out the bottle. "Anyone need a refill?"

Ellison takes it and inspects the label. "You remember the girl who used to sing for Southern Ophelia? She quit because she married a guy from Australia. A winemaker. This is from his vineyard. Do you know who I'm talking about, Bleu?"

"Yeah."

"I saw Southern Ophelia perform at Coyote Ugly when they were first starting out. Long before they hit it big. Do you have any of their old music when she was still singing with them?"

"Yeah, but I think they only put out one album before she left."

"Put it on. I haven't listened to them in a while."

I connect my phone via Bluetooth to the speaker on the bookcase. I scroll through my music and play my favorite Southern Ophelia song, "Without a Goodbye." I wore this song out while Sin and I were apart—it fit us so perfectly. "This is their best one, in my opinion."

"Yes! I remember this one. So good, so good."

I doubt Westlyn, Lorna, and Lainie are familiar with it. "Ladies, this is country music at its best."

"Turn it up, Bleu. Loud."

My three friends listen to me and Ellison sing the chorus in unison. I think it's very possible that Ellison is a worse singer than I am.

"You lasses look like you're having a lot of fun." Agnes comes into the living room and places a tray of food on the cocktail table. "Mini ham and haddie pies. Scotch eggs and barbecued piggy scallops. There's more in the kitchen when you finish these off."

"Thank you, Agnes. Everything looks delicious."

"I'll be off now. Enjoy your night, lasses."

Ellison examines the cuisine Agnes has prepared. I can tell she doesn't find it appealing. "What the hell is this? I've never heard of any of it. And it looks as fucked up as a bologna Pop-Tart."

Oh God. At least she waited until Agnes left to express her distaste. I'd shit twice and die if she heard her say that.

"These are bacon-wrapped scallops. Nothing weird. And those are Scotch eggs. Just boiled eggs wrapped in sausage meat and breadcrumbs. Sort of like an egg-stuffed meatball. Agnes's are really good. But I'm not sure about the ham and haddie pies. I've never had those before."

Westlyn grabs one and pops it into her mouth. "My mum cooks these at least once a month. They're made with smoked haddock and bacon. The pie portion is breadcrumbs and grated Scottish cheddar cheese. These are quite delicious—even better than my mum's, although I'll never tell her that."

I'm really looking forward to catching up with Westlyn. "I haven't seen you much this semester. Tell us everything about uni."

Westlyn puffs her cheeks out and crosses her eyes. "Economics is tough. I'm not really sure why I chose that as my contribution."

"What about life outside of studies?"

"That's actually pretty spectacular." I'm guessing that being at the university is probably Westlyn's first opportunity at socializing with people outside of The Fellowship.

I recognize her goofy expression. I saw it on my own face several months ago. "I only know of one thing that would make school spectacular."

Westlyn bites her bottom lip, likely to keep herself from grinning. It doesn't work.

"You've met someone," I say.

She shakes her head. "It's nothing."

People don't look the way she does over nothing. "Your smile says otherwise."

"He's just a guy I have some classes with. We've talked a few times. It's no big deal."

"Is he cute?"

"Extremely."

"Does he make a point to sit next to you?"

"Aye."

He sounds like he's into her. "But he hasn't asked you out?"

"No, but I get the feeling he wants to."

"Nothing is wrong with you asking him out," Ellison says. I'm not at all surprised she would encourage Westlyn to do so.

She shrugs. "I've never done that before. I wouldn't know what to say."

"There's nothing to it. Just ask him if he wants to go out sometime. He'll say yes. You'll go to dinner and a movie. Or whatever you do on dates here. Then you'll find somewhere to fool around," Ellison says.

Westlyn is all giggles. "I haven't fooled around with a guy in so long, I probably wouldn't remember what to do."

Lorna grabs one of the reds for a refill. "I bet it's been longer for me than any of you."

Westlyn cackles loudly. "I don't know about that. Can you top eight months? And it wasn't even full-on sex. That's been over a year."

"I can't but I'm at five months. That's a record for me. Definitely the longest I've gone since I started having sex. I'm miserable," Ellison admits.

Westlyn laughs. "Then I'm still winning."

"Not for long. Can someone give me a drum roll, please?" Lorna says.

Ellison leans forward and taps rapidly on the cocktail table.

"Duh duh duh duh," adds Lorna. "Well over … two years. Going on three, but I'm not exactly sure because I've stopped keeping up with it."

Ellison slaps the table. "Holy shit, Lorna. You need a broom to clear out the cobwebs between your legs."

"Tell me something I don't know."

"Why so long?"

I'm interested to see how she'll explain this. "I decided I was finished letting men use me for their pleasure. I want someone who loves and treasures me. The only way to get that kind of man is to become a woman worthy of those things."

She didn't come out and say it, but anyone can read between those lines.

Westlyn squeals. "Oh my God, Lorna. You're in love."

Lorna wears the same goofy smile I saw on Westlyn's face earlier. "Maybe."

"I don't think there's a maybe about it. You are. And you have to tell us who he is."

Lorna shakes her head. "My secret to keep."

Westlyn groans. "No! That's completely unfair. You can't admit you're in love with someone and then keep it from us."

"Trust me. I can."

"We'll get it out of you before the night's over."

"I assure you there's not enough wine here to make me talk."

"We'll see about that," Westlyn says.

I don't want anyone to ask Lainie about her last sexual encounter so I steer the topic in another direction. "We're going to miss you, Lainie."

"And I'll miss all of you too. But Dublin isn't that far. We'll still see one another."

We all jump when there's a sudden commotion at the front door. It sounds like someone trying to push his way into the flat. We all go still and silent. My heart immediately takes off in flight.

"Is someone trying to break in?" Lorna asks.

"It could be that mugger. Get your gun, Bleu," Ellison squeals.

I get up from the couch and fetch one of my Berettas from its hiding place in my new end table's drawer.

Kyle and Blare are on guard outside since we're having a girls' night in. Surely they didn't let anyone get past them.

I take aim at the door, prepared to annihilate any persons passing through the doorway. Whoever it is, I'm ready for him.

CHAPTER EIGHT

SINCLAIR BRECKENRIDGE

My father steps onto the rostrum located at the back of the pub. "Thank you all for coming tonight. My son and I called this meeting so we might discuss future dealings with The Order. I'm going to ask Sinclair to step forward and take the lead."

"As you all know, Torrence Grieve kidnapped and beat my wife until she almost miscarried our child. Your feature leader."

Low murmurs spread throughout the room. I'm sure there's a lot of speculation about the other things they may have done to Bleu. I'd very much like to clear the questions in their minds, but Bleu wouldn't have me discuss a private matter in such a public way.

"I killed Torrence and the two men who beat her. No man who harms my wife will live."

The brothers erupt in cheer.

"Torrence has no successor so The Order is without a leader. Should they appoint one, he will not have been properly trained. He'll be inadequate for the job. That places their brotherhood in a weakened state. There's no better time for us to make a strike against them."

"What about numbers? Those haven't changed," a brother calls out. It's a legitimate concern since The Order is bigger than we are.

"That's one of the topics we brought you here to discuss tonight. You're all aware of our new alliance with The Guild from Dublin. The Order has a firearms customer our Irish friends would very much like to make their own. But like us, The Guild is smaller in numbers, so they have asked for our help."

Leith stands in the corner, arms crossed. "Why should we stick our necks out to help a new alliance that hasn't yet proven its loyalty?"

Good question. "Because we need them as much as they need us. Together we can wipe out our enemy. It's a beautiful plan. The Guild gets the buyer they want. We get all of The Order's remaining business associates. But most of all, we get the joy of destroying them, which means they no longer attack the women of The Fellowship."

Leith should understand this. He saw them go after Lorna and Greer at his pub.

No one's wife, daughter, or sister is safe. They need not think they are. "If you believe my wife is the only woman in danger, you're wrong. It could've just as easily been yours they took had the circumstances been different. They won't stop using that tactic against us because they know we won't retaliate using the women from their brotherhood."

"You're asking us to go to battle," Hewie calls out.

"Not battle. As your leader, I'm telling you it's time to win the war and be done with this."

The room hums with low murmurs as the brothers talk amongst themselves. "When will we do this?" Leith asks.

"My father and I will be meeting with the leaders of The Guild over the next several weeks. We want everything to align perfectly so you shouldn't expect this to happen soon. You can anticipate a few months of planning to ensure everything falls into its proper place."

"Won't we be giving them time to recover from their loss and become stronger if we wait?"

"It takes years to train someone to lead an organization the size of The Order. They have no teacher. I have no fear of them gaining strength before we attack."

I look around the room. "Other concerns?"

The discussions last nearly an hour, ending on a positive note. "You are our trusted leader and we will follow you to the death."

I stand on the rostrum looking over my men spread throughout the pub. They're punching their fists into the air while chanting, "To the death!"

My men are loyal, just as I expect. "Then I declare this meeting adjourned."

Though the meeting is over, I can't go home. Bleu is having her girls' night in with her friends. I don't want to ruin her fun.

I sit with Leith and Jamie in our usual spot but tonight Mitch has joined us.

"You did a fine job of getting the brothers fired up. I haven't seen them that excited in years," my brother says.

"It's time their fires were stoked."

"You killed Torrence Grieve. They have nothing but admiration for you. They'd follow you into hell if it's where you led them."

Greer doesn't come by to take our order. She simply appears with our usuals. "Johnnie Walker Black Label. Ballantine's. And two Guinnesses. Anything else I can get ye?"

"I think we're all good here."

Jamie waits until Greer walks away to ask why Lorna isn't serving us.

"She asked off for the night," Leith answers.

"None of your lasses are ever off during Fellowship meetings, especially your head barmaid. Your rule," Jamie says.

Leith shrugs. "She had something she wanted to do tonight."

"Did she suck your dick to get you to go along with that?" Mitch says.

Lorna once had a reputation for such things but she isn't like that anymore. "Shut up, Mitch."

I wait for Leith to come to her defense. I can't say I'd be disappointed if he punches my brother in the face for a comment like that. "Yeah and she sucked me off good too. She's the champion of deep-throating. You should have her do you sometime."

I don't understand why Leith is going along with Mitch's arsholery where Lorna is concerned. "Fucking liar. Lorna didn't suck anything. She's one of my wife's best mates. Bleu wanted her at their girls' night. Leith couldn't refuse the request of his leader's wife even if Lorna is his head barmaid."

Leith and Mitch have pissed me off. "You're both dicks for talking about her that way. I'd make you apologize but then she'd know what you said. That would only accomplish hurting her and I won't do that."

"Damn, Sin. Are you on your period or what?" The two of them are laughing at me.

"Fuck both of you."

"Don't get pissed off. We were just bullshitting." Leith didn't sound like he was bullshitting to me.

"Actually, I thought you were serious about Lorna sucking you off," Mitch says.

Jamie looks as disgusted as I am by their immaturity. "You're both arseholes."

Greer comes by to check on us. "Anyone need anything?"

Leith glides his hand up the back of Greer's thigh until it's beneath her skirt. "Not right now but maybe later."

"Just let me know. I'm here to serve you."

Leith watches her arse sway as she walks away. I'm reminded of the way he did the same with Bleu when she worked for him. It pisses me off all over again remembering the way he once put his hands on my wife.

"Do you fuck all your barmaids?" Jamie asks.

"I do if I feel like it."

He's full of shite. I know for a fact that he doesn't shag Lorna.

Jamie changes the subject. I'm grateful. I don't want to hear Leith's and Mitch's bullshit anymore. "What's going on at your place tonight?"

"Lainie is leaving in a few days. I secured a place for her with The Guild. I thought tonight would be a good time for the lasses to get together before she goes."

"If my sister is involved, they're painting their nails and talking about sex. Guarantee it."

If so, they're doing those things while drinking plenty of alcohol. "They're probably steamin'. I left four bottles of wine for them."

"There are four single women, three of whom I'm not related to, drinking lots of alcohol at my brother's place. They're talking about the sex they aren't having but would like to. That's where we need to be. Not here talking about who is or isn't sucking Leith off." That's probably the brightest thing Mitch has said all night.

"Think Bleu will mind us crashing her party?" I suspect Jamie is eager to see Ellison again. It's been a while.

My drinking companions are eager to see Bleu's friends. I shouldn't stand in the way of potential matches since that is part of my job as leader.

"I guess we can find out."

ONE HOUR AND MANY DRINKS LATER, I'M AT HOME KNOCKING ON MY OWN front door. The three numpties with me are drunk and looking for female companionship. I'm fairly certain they'll be out of luck. I'm the only one who'll find a playmate tonight.

Instead, make that a mate since very little playing has been going on for the last couple of months.

No answer at the door. "They probably can't hear us if they've had all that wine I left for them."

I beat on the door again.

"Why are you knocking?"

I have no idea. This is my flat. I should just walk in like I own the place. 'Cause I do.

I turn the knob but it's locked. "I don't have my keys." I ring the bell. "You should know now I'm blaming all of you if Bleu gets pissed off about this."

Ellison swings the door open and Bleu is standing beside her, gun in hand. "What the hell are you doing, Sin? Sounds like you're trying to break down the door."

"Sorry, Bonny. I forgot my keys."

Ellison scans the crowd, her eyes stopping on Jamie. "What are y'all doing here? Crashing our party?"

"We hope to," Jamie says.

She and Bleu turn, leaving the door open for us to come in.

"Look at that fit arse," Leith whispers. "Those MacAllister sisters are well bred."

"Shut up." I punch Leith in the chest. "One of those MacAllister sisters is my wife. You'd be wise to remember that."

"Never fear, mate. It isn't possible for a one of us to forget that Bleu is your wife."

We find the rest of the lasses in the living room doing mostly what we expected—painting nails and drinking wine.

Bleu points to the food. "Agnes made hors d'oeuvres. There's plenty if anyone's hungry."

Mitch grabs a handful. "Men are always hungry. And horny."

"We've drunk most of the wine already. Well, they have." Bleu lifts her glass. "Sparkling white grape juice for me so I don't liquor these babies up."

"Aye. The twins." I hear the sarcasm in Leith's voice.

He holds up the full bottle of Ballantine's he swiped from the pub. "We must make a toast for our fierce leader."

Everyone but Bleu gets a huge shot of Scotch.

Leith lifts his glass, everyone mimicking his move. "To Sin, his beautiful wife, and their two babies on the way. May our leader's life always be as perfect as it is today. May he always, as usual, get everything he wants."

Those words coming from anyone else might be welcome, but not from Leith. He comes off sounding like a jackarse.

"Cheers." Everyone turns the bottoms of their drinks up.

I meet Leith in the hallway on the way to the bathroom. "You know what, Sin? You're incredible. You couldn't even be average and give your wife one bairn. You had to show off and knock her up with two."

I can't take the credit for that. "Bleu's pregnant with twins because we couldn't conceive on our own. She had to undergo an in vitro procedure for us to have a baby. It wasn't my prowess as a lover that got my wife pregnant with twins. Whoever was holding the petri dish did that."

"Oh."

"We were told we might not be able to have our own children if we didn't do it now. It was scary as hell for a while. So you're wrong about everything always being perfect for me."

"I didn't know."

"It's not something we were planning to advertise."

"I'm glad it worked out for you."

"Thank you. We're very happy to be getting two since we weren't sure we'd even get one."

Leith gives me a half hug slap on the back. "Congratulations.

You'll be excellent parents. I mean that."

My mates are steamin' but the lasses are even further ahead. They started drinking hours ago and now they've added Scotch on top of their wine. They are going to feel like shite tomorrow.

"You look tired, Bonny."

"I am. Would it be terribly rude to leave them and go to bed?"

"No. They've drunk a shit ton of liquor. They don't care."

Bleu gets up from the sofa. "Sorry, guys. I'm calling it a night. These babies steal all my energy. You guys stay up and drink as long as you like. Sterling can drive you home or you're welcome to spend the night. You can figure out the sleeping arrangements as long as none of them include my bed."

Bleu locks the door behind us. "Just in case. I don't want any drunk wanderers finding their way into our bedroom."

"Good idea."

We finish our nightly rituals side by side in the bathroom and get into bed. "Want the lamp off or are you going to read?"

"You can leave it on."

Over the last few weeks, we've gotten into a habit of reading when we go to bed. I admit that for me, it began as a form of distraction. I enjoy it but it's a poor substitute for sex.

I still have a little buzz from the whisky but I take my book from the nightstand anyway and fall back into the story. Maybe that's why I barely notice the bed dipping next to me. But Bleu pulling back the covers to kiss my stomach just above the band of my sleep pants while her hand caresses me through the thin fabric gains my attention.

I lower my book and peek over the top. "What's going on down there?"

"If you don't know, then it's definitely been too long since we fooled around." I won't argue with that.

"What kind of fooling around are you talking about?" We're both very aware that penetration is off the table until further notice.

"Just a little something I want to do for you." She pushes her hand down the front of my sleep pants. She grasps my cock firmly and glides her fist up and down the shaft. I'm not fully erect but getting there fast.

I close my eyes and lose myself in the moment. I imagine my dick sliding in and out of her body instead of her fist. It's nowhere near as good but it'll do.

"I want to make you come."

Jerking yourself off is nothing like having your hot wife do it for you. "No worries. You are. Soon."

She alternates between long, slow strokes and quick short ones. Just when I get into the rhythm of one motion, she changes the movement and inhibits my orgasm. It's in-fucking-credible.

She's added something new to the mix—rubbing my balls. She's never massaged them this way before. "You like that?"

"Fuck yeah."

"I want to make you feel good."

"No worries, Bonny. I'm definitely riding the feel-good train."

"Want me to suck you off? I will."

I was already feeling the early beginnings of my climax so hearing her ask that is almost enough to make me blow. "You have a dirty mouth tonight."

"It could be dirtier." She leans over and licks my shaft from base to tip before sucking the head into her mouth.

Dammit. I would love nothing more than to feel her mouth all over me but there's no time. I tense, trying to hold back but it's no use. This feel-good train is about to derail. "Ohh. Stop. Stop, Bleu. I'm about to come. Right now."

And I do, barely a second after putting my hands on the sides of her face and pulling her mouth off my cock.

That was close. Another second and I think I would have gotten off in her mouth. "I'm sorry. I should have had you to stop sooner." But it felt so damn good.

"One of these days I'm not going to quit when you tell me to." I don't want that and she needs to understand why.

I rub my thumb over her bottom lip. "You're my wife. You'll use this mouth to kiss our children. It's not a receptacle for that."

She kisses the pad of my finger. "I don't like that other women have done pleasurable things for you that I haven't. It bothers me."

I'd like to tell her that no woman has ever been dear to my heart because she let me come in her mouth, but I'm certain that won't go over well. "I set you apart because I hold you in a different regard than other women. You're very special to me and this is one way I treat you as such."

Bonny will never be just another woman to me. She's my life. My love. My heart. My everything. Always.

CHAPTER NINE

BLEU BRECKENRIDGE

IT'S BEEN FIVE WEEKS SINCE MY THREATENED MISCARRIAGE. DR. KERR ASSURES US the danger of losing the babies to what he calls a marginal abruption has passed. The placenta has grown over the tear as he predicted. Everything appears normal on ultrasound and growing right on schedule.

I've had weekly scans for more than a month so we're watching our babies grow and develop from one week to the next. Without doubt, it is one of the most surreal moments of my life. "Oh my God. Look at that, Breck. They've grown so much."

He's glued to the screen. "It's amazing how much they've changed in seven days. They look more like tiny humans instead of tadpoles."

"Look at their tiny little hands and feet." It's unbelievable.

Sin gets up for a better look at the monitor. "Both look healthy?"

"Aye, from what I can tell. We should be able to determine their genders in a few weeks. Maybe not that long."

We haven't talked about finding out. "That seems really soon."

"Ye're slim so I'm able to see yer wee ones well."

It seems like it would be so much more special to discover their genders in the delivery room when we meet them for the first time. "I'm not sure I want to know what they are. How do you feel about being surprised?"

"I assumed we would find out, so I haven't considered the alternative," Sin says.

"I think the element of surprise times two would be so much fun."

"We have time to think it over." I'm not sure Sin's on board with me on this one.

"Dr. Kerr wants to see the results of the ultrasound before yer exam. I'll dictate a report for him now and send it over as soon as possible so we can get ye out of here at a reasonable time. Leave yer bottoms off in case he needs to do a physical assessment."

Ugh! I love coming to my appointments so I can see my babies but I hate the exam part. And I don't think Sin is excited to see another man touch me that way, even if it is for medical reasons.

I slide up the exam table to get more comfortable while we wait.

"I think Dr. Grabby Hands enjoys seeing you without your knickers a little more than he should."

"He has to check me to be sure everything is all right. It's nothing more than a job to him. He probably gets tired of looking at vaginas all day. I'm sure once you've seen one, they probably all look alike."

"I happen to think yours is pretty special."

"It pleases me to know you have fond memories of it."

"I'm really hoping Dr. Kerr tells us I can get reacquainted with it soon. Twelve weeks is a long time to be parted from my favorite playmate."

"I think I've been highly accommodating."

"Exceptionally so—and I'm damn appreciative of your generosity—but it's not the same. I miss the connection we have when we make love."

He's right. We share so much more than a physical bond. "Me too. But at least you get to have an orgasm. I get nothing."

"Don't forget that anticipation is the best form of foreplay, Bonny."

I think he enjoys saying that more than he should. "Says the husband who's getting hand and blow jobs while his wife's sexual frustration is escalating out of control."

"You're entering your fourth month. With any luck he'll give us the go-ahead since everything has been back to normal for several weeks."

"Fingers crossed." I want off bed rest even more than I want sex, but I keep that little tidbit to myself.

Dr. Kerr comes into the exam room. "Mrs. Breckenridge. How are you this week?"

"Excellent. I feel wonderful."

"Very good to hear. Nausea has subsided?"

"Haven't had any in two weeks."

"Good." He pulls on exam gloves—I know what's coming next. "Cold wet touch to your bottom and then some pressure." It's the same thing he says every week before checking me.

I lie on my back staring upward while Dr. Kerr does my pelvic exam. I distract myself by counting the ceiling tiles until Sin gains my attention by squeezing my hand. My grinning husband mouths, "Lucky bastard."

I mouth back one simple word I'm certain he'll understand. "Stop."

He's laughing at me. Again.

"Cervix is closed and thick as I would expect. No bleeding. Ultrasound is normal. I think you're fine to return to your normal level of activity."

He has no idea what my normal activities consist of or he wouldn't say that.

"No more pelvic rest?"

"It's fine to resume sexual activity."

I'm embarrassed to ask but I do anyway. "With orgasms?" Please, please, please say yes.

"Aye. Orgasms are fine but you should avoid vigorous intercourse to be safe."

Sin waggles his brows at me.

"I think we can schedule your next visit for two weeks since you've been complication-free."

I'm waiting in line to schedule my next prenatal appointment when Sin leans over to whisper in my ear. "Linsey can manage without me. I'm going to have her clear the rest of my workday."

This isn't surprising. "I thought you might."

"I want to spend the rest of the day reacquainting myself with you."

"I'm not sure how much reacquainting we'll get done. We have a houseguest and thin walls. You know neither of us do a great job being quiet." I'd die a thousand deaths if Ellison heard us making up for lost time.

"Fuck it. We'll get a room."

"And room service. I'm starving."

"Aye. You'll need plenty of fuel for what we're going to be doing."

I WATCH THE NUMBER ABOVE THE ELEVATOR DOORS INCREASE AS THE LIFT RISES TO our floor. Twelve. Thirteen. Fourteen. Three more to go. It's too many when your husband pins your body against him while his hand roams downward to rub between your legs.

He's fervent to say the least.

Warm breath moves over my ear. A tingle races down my spine and goosebumps erupt over my skin. I'm sure there's a camera on us right now. All elevators have them. "We're probably giving a thrill to whoever is watching the security footage."

"Don't give a fuck. The thrill I'm feeling is much more important to me right now."

The doors open and we sprint toward our room. Sin is so anxious his first three attempts at unlocking the door are unsuccessful. "Son of a bitch. The keycard isn't working."

I hold out my hand and he places the card in my palm. I slide it in and pull it slower. Click. "Open sesame."

"Fuck. That was sexy."

All I did was open a door. "I put the keycard in the hole and pulled it out."

"I know," he growls while pulling me through the door toward the bed.

We shed our coats and go to work on all fabric barriers preventing our bodies from being bare against one another. He undresses himself while I do the same, his eyes never leaving my body. "Shite. I may come before you get naked."

My eyes immediately drop to the crotch of his boxer briefs. He has a huge erection tenting his underwear with a wet spot covering the tip. "Don't you dare."

I undress faster. More than one stitch pops as I pull my dress over my head. Articles of clothing drop randomly to the floor with no regard for wrinkling.

I'm reaching behind my back to unfasten my bra when Sin comes to me. He grasps my panties and pushes downward until they fall to my feet. I kick them away and drop my bra next to them.

I glide my hands up Sin's arms until they meet behind his neck. His mouth possesses mine as we move toward the bed. In one fluid motion I sit and slide backwards. I lift my hair from my back and shoulders before lying down so it's spilling around me. He loves that.

I'm stretched side to side across the bed. Wet and wanting. Knees bent. Thighs spread wide.

Sin grabs my ankle and brings it to his mouth. He kisses the inner side. His hand glides up my calf to my thigh. "I love your legs."

"I love my legs when they're wrapped around you."

His mouth moves up my calf, spreading kisses in its path. "These are going to get a lot of exercise chasing after two bairns."

"I'm sure they will, but I hope they get a lot of exercise tonight keeping up with you."

"You'll get all the workout you want, but first I'd like to show my gratitude for your very generous mouth during our period of abstinence." His lips trail kisses up my inner thighs. "You were very good to me. Now I'm going to be good to you."

Sin crawls on to the mattress and grabs two of the extra pillows. "You know what I need you to do."

I absolutely do. He's going to wedge my bottom upward so his mouth can perform its duties to the fullest potential. He's full-service when it comes to oral. "Whatever you say."

He pushes my legs apart and nibbles each side of my groin. I think I may convulse from the ecstasy.

I've never wanted to feel his mouth on me so badly. I'll beg if it's what he wants. "Please."

"Please what?"

I'm trembling. "The teasing is killing me, Breck. No more. Please put your mouth on me before I die."

His warm wet tongue glides up my center slowly. "Ohh."

I fist his hair when he does it a second time.

"Is that what you want from me?"

"Yes! It feels so different from before. So much more sensitive." I read that a pregnant woman's erogenous zones are heightened during pregnancy. I thought it was bullshit. But now I see that I was wrong.

He continues licking me but it isn't just the center. He nibbles and sucks my outer lips, teasing me before moving back to the middle. I can't stop myself from rocking against his mouth. "Ho-ly shit!"

He wraps his arms around my thighs and holds me still while sucking my clit. First soft and then hard, alternating back and forth between the two.

Sweet torture.

It's been months since my last orgasm but I easily recognize the signs of its approach. "Oh. Oh. Oh. It's starting."

Sin sucks harder, making me come faster. I fist his hair and rock my hips to ride out the warm pulsations of pleasure. "Ohhh!"

Sin puts my legs over his shoulders and my toes dig into the muscles of his back. I tense, pulling him against me even harder. I can't get enough. I crave more. Need it.

When I spiral down from the high, my body goes limp. My face pulsates. Euphoric waves of warmth spread down my legs and arms. My hands tingle. All signs of a magnificent climax. "That was incredible."

I'm boneless, unmoving.

"We aren't done yet." He crawls over me and kisses my face. "Not even close."

He pushes his body away from mine and looks down at my belly. He caresses it with his hand. "Your baby bump feels like a grapefruit pushing against my stomach. You didn't have that the last time we did this."

Hearing him say that is a reminder of how long it's been. It seems like forever ago.

He adjusts so he's holding most of his weight off me using his arms. "Is it too much pressure? Am I hurting you?"

"No."

"Are you uncomfortable?"

I reach behind his neck and pull him down so our bodies are pressed together again. "I'm fine, Breck. I'll tell you if that changes."

He kisses me hard. I part my thighs so his erection is pushing against my entrance. I cross my ankles behind his back and squeeze him closer. I lift my pelvis and his tip barely enters me. It isn't enough. I'm desperate to have him inside me to the hilt. "I really want you to fuck me."

He pulls out. Not the direction I'm looking for. "I'm terrified that fucking will hurt you or the babies."

"Not going to happen."

"You're my china doll. It would kill me to harm you in any way."

I grab his face, forcing him to look at me. "Listen to what I'm saying. I won't break."

He doesn't look convinced.

"Okay. It probably isn't a good idea to bend me over the arm of the sofa or put me face down on the bed with my ass in the air. But we'll find what works." I reach between us and grasp his cock. I position it at my entrance and wrap my legs around him again. "Ease in if it scares you. Start out slow and shallow and build up to deeper and faster as you become more comfortable with it."

He's unmoving.

"Please, Breck. It's safe. Dr. Kerr said we could do it and we both want to. Making love is a huge part of who we are. We need this."

"You will immediately tell me if anything hurts or doesn't feel right."

"Absolutely."

He relaxes and breathes deeply. "Okay. I'll try slow."

I glide my fingertips down his face. "Into me … you see."

He catches my hand with his and presses it against his cheek. "Into me … you see."

He enters me slowly and squeezes his eyes shut. "Oh fuck, you feel so good." He thrusts slowly several times. "So wet and tight."

I rock my hips with him slowly. I'm afraid of spooking him if I'm too aggressive.

What they say is true. You don't know what you've got until it's gone. "God, I've missed this."

His face is buried in the bend between my neck and shoulder. All of his weight is supported by his arms pressed into the mattress on each side of my head. "I'm not going to last long."

"I'm pretty sure we didn't rent this room with the intention of doing it once."

Sin tenses and groans. It's the only sign of his climax since he doesn't thrust deep or hard as per his usual finale.

Neither of us is out of breath or slick with sweat. I wish we were.

He rises and throws the covers back, patting the side of my hip. "Lift."

"What are you doing?"

"It feels like something's oozing out."

"I'm sure it is. It's called semen. And probably a lot of it since we haven't had sex in so long."

He lowers himself and hovers above me, our bodies barely touching. It's maddening. "I just needed to be sure it wasn't blood."

I pull him closer but he holds himself steady. "I love that you're concerned for our safety but I really hope you get over this fear soon."

"Forget it. I'll never get over my worry or fear for your well-being or that of our children."

He kisses me quickly and rolls to lie beside me. He laces his fingers through mine before resting our clasped hands on his chest.

"There's so much more to us than sex, but I must admit, I've missed doing that terribly." He brings my hand to his mouth for a kiss.

"Me too."

We lie side by side, simply enjoying post-orgasmic bliss. It's more relaxing than any pill or drink.

My mind wanders from one topic to the next but lands on my sister. "I've been thinking of Ellison a lot lately."

"She appears to love being in Edinburgh. I'm under the impression she doesn't intend on leaving anytime soon."

"Not before these two make an appearance."

"Realistically, do you think your sister will be able to leave after they come?"

The babies and I are the only family Ellison has. And there's nothing waiting for her at home. I know where this conversation is going. "I'm not sure how to tell her about The Fellowship so she doesn't flip out."

"Is it possible you're giving Ellison too little credit, just as you did Harry?"

Sin was right about my dad, which means I was wrong. I can admit that. "Maybe."

"It's your choice but I think you should do it soon if that's the direction you're leaning toward. Telling her after our hand has been forced won't go as well."

"I think my decision has evolved into how to tell her rather than if I will."

"Do you want me to help you explain everything to her?"

"No. It's probably best if I do it alone. She's going to have a lot of questions. It's important for us to be able to speak freely. I'm afraid she'll feel uncomfortable if you're there."

"That's understandable, but I'm always willing to take care of it if you should decide it's what you want."

"Right now, there's only one thing I want." I rise and put my leg over Sin so I'm straddling him.

He's afraid of hurting us—and I understand that—but he needs to see that I'm durable. That's why I'm taking control this time.

I lean down and kiss the side of his neck. "Been long enough for round two?"

He thrusts his hips up so his erection pokes me. "You tell me."

Good. He sounds more confident. And playful.

I reach between us and grasp his cock, positioning it at my entrance. "Easy, Bonny."

"I'll be careful." I sink down slowly and he grabs my hips, preventing me from going all the way.

I put my hands on top of his. "I'm in control."

I lean down to feather kisses over his face and he becomes less tense. I sink deeper before lifting my hips to slide him out. "That's it. Just lie back and enjoy the ride."

Four rounds of sex over six hours. The last time was a concession on Sin's part—because I begged. He's satiated but I'm not. My hormones are raging.

He sits on the edge of the bed to put on his prosthesis. I'll never get him to agree to another go once he secures his leg. "One more before we have to leave?" I kiss the side of his neck to encourage an affirmative. "Please, Breck."

"No, Bonny. We did it three times more than we should have."

"I beg to differ."

He twists around to kiss me. "I need to take you home. I have a meeting in an hour."

He hasn't mentioned a meeting. "I thought you cleared your workday for us."

"I cleared my day at the office. I have Fellowship business to tend tonight."

I don't always love the affairs he's in charge of. "I hope it's not another meeting about a gentlemen's club."

"Nothing like that. A brother has asked me to meet with him at Duncan's about a match with Lorna."

"In the pub of the man in love with her?"

"You don't have to tell me how fucked up it is. But maybe Leith's eyes will be opened to see what's right in front of him."

I'm confused about so many things when it comes to Sin's friendship with Leith. It's different from his with Jamie. Something happened and I'm guessing it has everything to do with Lorna since that tends to be a sore topic between the two. "You said that there was history with you, Jamie, Leith and Lorna but you never told me what it was."

"There's a reason for that."

I hug him from behind. "It can't be so bad."

He sighs. "You're wrong. What we did was fucked up."

"I can always handle the truth. The not knowing is what kills me." I say the words but my heart pounds. He's told me it's bad. Do I really want to know this secret they share?

He drops his head as though he's ashamed. I've never seen this reaction from him. "It isn't pretty. I don't want my past with Lorna to change the way you feel about me. Or her. She's one of your best friends. You treasure that friendship, and she does as well. I don't want to see a problem develop between you."

"What's passed is past."

"You say that now."

Okay. They've had sex. It happened before me so I can move beyond that. "Can't you see that you're choosing to be loyal to them by keeping this secret from me?"

"I'm not. I'm making the decision to shield you from something that is so very ugly. Protecting you is what I do. Never mistake that as me being loyal to someone else. My devotion belongs only to you.

Always."

That's not how it feels. "I'm a rational adult. I swear I will not hold your past against you."

"Leith, Jamie, and I were young and stupid. We were boys trying to be men. Lorna was starved for attention. So we gave it to her."

"In the form of sex."

"No. In the form of fucking. A lot."

It's not something I'm proud to hear but I'm not sure why he thought I couldn't handle this. "I guessed as much judging by the things you've said."

"You haven't nearly guessed all of it. When it was happening, I wasn't thinking of anything but the present. I never considered the possibility that I'd one day have this beautiful woman in my life that I adore. By some miracle she'd agree to be my wife and become the mother of my children. I never imagined I'd be sitting here searching for the words to explain the things I did with one of her best friends."

I don't know what to say to that.

He breathes in deeply and releases it slowly. "We took it much further than we should have."

I will be sick if he's talking about rape. "As in what?"

"We were all with Lorna at the same time."

I need a clearer explanation. "When you say at the same time, do you mean the three of you were sleeping with her over the same period of time or do you mean she let the three of you gangbang her?"

He doesn't answer right away. "It sounds even worse when you use that word but aye. We had lots of three-on-one sex. But it was always voluntary."

This isn't what I was expecting. I feel queasy.

"It was her suggestion. Of course the three of us were numpties and thought it was a fantastic idea. But it was after her parents were killed. She was hurting and looking for love and security. We used her for sex. Not my proudest moment." He shakes his head. "If we have a daughter and any man did to her what we did with Lorna, I would kill him."

I feel minimally better knowing it was Lorna's idea instead of them talking her into it. "I hope you all used condoms."

"Every time." At least they used some intelligence.

My God. What was Lorna thinking she would accomplish by doing that?

"I don't need details but explain how the foursome came to an end."

"Jamie lost interest. So it was me, Leith, and Lorna. After that, the dynamics changed among the three of us."

This is totally predictable. "Anyone knows that you put two males and one female together in a sexual situation and there's going to be a pissing contest. It's the nature of testosterone."

"That sounds like a fair assessment of what happened. Leith began competing with me for Lorna. He wanted all of her attention."

I know my husband. He doesn't like losing. "So a rivalry was born among best friends."

"Aye. A rivalry to see who she'd choose for sex. That's all it was for me. Never a battle for her heart."

"But you think it was more for him? A duel for her love?"

"I do now. I think he fell in love with her and saw me as the one keeping them apart."

Even then, Leith and Lorna knew Sin would one day be their leader. I highly doubt either of them would have told him to bow out so they could be together. "What brought it to a head?"

"Ugh," he groans. "These aren't things a husband is supposed to tell his wife."

He has this wrong. "They are when you're my husband."

He puffs his cheeks out as he exhales. "Leith walked in on me and Lorna in the stockroom at the pub. He'd seen us have sex on many occasions so I didn't think a thing of it. But Leith was never the same after that. Even today, it's like we pretend to still be best mates but he hates me."

Men are so stupid sometimes. "That's because you were having sex with the woman he loves."

"That was more than two years ago. Never again after that night. I swear."

This is a damn mess. "What do you plan to do about this brother proposing a match with her?"

"I want to make this right for Leith and Lorna. I'm going to give him one final chance to do what he should've done years ago. If he doesn't, then that's on him. I can't spend the rest of my life blaming myself because they aren't together."

What Sin did was wrong. No doubt about it, but he shouldn't continue holding himself responsible for Leith and Lorna being apart. "They're mature adults now. They can make their own decisions about what they want from one another. That's why I'm calling her. She should know what's happening so she can make an informed decision about her destiny. Clearly, fate shouldn't be left solely in Leith's hands in case he decides to fuck it up again."

CHAPTER TEN

SINCLAIR BRECKENRIDGE

We drop Bleu at home and Sterling drives me to Duncan's. I'm not scheduled to meet with Noah Wallace for another hour. I'm intentionally early since I have business to discuss with Leith. I'm giving him another chance to claim what he wants before I move on to another suitor for Lorna.

I sit at our triad's table. The vinyl-covered seat beneath my arse doesn't have time to warm before Lorna plops down across from me. "Bleu called."

"I know. She told me she would."

"Please tell me why it is that I've known you my entire life but it's your wife who calls to inform me that you have a meeting with Noah Wallace to discuss a possible match between us."

She's angry. I wonder if it's because I haven't told her about the meeting with a brother concerning her future or because it's not Leith who has approached me.

"Noah asked to set up a meeting to discuss his interest in you. You aren't involved with anyone so I'm obligated to hear him out."

"You aren't my father."

"But I am your leader and no one has claimed you."

Her mouth twists. "As much as I appreciate you pointing that out, I'm already quite aware."

I'm handling this all wrong. "I wasn't trying to be unkind. I only meant that if there's interest in you by a brother, I have to explore it. It's part of my duty. My father and I are accountable for securing a good match for you because you don't have a father to do so. I think you'd prefer I make the arrangement rather than my dad."

My father's marriage was arranged. Although he and my mother aren't in love, he still firmly believes in arranged marriages because they often benefit The Fellowship. If things don't work out with Leith, at least I would try to find Lorna a match where there was some kind of affection.

"Maybe I don't want a husband. Have you ever considered that perhaps I'm happy with the way my life is?"

She forgets she's already confided her discontent. "But you aren't. And I feel I'm to blame for that."

"How could you be the cause for my unhappiness?"

It's time to get real about what happened. "I think you and Leith fell in love after Jamie left the group, but I fucked it up by being the third wheel."

Lorna's eyes grow large. I've caught her off guard. "I loved Leith but he didn't love me back."

The more I learn about love from Bleu, the more I see things for how they really are. "He loved you then and I think he still does."

She's shaking her head. "No man would sit back and watch his best mate have sex with the woman he loves. It doesn't work like that."

She's exactly right. "That's why it all ended. He couldn't stand it anymore."

"Well, he's not the only one. I couldn't stand it anymore, either."

She's referring to me. "I'm sorry for everything. What we did was wrong, but I want to make it right for you now."

Her eyes well with tears. "I disgust him. Did you know that I work with him five, sometimes six days a week and most of the time he can't even look me in the eyes?"

I've never noticed Leith being that way with her.

"I'm going to give you a bit of advice, Sin. Make sure Bleu never finds out what we did because I can promise you this. You never want to see revulsion in the eyes of the person you love when they look at you."

"Bleu knows."

"No!" Lorna slaps her hand on the table several times. "No!

How?"

"I told her."

"No!" Her mouth gapes as she shakes her head. "Why the hell would you do that?"

Lorna doesn't yet understand the relationship between spouses. "She knew we had history and asked me to tell her about it."

Lorna puts her head down on the table. "That was a dumb, ignorant, stupid move."

I disagree. It's probably one of the best I could've made for my marriage. "I'm glad she knows. I never have to worry about someone else telling her."

Lorna kicks me beneath the table—in my prosthesis. "Fuck you, Sin! Fuck you!"

I reach down to ensure it's still in place. "Why are you so angry?"

"Because Bleu's a dear friend who now hates my guts."

If I were married to any other woman, Lorna would probably be right. Most wives wouldn't so easily forgive what we did. "She doesn't hate you."

Lorna lowers her voice to a whisper. "She just found out one of her best friends slept with multiple men at the same time and one of them was her husband. How could she not despise me?"

It indeed sounds bad when she says it like that. "You spoke to her less than an hour ago. Did she sound angry or say anything to make you believe she hated you?"

"No."

"Because you're a beloved friend to her. She doesn't like the things we did but she harbors no ill feelings toward either of us about it. What has passed is past. That's what she said."

Lorna covers her hands with her face. "I don't know how I'll ever face her again."

"You'll act no differently because she'll have it no other way."

"Oh God. I hate this. I wish we'd not done any of those things."

She isn't the only one who wishes we could take it back. But we can't, so we must make the best of a bad situation. "Do you still love Leith?"

She places her hand in the center of her chest. "With all of my heart and soul."

I can work with that. "Will you let me fix this?"

"I'd love nothing more but I'm not holding my breath."

"If it doesn't work out, then you're no worse off."

"Except you will have given me hope and then yanked it out from beneath me."

I'll only do this if it's what she wants. "It's your decision."

"What would you say to him?"

"I'm going to tell him about Noah asking to meet to discuss a match with you but that I think he would be a better fit."

Lorna leans back and moves her hand to her stomach. "Oh God. I feel like I may throw up."

It's a sure sign she's in love with him. "Is he in the office?"

"Aye. He's closing out the books for the month."

I get up to leave the table. Lorna looks as though she may pass out. "You might want to consider having a whisky. You look pale."

"You would be too if you were in my shoes. My entire life is riding on what you say to Leith."

"Trust me when I say I understand the feelings you're having. I'm on your side. I promise I'll do all I can to make Leith see that you belong together."

I knock on the office door because it's closed. And locked. "Leith."

He calls out from the other side. "Go away."

Leith is my best mate, but even on his best day he doesn't get to tell me to leave him alone. I knock again much louder. "Come on, Leith. We have business to discuss and I'm running short on time."

"Hold the fuck on." I can hear him muttering on the other side. "Mother. Fucker."

He yanks the door open. "What!"

I step out of the way so Greer can exit. It doesn't escape my attention that she's straightening her blouse as she passes through the door. "Hi, Sinclair."

"Greer."

Leith plops down in his office chair. "Whatever business you're here to tend better be important. You just cost me a shag."

"Are you in some kind of relationship with Greer?"

"No. We fuck when we feel like it. That's all."

He reaches for a bottle of Ballantine's and pours a glass. "Want one?"

"Sure."

"You said we had business to tend?"

"Aye. Noah Wallace asked me to meet with him about a potential match he has in mind."

"Let me guess. He's after Declan Stuart's sister."

He's going to wish it were her when I tell him who it really is. "No. He's interested in Lorna."

He's bringing his glass of whisky to his mouth but stops before taking a drink. "He wants to claim Lorna?"

He wouldn't ask to meet with me if he were only interested in claiming her. He doesn't need my permission for that. "I think he means to make her his wife. We're meeting at nine to discuss the details so I'll know more then."

"You're her leader. You have the right to refuse him on her behalf."

"I could, but why would I if they're both agreeable?"

He perks up. That caught his attention. "Have you asked Lorna how she feels about a match with Wallace?"

"I don't have to because she's in love with someone else. Has been for years."

He tosses back his whisky and reaches to pour another. "We work together almost every day and I've seen nothing that suggests she's in love with anyone. Yet you seem very clear about it." He sounds pissed off, like he suspects I'm talking about myself.

"That's because you've been blind to it."

"What is that supposed to mean?"

I'm not sure he sees what he does to her. "You keep Lorna close, yet you're careful to maintain distance. But every once in a while when you've had a little too much whisky, you let down that wall that separates the two of you."

"You're confusing the hell out of me."

"Lorna is in love with you. She has been for years."

"I think you're wrong about that."

"I'm not."

"Then explain this. If she was in love with me, how could she keep fucking you?"

This is so much harder than I thought it would be. "I think she realized it that night you walked in on us because it never happened again after that. I swear. And she's been suffering in silence since."

"Did you know Lorna and I were having one-on-ones without you?"

That's news to me. "No."

"I thought I had won Lorna—until I found you with her in the storage room. I was completely wrecked, so please excuse me if I'm a little insensitive to the degree of suffering she has experienced."

"She never had one-on-ones with me until that night. It was the first and last time."

"I don't really want to hear this right now."

He has to. It's time to get it all out in the open. "Lorna hasn't been with a man since then because she's in love with you."

"She fucked the three of us enough that her pussy needed a vacation."

That was completely uncalled for. "You're being a pure arse."

"What do you expect? That I'd go out there and fall to one knee and propose because Noah Wallace wants her?"

Actually, yes. That's sort of what I was hoping for. "I thought you loved her and would be happy to find out she felt the same."

"Are you out of your damn mind, Sin? I've watched her fuck you and Jamie in every position imaginable. The last thing I want is a whore like that for a wife. And I damn sure don't want that as the mother of my children."

"If you don't love her, fine! But she's our friend and you don't get to talk about her like that."

"I'm just speaking the truth."

He's being a hypocrite. "We were all there making the same mistakes so don't count yourself out when you pass judgment." This is going nowhere and I've had enough of his shite. "You know what? You're a total dick!"

"Well, Lorna does love some dick. Guess that explains why she wants me."

"Fuck you, Leith!"

I have to get out of here before I go across the desk after him.

I'm walking toward the door when he calls out to me. "Just

because you got your happily ever after with your perfect life doesn't mean everyone else does."

I jerk the door open and come face to face with Lorna, huge tears streaming down her face. "I decided I wanted to be the one to tell him—until I heard the things he said about me."

She reaches up to wipe the tears rolling from her eyes. "I'm not feeling very well. I think I should go home. It's not busy so I'll have … Greer pick up … my tables."

"I'm so sorry." I wanted to make things right for her but all I've done is mess everything up.

I move toward her but she steps away, holding her hands up to stop me. "No. Don't. It was stupid to think he could have feelings for me. Brothers fuck women like me. They don't marry them."

"That's not true." Lorna is worthy of someone's love. Leith doesn't deserve her. "Don't go." I don't want her to leave like this.

"I can't stay." She squeezes her eyes shut. "I have to get out of here."

I let her go because there's nothing I can do to make this better for her.

Leith has pissed me off over the years but I've never wanted to beat him into the floor so badly in my life. And I may.

I go back into his office. "You should know that I just met Lorna in the hallway. She was coming to tell you that she loved you but was interrupted when she overheard you calling her a whore who was unworthy of being your wife or the mother of your children. Congratulations! You win the arsehole of eternity award."

"Shite!"

"You'll never have to worry about her being in love with you because I'm certain that just ended. And I'm guessing you should start looking for a new barmaid to manage this place because it will be a miracle if she comes back to work for you."

"Son of a bitch!" He gets up and moves toward the door. "I have to talk to her."

"I'm not sure now's the right time." He didn't see the hurt in her eyes.

He's panicked. "I have to do something to fix this."

He's not grasping the severity of the situation. "Leith. I'm not sure there's a fix for this."

"I have to try."

I'm going to make him admit he loves her. "You said she's an unworthy whore. Why go after her? It's no skin off your back if she's gone for good."

"Because I lied, okay? Everything I said about her was rubbish."

"Then why did you say them?"

He doesn't reply.

"Tell me."

"Because I love the fuck out of her." He drops his head. "But she has cut me to the bone deeper than you can imagine. Both of you."

It's time for this to end. He must figure out what he wants. If it isn't Lorna, he needs to let her go. "What do you want, Leith?"

"I don't know."

"You do know but you're fighting it."

He says nothing.

"You can love her or hate her but not both. Your decision. Which is it going to be?"

"God knows I don't want to but I can't help myself from loving her."

"Then go after her and tell her how you feel."

Leith grabs his coat from his desk and dashes out the door.

I return to the triad table to wait on Noah. Greer comes by and places a Johnnie Walker in front of me. "How are Bleu and the baby?"

I can't stop the corner of my mouth from tugging upward concerning our well-kept secret. I can't wait to make the announcement about the twins at my swearing-in. "Mom and baby are doing well. She's been a little nauseated but otherwise …" I stop midsentence when I hear a shot fired outside the pub.

I grab Greer's arm and pull. "Get down."

I rush toward the door and scan the front of the building, Beretta in hand. I see no one.

"Sin! Sin!" It's a high-pitched, panicked female voice. Lorna's.

Four of my brothers and I exit the pub. "Cover me."

I dart around the corner of the building and find Leith lying face down on the ground, Lorna sprawled under him. Blood is pooling on the cobblestones beneath them.

"Are you shot?"

"No, but Leith is!"

I roll him off Lorna and look for his wound, seeing it in his shoulder. Maybe a second in his arm. There's too much blood to be certain but neither appear life threatening. "Not too impressive, mate. Jamie can fix this in a snap."

Bystanders are on the street staring at us. "We need to get him out of here before someone calls the authorities."

I phone Sterling to pick us up while one of my men calls Jamie. "Tell him to meet us at my place."

We move Leith into the back seat of my car.

Lorna climbs in with Leith, placing his head in her lap. "I'm coming with you. No argument."

"I'm so sorry, Lorna," Leith says.

"Don't talk."

"But I need you to know that I didn't mean any of those things I said to Sin."

"Shut up. You've been shot. Now isn't the time to discuss what you did or didn't mean." Good for her. She isn't going to let him off the hook because he's taken a bullet or two. I hope she gives him hell.

"What happened?" I ask.

"An Order member grabbed me from behind and tried to shove me into the back of a car. Leith came out and saw what was happening. They struggled and he shot Leith.

This is another cowardly attack. They aren't going to quit until they're made to stop.

The Order is in complete chaos. That's good yet also bad for us. At least with Torrence in charge, they were typically predictable. That means we can probably expect more of these random attacks as a show to prove they've not been weakened by their leader's death.

Jamie's waiting in the drive when we arrive at my flat. "Let me have a look before we move him."

Jamie takes out bandage scissors and cuts Leith's shirt down the center. "Dammit. You know this is my favorite Johnny Cash T-shirt."

"Aye. I know."

Jamie inspects his wound. "Doesn't look serious but I can't tell if there's an exit wound without turning him. Take him to the guest room."

We're passing through the front door when Bleu meets us in the foyer. "What in the world is going on?"

"Leith was shot."

"Boss. There's a woman in your guest room."

Ellison rushes into the foyer. She's pointing in the direction of her room. "Jamie and two other men just put Leith on my bed. He's been shot!"

"Jamie's going to treat him here."

Ellison's mouth gapes. "Physicians treat gunshot wounds in a medical facility. They don't make house calls for trauma like that."

I look at Bleu. "I don't think we have any choice but to tell her now."

"No."

"Tell me what!"

The three of us go silent, Bleu and I looking at one another. She's making eyes at me. I shrug and mimic her expression. "I don't know what that means."

"Well, somebody needs to tell me what the hell is going on around here."

We have no choice. "Is it going to be you or me?" Sin asks.

Kyle comes into the foyer. "Sorry to interrupt, boss. Jamie told me to get help for Lorna. She's passed out."

Great. This night couldn't be more perfect.

We go to the guest room and find Lorna out cold in the arms of Blare. "I caught her as she was going down."

Jamie doesn't look up from working on Leith's wound. "She'll be fine. Move her to the couch in the office."

Ellison moves to look over Jamie's shoulder. "The skin has an abrasion collar around the entrance wound so he was shot from a distance with a small caliber handgun."

"Very good assessment."

Jamie holds out a pair of latex gloves for Ellison. "Help me roll him over so I can look for an exit wound."

Leith groans loudly when they flip him onto his side.

Ellison points at Leith's back. "There it is. Slit-like and marginally larger than the entrance. That's good. It means the bullet didn't hit anything to slow down its momentum. Those can be some nasty injuries to treat."

"How do you know so much about trauma?"

"I worked in the ER in a town with a ridiculously high crime rate. We saw at least one of these every night." Ellison holds out her hand. "I'll clean and dress this while he's on his side. No need to roll him again since it seems to be causing him quite a bit of discomfort."

Leith chuckles, followed by a loud groan. "It's a little more than discomfort, lass."

I'm back to being pissed at Leith now that I know he'll be all right. "Discomfort is the least of what you deserve."

"Please don't let her leave without seeing me. I have to talk to her." His voice is desperate. Good.

"We'll see."

I'm in no mood to offer him comfort by promising I'll have her come to him. Let him worry she'll slip away.

Jamie and Ellison work as a team to quickly dress Leith's wounds. "You know the drill. Antibiotics for prophylaxis and let me know immediately if you run fever. We don't need another case of sepsis."

"Another?" Ellison asks.

"Aye. Sin nearly died from a bad case a few months ago."

Ellison stalks toward the door. "Bleu. I need to see you. In private."

This isn't going to be easy for Bonny. "Want me to be with you?"

She nods. "Please. I can't do this by myself."

We follow Ellison into our bedroom and shut the door. "Somebody better start talking."

I cross my arms and lean against the wall. "She's your sister. The floor is all yours."

CHAPTER ELEVEN

BLEU BRECKENRIDGE

I'VE HAD MORE THAN A MONTH TO PREPARE MYSELF FOR HOW I'LL TELL ELLISON about my life within The Fellowship. I'm not a damn bit closer to finding the words than I was five weeks ago when she unexpectedly appeared in my hospital room. "You should probably sit since there is no short version to this story. It goes back almost nineteen years."

She retreats into the corner chair. "You're scaring me."

She should be frightened.

"When I woke in the hospital after my mother's murder, I was afraid. I knew the man who killed her would find out I didn't die and possibly come back for me. So my seven-year-old mind decided I should pretend to remember nothing about that night's events. I thought he might spare my life if he believed I couldn't identify him. I was a child who'd undergone a traumatic experience so no one pushed me to remember anything."

Ellison looks pained. "Oh God, Bleu. You remember that?"

"Every terrifying second."

"And you bottled it, never telling anyone."

Here we go. "I spent my entire childhood fixating on how I would make my mother's killer pay for what he'd done to us. When I turned twelve, I was ready to begin learning how to make that happen."

"I don't understand." Of course she doesn't. No normal person could fathom what I'm about to tell her.

"I told Dad I remembered everything and that I was going after my mom's killer."

"You can't be serious."

"My intentions were to murder her killer—shoot him exactly the way he did my mother. I told Dad I was doing it with or without his training. He feared for my safety so he agreed to teach me."

Ellison's brows are scrunched. I know her so well, I easily recognize it as her "thinking hard" look. "You expect me to believe that Dad taught his twelve-year-old daughter how to kill? Do you even know how crazy that sounds?"

This story has so much more crazy to it than she can possibly imagine. "He trained me until I entered the police academy. My entire career as an officer and then as an agent was so I could further my education to learn how to infiltrate an organized criminal organization called The Fellowship. Everything I did was so I could get close to her killer, Thane Breckenridge. The plan was to do that through his son, Sinclair. Which I did."

Breck takes my hand and squeezes it. "But then I fell in love with Sin and couldn't go through with any of it."

"Your father-in-law is your mother's killer?"

"I thought so, but I was wrong. We still haven't figured out who he is but we're getting closer every day."

I put my hand on my belly. "I've hired Dad's old partner Debra to take over the investigation since it isn't safe for me to be out tailing potential killers while I'm pregnant."

"What is Fellowship?"

This part is going to be trickier. "A group of people, much like a family, with designated leaders. Thane is the head authority. His son, Sin, is second in charge and will one day step into his shoes as leader when Thane decides to retire."

Sugarcoating what we are will be lying. I won't do that to my sister. She needs to understand everything about The Fellowship if she's to consider staying. "We're similar to what you know as the Mafia, but not Italian. The Scottish version."

"They're criminals and you're part of it?"

"Sin is my husband and this is his way of life. As his wife, I'm a part of everything he does."

"You're an FBI agent and you've chosen to marry into a family of criminals? That doesn't make sense."

She's stuck on the criminal part. "We're more than that. These people are my family. I love them dearly."

"I am your family." She looks hurt. That's not at all what I want.

"You are and always will be, but my place is here with my husband within The Fellowship."

"Dad is rolling in his grave."

I'm about to burst her bubble—and I hate that. "Dad knew. We told him everything before he died."

"You're lying."

"I'm not. Dad gave us his blessing."

"He wouldn't have if he'd understood what this was all about."

"He understood everything. We watched The Fellowship for years so we could find the best way for me to infiltrate. Dad knew every detail about the Breckenridges and their circle. He came to like Sin very much and was happy to see us marry."

The next hour consists of a lot of things: honesty. Tears. Yelling. Lots of explanations about what The Fellowship does or does not believe in or practice. What becoming a part of this world really means.

The conversation with my sister isn't pretty but Sin never leaves my side. He clarifies things about The Fellowship that I cannot.

"I feel like I don't know who you are anymore."

The truth is Ellison never knew the real me, but this is my opportunity to show her. "I'm the sister who loves you. The one who wants you to stay and become a part of my world. I need you. And my babies need you. You're the only Auntie Elli they'll ever have."

Yeah. It may be a low blow to use my babies as a means to convince her to stay but I don't care. I'm prepared to be a little selfish if it means I get to have her in my life.

"Becoming a part of your world means accepting this culture as my own. I'm not sure I can do that."

I understand her hesitation. This is a lot to learn about in one sitting. I've had years for it to sink in. "I have a wonderful life, Ellison. I couldn't be happier."

"You're on cloud nine. I don't dispute that at all, but we're very different people. I'm not sure I'm cut out for this."

"I wasn't certain I could do it, either, but now I can't imagine being anywhere else in the world."

"It's bizarre that a man would volunteer himself to be beaten in my place so I can become his. And part of this."

I understand her confusion. I was once the outsider looking in. It isn't an easy thing to comprehend. "It's extreme for a reason—so the act of bringing a person into the brotherhood isn't taken likely. Only a man who truly loves you would volunteer to do it. It's a huge sacrifice but I can promise you this: you'd never doubt his love for you and no one within The Fellowship would, either."

"It's barbaric."

Sin bursts into laughter. "I think your sister is understanding our ways perfectly."

I punch Sin's arm. "Not helping."

"If I loved the man back, how could I let him put himself through that?"

"If he's anything like Sin, he'd do it without telling you." Which is probably best. I don't think I would've gone along with it had I known. Especially since I wasn't planning to become a member of The Fellowship at that time.

"You found out after the fact?"

Boy, did I ever. "Yeah. Sin looked like he'd been run through a meat grinder."

Ellison shakes her head. "That's horrible."

"You'd think it would be, but it's not. When you're over the shock of it, you're able to see his sacrifice for the beautiful thing it is—his choice to suffer in your place."

Ellison looks at Sin. "You got him. I'd probably get some old fart in a kilt."

"First of all, your consent would be necessary for Sin to make any kind of match on your behalf. Secondly, there are some seriously hot Scotties in The Fellowship."

I look at Sin and shrug. "Sorry, but it's true."

Ellison sighs. "Jamie is so beautiful. I go completely stupid whenever I try to talk to him."

"And he's a great guy. I've come to love him dearly." I wouldn't mind seeing my sister with him at all.

"You don't view being in this world as a sacrifice, but to me it is. It would be a huge concession on my part. I'd be leaving my whole life behind. I need time to think about this."

I'm asking Ellison to change her entire existence. I don't take that lightly and neither should she. "Of course. Take all the time you need. No pressure. Sin and I are both here if you have any questions."

"We've been in here a long time. We should probably check on Leith." Sin's right. Time has gotten away from me. "And Lorna too."

I poke my head into the office but no Lorna. We go to the guest room where Leith is but the door is shut. I'm not sure what's happening on the other side but my gut tells me to walk away.

We go into the living room and find Jamie. "Is Lorna all right?"

"She's fine. She's in with Leith now."

Oh. That sounds promising. My husband's plan must have worked.

Ellison goes to the coat rack and puts on her wool peacoat. "I'm going to take a walk. I have a lot to think about."

Oh dear. I don't want to tell her it isn't safe, but I have to. "I'm sorry, Elli. You can't go out alone."

"I'll walk with you, if you don't mind my company," Jamie says.

"I'd like that." Ellison looks at me for approval. "Is that all right?"

I trust Jamie to protect my sister. "Absolutely."

"Call if there are any changes with Leith. We won't go far."

I'm dying to know what Leith said when Sin told him about Lorna. "The guest room door is shut. I take that as a sign things went well with Leith."

"Oh, Bonny. It didn't go well at all. The whole thing went sideways."

I recount the events of the night for Bleu.

"Oh no." She must be completely heartbroken.

"I've never wanted to hurt him so badly in all my life."

"I want to hurt him now." Had I known this an hour ago, I'm not sure I would have allowed him in my home to be treated. I might have told Sin to leave him on the sidewalk.

Sin and I go silent when we hear Leith's voice carry down the hall. "Please don't go!"

No reply.

Lorna comes into the living room. "I'm sorry to trouble you but I need a ride. Would you mind asking Sterling to take me home?"

"Of course. It's no problem at all, but you're welcome to stay as long as you like."

She's covered in Leith's blood. "Let me get you a change of clothes," I say.

She puts her hand up. "No. I really just want to get out of here now that I know he's going to be fine."

I feel like I should say something about Leith's reaction. "Sin told me what happened. I'm sorry."

This isn't my friend I'm used to seeing. This person is shrinking into herself, her posture telling the story of how she feels. "I've never been so hurt or humiliated in my life."

I want Sin to say something to make her feel better so I nudge him with my foot.

"I know he acted a fool but he loves you. He told me so after you left."

"Not possible. A man would never say things like that about the woman he loves."

I don't have an argument for that and I'm certain Sin doesn't, either.

Leith appears in the entrance to the living room. He's shirtless with a large white dressing over his upper left shoulder. There's a small amount of blood seeping through. "Thank God I caught you before you left."

"I'm on my way out the door right now."

He moves closer to her, holding the wall for support. "Don't go. We're not finished talking."

"I'm done."

"I didn't mean any of it. Not a word."

"When Sin proposed a match between us, all you had to say was that you weren't interested. Instead you were cruel. You humiliated me and it broke my heart into a million pieces. If nothing else, I thought we were at least friends. But a friend would never be so heartless."

"How can I fix this?" Leith's voice is desperate.

"You can't be fixed by the same person who broke you."

Lorna takes a ring of keys from her purse and holds them out to

Leith. "You should give my position to Greer. She's the most capable."

Leith refuses the keys. "No. I'm not taking those from you because you're not quitting the pub."

"I am. Doesn't matter if you take these or not. I won't be back."

"Where will you go?"

"I hear Leon is hiring at the club and the pay is good."

Leith's jaw becomes rigid. "Absolutely not. There's no way I'm letting you dance naked."

"Guess what, Leith? Whores are pretty limited in what their job description includes."

Lorna drops the keys on the cocktail table and walks out the front door without looking back.

Leith fists the front of his hair while both hands rest on his forehead. "I'm so stupid."

I hope he feels like a piece of shit for what he did to Lorna.

He stumbles and Sin rushes toward him. "You look like shite. You need to go back to bed before you collapse."

"I have to go after her."

He looks like he could crumple at any moment. "No. The only thing you have to do is lie down before you cause yourself to hemorrhage."

Leith sways as he closes his eyes and holds the front of his head. "That may not be the worst idea you've ever had."

Sin and I help Leith back to bed. "Bleu. Tell me how to mend this."

I assume he's asking me because I'm a woman, but I'm not experienced in relationship drama. All I can do is tell him how I'd feel. "It's a fresh hurt. You can tell her over and over that you're sorry but words are meaningless to her right now. All she's going to hear is the echo of you calling her a whore."

"You're saying she's never going to forgive me?"

I can't speak for Lorna. "Maybe. Maybe not. I'd bet money that even if she does, she'll never forget. I know I wouldn't."

"I've ruined my relationship with her forever." At least he sounds remorseful.

"You confuse me, Leith. I'm not sure what kind of relationship you think you have with her. From where I stand, all I ever see is you ignoring her."

"We work together all the time. It isn't possible for me to ignore her."

"Yet you do. You may occupy the same room but you look straight through her as though she isn't there."

"Is that how she feels?"

"Every day, all day long. She feels invisible to you."

"I had no idea."

"You've been thoughtless where Lorna is concerned."

"I've never done anything to hurt her. She's the one who hurt me."

Cry me a fucking river.

There's no way I'm going to let him off easy. "You parade women in and out of your office in her face. She isn't stupid. She knows you're screwing them yet she chooses to not let a man touch her in more than two years. She did that for you—to change the way you saw her. But her self-denial didn't change anything. You've been too busy fucking around to notice. It's time to stop punishing her because you can't get over what happened with the three of you."

Leith jerks around to look at Sin. "You told her?"

"We don't keep secrets from one another."

"It's in the past, Leith. You can't keep punishing Sin and Lorna for what happened."

"I'm not good at letting things go."

"Then learn to be good at it. Or risk spending the rest of your life being miserable without Lorna. Your choice."

"You're my best mate," he says to Sin. "You knew I loved her."

"I do now, but not back then. I swear."

They need to talk and I have no business being part of the conversation. "This is for the two of you to work out."

I shut the door behind me. I consider going to bed but it's early yet so I plant myself on the sofa in the living room. I turn on the television but it literally takes nothing more than a slow blink for me to fall asleep. This pregnancy and the accompanying anemia continue to rob me of energy despite the vitamins and iron.

I'm dozing on the couch when Ellison and Jamie return from their stroll. "That wasn't a long walk."

"Brrr. It's so cold out there, the hookers are blowing on their hands." Classic Ellison comment. And I love it. I've missed her sense of humor.

"You two act like we're in Antarctica. It isn't that cold."

"It's cold compared to where we come from. Which gives me something else to consider while making my decision to stay. You know how much I love being in a bikini on a boat drinking a cold beer in the middle of a lake on a hot day."

Jamie's eyes blatantly roam Ellison's body. Yep. He's totally imagining what that might look like.

"Nope. That won't happen here."

I have no doubt that Jamie is attracted to my sister. Perhaps I should have Sin speak with him about a match with Ellison. I already know she'd be keen. That is, if she decides to stay.

"I assume Leith did all right while I was out since you didn't call."

"Fine, if you don't count when he got up and tried to go after Lorna when she left."

Jamie looks irritated. "What a dumb arse. He could have caused himself to hemorrhage."

"We put him back to bed."

"I should check on him before I go to make sure he didn't cause his wound to start bleeding again."

Sin and Leith have been talking for a long time but I don't want Jamie to interrupt. "It might not be the best time to check on him. Sin and Leith are hashing out the problem they have after what happened with Lorna a couple of years ago."

I lift my brows at Jamie and hope he gets my drift since that's all I can say in front of Ellison.

"I can check Leith's wound when they finish talking if you'd like to go home," Ellison says.

Jamie doesn't look convinced. "Sure you don't mind?"

"It's no problem. I know what complications to look for and I'm here anyway. I might as well be useful."

"It would be nice to get some sleep. I start a twenty-four-hour shift tomorrow."

I figure Sin and Leith will be a while. "All the more reason for you to go. Don't worry. Ellison's a seasoned nurse."

"Aye. She told me about her experience while we were out. Time wise, she has more hands-on experience than I do. She's seen a lot."

Ellison can be humorous and immature at times but she's a damn good nurse. "She's very competent and will have us call you if there's a problem."

"Okay. I'll check in before my shift starts in the morning."

Ellison's willingness to help and Jamie's ability to accept it is a good sign. There are going to be times when Jamie will need assistance and I can't think of a better candidate.

I'd like to ask her what they talked about during their walk but I don't want to push. The choice to stay must be hers. I can't have her blame me for pushing her into a decision she'll regret later. It's no different than when Sin proposed. He was right to back away so I could weigh the pros and cons, so I'm going to do the same with my sister.

CHAPTER TWELVE

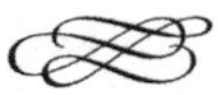

SINCLAIR BRECKENRIDGE

"WELL, HELL. I BOUGHT THIS DRESS TWO WEEKS AGO FOR YOUR SWEARING-IN ceremony and it fit fine. I put it on tonight and I'll be damned if it's not almost too tight."

Bleu turns to study her profile in the full-length mirror. She cups her hand beneath her small baby bump. "Do I look like I've grown that much in two weeks?"

I wrap my arms around her from behind, my hands covering her lower abdomen. "I think they're the ones who have grown. Not you."

"Good answer."

She weaves her fingers with mine. "It won't be long until you hug me like this and your arms will barely be able to fit around me."

I look forward to it. "Only means our babies are getting strong and healthy."

"If I keep growing like this, I'm going to be huge."

I don't like the worry in her voice. "Your body is expanding to accommodate the growth of our babies. That's the goal. We want them to stay in for as long as possible so they're not sick or scrawny when they're born."

"I know. I want them to be big healthy babies."

I kiss the side of her neck. "Never worry that I don't think your body is attractive. You're carrying my children—a part of me inside you. Nothing is more appealing than that. And I plan to show you just how sexy I think you are when we get home tonight."

She turns in my arms and glides her hands up to my shoulders. "I really want to kiss you right now."

I take note of the perfect coat of red shimmer on her lips. "But you won't."

She points to her mouth. "I don't want to smear this and look like The Joker."

"I intend on having this mouth later but there's something else I want right now."

I remove her hands from my shoulders. "Turn around."

I lift the hem of her dress. "What do you think you're doing?"

I push my hand down the front of her knickers. "Giving my wife a taste of what's to come later tonight."

She's completely smooth except for the small narrow strip of short hair down the center. Fuck. It's a turn-on every time.

I place my foot between hers and tap the insides of her ankles. "Spread 'em, Bonny."

She steps apart and my fingers find her sensitive nub. Her arse squirms in a circular motion against my cock as I stroke her clit. I didn't intend on this being about me but she's making me rock hard.

I saw a hint of insecurity so my intention was to make her feel sexy. I thought I could rub her off now and we'd worry about me later. But I'm not so sure I can wait until tonight to have her. She's turning me on too much.

I pull her against me and thrust my cock against her arse. "You have no idea how fucking fit you are."

She grabs my hand and grinds against it. "Make me come." Her voice sounds breathless, likes she's been running a marathon.

I rub her clit faster and harder. "Does that feel good?"

"Yes. Keep doing it just like that."

She reaches over her shoulder and grasps the back of my neck firmly while riding out the waves of her orgasm. "Oh God. That is so good." She squeezes her eyes shut and leans into me. "I'm coming."

She's so slick. My cock would slide into her so easily right now.

"Bonny ..." I don't even know what I want to say. Or ask. I only know I'm hard and I'll be miserable if I don't get off.

"I'm dying to bend you over and fuck you like crazy, but I'd never forgive myself if I caused something bad to happen."

"We'll be careful." She holds the hem of her dress at her waist and pushes her knickers down. "Undo your trousers."

I unbutton and await further instructions. I'd probably never admit it but I sort of like hearing her boss me around during sex.

She moves to the dresser and plants her palms on the top. She looks over her shoulder. "Come here, Mr. Breckenridge. We can't run behind for your ceremony. It wouldn't look very good for The Fellowship's new leader to stroll in late because he was busy fucking his wife."

I'm such a lucky bastard. "Yes, ma'am."

I position my erection at her entrance. I push it in a little and pull back, making the tip slick before advancing further. I stand upright and grasp her hips as I push into her slowly. "Good?"

"Mmm-hmm."

I pull back and plunge again. "You're all right?"

"Yes, but this is going to take a while if you ask if I'm okay every time you move."

I wish I had her confidence. "I can't help it. Being inside you still makes me nervous."

"How about you assume all is well unless I say otherwise?"

"That'll work."

I thrust into her and she says nothing. So I do it again. And again. I watch my cock sliding in and out of her. The sight alone is almost enough to make me explode.

I move my thumb to the cleft of her arse and drag my finger down. "I want to get inside this. But not now. After the babies come."

I read that anal sex is discouraged during pregnancy. That's fine. It isn't a spur-of-the-moment thing to try. It'll take some work so it's good for her.

"A deed so dirty, it shouldn't be done in the light of day?"

"Exactly."

I was already close to coming but talking about anal sex—and Bleu not telling me no—pushes me over the edge.

We're attending a formal occasion in thirty minutes. I don't want her walking around smelling like sex.

"I'm not coming inside you." I reach into the top drawer of the dresser and take out the first thing I see—one of Bleu's cotton nightgowns. "Sorry. Hope you weren't planning to wear this to bed tonight."

"It'll wash."

She pulls her formal gown down and turns. "Maybe you can't fuck me hard but you can still fuck me good."

"Who are you kidding? I fucked you great."

"You certainly did. Are you beginning to see that we can have great sex without something bad happening?"

My confidence has improved. "You were right."

"Corporate has approved a new policy. Assume I'm fine unless otherwise stated. Got it?"

"Understood."

I'm buttoning up when she slaps me on my arse. I jerk because I wasn't expecting it. "You said that was a taste of what was to come later. I'm anticipating impressive things."

"Expect to be dazzled."

My swearing-in ceremony is being held at a banquet room inside a hotel owned by one of the brothers. Every Fellowship member not working on assignment tonight is in attendance, making for a large crowd.

Our people are unaware that tonight is doubling as a twofold ceremony. Bleu and I plan to formally announce the upcoming arrival of not one but two future Fellowship leaders.

I know she wishes Ellison could have come but her sister can't participate in ceremonial Fellowship functions until she is one of us.

We're sitting front and center at the leadership table with my parents, Abram, and his wife Torrie. I'm surprised they showed since Abram hasn't taken the loss of his leadership role well. I'm not sure what my uncle expected. We agreed on the terms of his interim role and he fulfilled them. There was no reason for him to think I'd never take my place at my father's side.

Bleu is earning her badge of misery. She's irritated she's being forced to endure Abram's company. Can't say I blame her. At least she has my mum at our table and Westlyn at the neighboring one.

"I'm sorry. He isn't in a leadership role anymore, but he's still family. The Breckenridges always sit together at formal functions."

She won't even look in his direction. It's probably best. "It is what it is. I'll survive. And maybe he will too, unless he decides to harass me."

"I told him I wouldn't tolerate him badgering you. He's had fair warning."

Bleu looks in the direction of her friends. "I may disappear for a while after the official stuff. I plan on talking to Lorna about that job at the gentlemen's club."

Lorna needs to be told by someone other than Leith or me that dancing topless is not the best decision. "I think that's an excellent idea."

"I'll probably recruit Westlyn to help me."

Dinner is served and Bleu is immediately inspecting the plates around her. She has a big appetite now that the first trimester nausea has passed.

Bleu studies my plate for a moment and uses her fork to point at it. "That looks good. What is it?"

"Venison." I'm going to enjoy telling her the next part. "With haggis."

"Liar." She pokes it with her fork. "It doesn't look like the haggis I've seen before."

"This one is wrapped in a puff pastry."

She studies the nontraditional form of haggis, showing a lot of interest in it. "Are you thinking of trying it?"

"It looks really good."

"You're welcome to some if you'd like."

"My appetite and tastes are evolving. I think I will."

My mum leans over. "Yer wife is carrying a pair of Scottish weans who are determined to have their haggis. Boys. Both of them. Mark my word."

"We'll see in about five months."

"I thought you were finding out their genders at Bleu's next appointment." I hear the disappointment in Mum's voice.

"We talked about it and decided we want it to be a surprise when they're born."

"We can't prepare if we don't know what they are."

Decision's been made. There's no persuading us. "They're babies. We'll get the necessities. The pink or blue stuff can wait."

"I may explode from the anticipation of not knowing."

"Please don't. Bleu is going to need your help with them."

I notice Bleu isn't contributing anything to the conversation. "Bonny. You've eaten half of my plate."

She wipes her mouth, no doubt hiding a grin behind her napkin. "Sorry. I was going to get a taste and next thing I knew, half was gone. It's really good."

I swap out my plate of venison for her chicken. "You're welcome to it. Unless you're planning to eat mine and yours."

She punches my bicep. Hard. "Shut up."

We finish dinner and Bleu leans back in her chair, her hands cupping her small bulge. "Woo. I thought this dress was a snug fit before."

"I love it on you. It's sexy."

I spot someone very special across the room. "Come with me. There's someone I'd like you to meet."

I take Bleu's hand and lead her through the crowd. "This is Brooke Drummond, Callum's widow."

Although Bleu has yet to meet Brooke, she's aware of my pledge to personally see to the care and safety of her and her unborn child.

Bleu's eyes flash with acknowledgement. I'm pleased she remembers.

She embraces Brooke. "Sin has told me wonderful things about you and Callum. It's so nice to finally meet you."

"I'm glad to meet you too. And happy to see you're off bed rest."

"That was brutal."

"My doctor placed me on it for a while when Callum died. Afraid the stress would cause me to lose the baby." She places her hand on her tummy. It's twice as big as mine. "But I didn't."

My father cues me it's time. "We're up."

Bleu places a hand on Brooke's shoulder. "Our presence is requested but we'll definitely talk later."

Bleu and I join my father on the rostrum behind a podium. Tonight's event has felt like nothing more than a large dinner party until now. This is where the commitment gets real. There's no going back after this. And I'm ready.

My father makes the opening statements, recites The Fellowship creed, and then instructs me to repeat after him. The formalities are still familiar in my mind from when I attended Abram's swearing-in as my interim replacement almost six years ago.

"I, Liam Sinclair Breckenridge, freely and willingly accept my role as leader of this organization known as The Fellowship." That's how it begins. The lengthy pledge that follows mostly pertains to declaring absolute and unwavering loyalty to the people of my brotherhood.

My father included Bleu in the rites, which I wasn't expecting. He had her repeat similar declarations, vowing her complete and unfaltering loyalty in support of me as her husband and leader of The Fellowship. She vowed to be steadfast at my side, supporting me in all of my decisions.

Once the swearing-in is complete, our people wait for a word from me. I understand it's part of my duty but I hate giving speeches. "I've been trained for this job since the day I was born so this has been a long time coming. I want you all to know I'm both ready and prepared to be your leader."

I gesture toward Bleu so all attention is focused on her. "Many of you aren't yet acquainted with my wife. As you come to know her, I'm positive you'll see her for the amazing person she is. She's the strongest woman I've ever known and I'm certain I'll be a fiercer leader for you because she's by my side."

I take her hand in mine. "One of our duties as your leaders is to provide an heir. As you already know, we are expecting our first child in September. What we haven't told you is that Bleu is carrying twins."

The crowd applauds and yelps so loudly I'm forced to let the noise die down before I'm able to continue. "We anxiously await the arrival of these children and look forward to raising them in the way of The Fellowship."

I debate telling them our plans for the way any sons of ours will be reared but decide to tackle that at a later time.

"As leader to the women of The Fellowship, Bleu has been hard at work creating and organizing many new opportunities for those she'll be presiding over. I'll let her expand on what those things include."

Bonny steps to the podium and adjusts the mic. "Good evening. First of all, I want to express my sincerest appreciation to you for welcoming me into your circle. I understand that isn't an easy thing to do within The Fellowship, but you've been so kind and hospitable. Thank you from the bottom of my heart."

Bleu removes the mic from its stand. "I'm sorry. This podium is too formal for me."

She crosses the floor of the rostrum, microphone in hand. "My husband and father-in-law are in charge of the brothers. My role is to minister to the females of the brotherhood so I want to talk about women's services—or rather the lack of them. I have many things I'm considering but my biggest concern for now is the women's inability to protect themselves. They've not been taught any defense skills. We're all aware that The Order has a habit of targeting our women so I want to work toward putting a solution into place to combat that problem.

"I was kidnapped by them. Torrence Grieve tried to sexually assault me. I stress the word 'tried.' He was unsuccessful because I had the skills to fend him off. I want that for all of our women. They deserve that power."

It's selfish but a part of me is glad Bonny addressed this issue so my men are clear about what happened. It bothered me that they were probably questioning if she was raped.

"A good shepherd protects his flock but a better one teaches his sheep to become lions when attacked. Male or female, we all deserve equal training to protect ourselves. The Order is in a state of panic. They're desperate to prove they've not been weakened by their leader's death. Who do you think they'll come for? Our men who can defeat them or women they can overpower? How great would it be for them to come expecting to attack a sheep and find a lion in its place?"

The daughter of a trusted brother lifts her hand. "You have a question?" Bleu asks.

The young woman stands. "Hello. I'm Lacey Taggart."

"Very good to meet you."

"What do you mean when you say you want to make us lions?"

"I'm proposing basic self-defense classes be offered to those who are interested. For the women who'd like to take it further, I would recommend Muay Thai. The skills taught enable even the smallest woman to take down a larger male opponent. You're welcome to verify that fact with Leith Duncan if you'd like."

"True story," Leith calls out and laughs. "The lass put me on the floor of the ring with one punch."

"I have the perfect person in mind to help me teach the self-defense classes, but I'll need to find someone for the Muay Thai classes. The required physical combat will be too much for me during my pregnancy. But physical defense can't be the end of it. You need to know how to use firearms. I'd like a show of hands—women only—if you know how to properly fire a gun."

Only three. And one of them isn't my own mother. It's a shame. I'm glad Bleu sees this problem and wants to fix it.

"I only see a few hands. That astounds me. Let's pretend for a moment that a member of The Order is after you with malicious intent. Kidnap. Rape. Murder. Whatever. By show of hands, how many of you would like to learn how to defend yourself against him?"

Every woman in the room lifts her hand—including Torrie, Evanna, and Westlyn. I'm sure that pisses Abram off.

"Moving beyond learning to defend yourself, I want to find ways to offer more opportunities in the workforce. Perhaps you're in a marriage or you've been claimed and you don't have to work. Maybe you like it that way. That's fine, so this isn't for you. But if you are interested in independence, then this opportunity could be of interest. Brothers must select how they'll contribute to The Fellowship. Many choose to become professionals, go to college, and learn a trade or service. Women should be given the same opportunity."

Abram lifts his hand but doesn't wait to be acknowledged. "I'm unclear about something. Did you learn your defense skills and how to shoot a gun while you worked as an FBI agent for the US government, or were you taught elsewhere?"

Motherfucker just won't stop.

Bleu doesn't miss a beat. "I was initially taught by my father. It was important to him that I have the necessary skills to protect myself against those attempting to harm me. I learned to shoot a handgun when I was twelve. I never miss my target. But I didn't master the use of high-powered rifles until I was in the academy."

"You don't deny that you once worked for the FBI?"

"No. It's true, so why would I deny it?"

Good girl. She's making herself transparent. It's her only defense.

"You were an FBI agent and now you're part of The Fellowship. That's suspicious. Doesn't anyone else find Bleu's motives questionable?" His tone is contemptuous.

He's trying to place doubt about Bleu in the minds of our people.

"Sin is a lawyer. His professional career places him on one side of the law but his loyalty lies with The Fellowship. The same is true for me. I once had a career in law enforcement for the US but my allegiance now belongs to The Fellowship. My previous employment is nothing but beneficial for our brotherhood."

"You left the FBI less than a year ago. Your father was an agent so you were raised to have respect for the law. Do you really expect us to believe that you have no regard for it anymore?"

Bleu remains cool, seemingly unaffected by Abram's accusations. "I entered into the oath of marriage with the next leader of The Fellowship. I'm pregnant with his children, the future leaders of the brotherhood. Do you really think it's a valid argument to propose that I have sacrificed myself and the lives of my offspring because I have such a high regard for the law? I think not. Furthermore, I'm American. Even if I were still an agent, I would have zero jurisdiction in Scotland. It would be useless for me to come to Edinburgh to infiltrate an organization I can't prosecute. What you're proposing simply doesn't make sense. Not a single agency in the US cares about The Fellowship."

"You haven't addressed your motive."

"I have only one. Love. I love Sinclair and our children, not the law. Is anyone else unclear on this or is Abram the only one?"

The room remains silent.

"I'm very happy to answer any questions you may have. I actually prefer to get all of them cleared up now so there's no confusion later."

The room is quiet for another minute before a man toward the back lifts his hand. "I have three daughters. Fourteen, twelve, and ten. I worry for their safety so at what age do you recommend that they are taught these things you plan to offer?"

I lean over and whisper to Bleu. "He's the father of the girl who was beaten and raped by The Order several months ago."

"Twelve is the recommended age but girls' bodies mature at different rates. I probably wouldn't recommend waiting that late if the girl matures early. No Order member is going to ask her how old she is before attacking."

Abram has been unsuccessful in planting suspicion against Bleu. Our people don't seem at all concerned about her past. Women and parents of daughters are more interested in hearing about what my wife has planned for their safety rather than who she once was.

My gut told me Abram wouldn't be able to control himself so I was prepared for him to act out. I ordered security to be in place in case he got out of control. Now that the attention is no longer on him, I think it's time he's escorted from the ceremony.

I motion for my security men to come forward for him. Orders are already in place to take him to the black site.

Abram has fucked this night up for me. Instead of going home to make love to my wife, I'll be tied up carrying out penance against him. He's going to rue the day he chose to go after Bleu.

The Q&A runs longer than anticipated but I eventually get Bleu on the dance floor. "My dear Mrs. Breckenridge. The Fellowship is exceptionally happy with you right now."

She runs her fingers over the front of my hair, smoothing it into place. "Perhaps. I think they're highly pleased with their newest Breckenridge leader as well."

Our people don't get a choice about liking me. I'm their leader so they must do as I say. It's a done deal. But they get to decide if they are fond of my wife. And they are. Very much. I saw something more in their eyes and expressions—respect and admiration. "They really liked the things you had to say."

"I think so too but I'm sorry I stole the spotlight from you. Our plans were so well received that I couldn't stop once I started talking about them."

I knew Bleu was intelligent but she absolutely blew me away tonight. "Those aren't our plans. They're yours. Each idea was born through your vision of what you see for the future. You get all the credit for that."

"I don't care about or need credit. All I want is to see change for our women."

"You're making it happen and they're going to love you for it." I know I do.

I hold her close as we sway through two more songs. She places her head against my chest and becomes quiet. She isn't saying so but she's drained. "Things are dying down so I'm going to have Sterling drive you home. Kyle and Blare will go with you because I have a matter to take care of."

She cradles my face with her palm. "You told me earlier that I was only getting a small taste of what was to come when we got home."

"You still will." I kiss her forehead. "You're tired. Go home and rest. I'll be there in a little while to wow you."

"Has something bad happened?"

"Aye. Abram happened, so I had him sent to the black site for me to deal with in private." Which I happen to think is pretty generous considering what he did to Bleu was so public.

"I handled him. And he didn't even come close to succeeding at what he was trying to do."

True. "You made me proud, but he acted against you in front of the entire brotherhood. Because you're my wife, what he did is an act of betrayal against me. He's going to pay penance for that."

"You're going to have him beaten?"

"Within an inch of his life." And I shall delight in it.

"What does Thane have to say about that?" He grew tired of Abram's antics a while ago. He ignored them because he loves his brother but he won't overlook Abram attacking the mother of his grandchildren.

"He won't go against me on it."

"Do you expect to be long?"

"Two hours. Maybe three."

"Then I shall be naked, wet, and wanting when you come home to me."

Perfect. Just the way I want her.

ABRAM IS TIED FACED DOWN , HIS BACK BARED. HE'S FIGHTING TO FREE HIMSELF but it's useless. He should know that. "What the fuck do you think you're doing, Sinclair?"

I stand over Abram looking at the man I once adored as a most beloved uncle. That was before my immature mind could conceive of the evil things he was capable of. "I told you I wouldn't tolerate any more acts against my wife. This is the consequence of ignoring my warning."

"You're a fool if you believe your wife's loyalty lies with us."

"She married me. She's carrying the next leaders of The Fellowship. What is it going to take for you to accept that she's one of us and is here to stay for good?"

"Nothing will ever convince me of that."

"Then perhaps a good flogging will persuade you otherwise."

I nod at Sangster. "You may begin."

I see the hint of a smirk on Sangster's face. I'm grinning on the inside. Bringing Abram to his knees for all he's done to Bleu instills joy in me.

The multitailed whip strikes Abram's back and he yells out in pain. It's just as I thought. He can dish it but can't take it.

"How many lashes do you think is suitable for the things you've done to my wife? Let's begin with ten per incident? I think that's fair."

"Stop this, Sinclair. Can't you see what she's doing? She's a little bitch who's turning us against one another."

"No. You're the one who did that."

I hold out my hand to seize the whip from Sangster. "I'll take that."

I've said it more than once. Bonny is the only reason the light in me bothers to battle the darkness. But there's no light inside me now. I look at Abram and all I feel is hate. I'm glad because I'm going to need it for what I'm about to do.

"Each lash you feel is a consequence of your offenses against my wife. When I'm finished with you, you won't entertain the idea of crossing her again."

CHAPTER THIRTEEN

BLEU BRECKENRIDGE

DEBRA AND I HAVE BEEN WORKING WITH OUR FIRST SELF-DEFENSE CLASS FOR AN hour. We're both instructing but she's the physical machine behind this. She has to be at least fifty and hasn't broken a sweat. Total badass. I hope I'm in that kind of shape when I'm her age.

Sin gave us one of the vacant warehouses to turn into our training center. He had a small training arena constructed in the center of the building. Seating surrounds the ring on all sides so all of our trainees can observe no matter where they're sitting.

He has supplied us with weights and fitness equipment as well. And a daycare for the children. Totally unexpected. He's earning some serious points with the women of The Fellowship. And me.

It's time to begin the extreme physical part of the training so Debra is dressed out in a self-defense instructor suit. She looks like a red Michelin Man. "Who wants to be first?"

No one volunteers.

I'm happy my sister and best friends are in attendance. I can pick on them.

I look at Ellison, cueing her to come forward, but she shakes her head. Westlyn and Lorna do the same.

"Come on. Don't be shy. You're all going to do this part at some point."

The least likely person in the room stands to volunteer. Alanna Studwick. "I will."

Debra watches her approach the arena. "I thought today's class was supposed to be adults only."

"That was the plan, but I had to let this girl in when her father asked. She has a powerful backstory."

Our youngest trainee approaches Debra. "Tell me your name and how old you are."

"Alanna, and I'm fourteen. But don't take it easy on me because of my age. The Order members who took me from my bedroom didn't when they beat and raped me."

Debra doesn't appear shocked by Alanna's statement. I don't know if that's because she really isn't or if she's keeping her cool for the girl. "All right. I won't."

I approach her. "I'll help you into the protective headgear and padding."

Alanna holds out her hand and I slip the glove over it. "When I was seven, I was attacked by a man. I wasn't raped but I was left for dead. I understand some of the feelings you're having."

She holds out her second hand when I finish with the first. "People act like I should magically get over what happened because Sinclair killed the men who attacked me. I can't. I think about it all the time."

No one understands obsession better than I do. "It's okay to still be pissed off about what happened to you. Use your anger for good. Use it to your advantage. Let it be your motivator. A catalyst driving you to learn the skills you need so it never happens again."

"Is that what you did?"

I nod. "Men are bigger. Stronger. Can't change that so we must train to be faster and smarter."

"I want you to teach me those things so I can be like you."

I finish lacing the second glove and push the protective gear over her head. "Become proficient at what you learn in this class. We'll move toward Muay Thai once you've mastered self-defense."

I'm not surprised by the drive I see in Alanna. She reminds me of myself at that age.

We're able to work with six women before break time. "Good work, ladies. Let's meet back here on the mat in twenty."

Debra, Ellison, Lorna, Westlyn, and I go into the office space Sin had constructed especially for me. My place for scheduling classes or getting away when I need a moment of privacy.

"Alanna is one pissed-off kid," Ellison says. I assume she's referring to the aggression she saw in her.

"It's good for her to get that out." I know how important it is for her to find an outlet. "She did better than women twice her age. I have exceptionally high hopes for how well she'll click with martial arts."

"I hear the things The Fellowship women are saying about you. They think you're a wonderful leader. No one has ever done the things you're doing for them. They love you," Ellison says.

"I love them too. I want nothing but the best for all of them."

That's why I won't stop pushing for their safety and equality.

Sin had a last-minute trip to Dublin to meet with The Guild. He won't be back until late tonight. I'm sort of pissed off because that means he's missing my eighteen-week ultrasound today.

Sin's leadership role means he's going to miss a lot of things where the babies and I are concerned. I should accept it now.

I have Ellison. At least today and until she decides to stay or go.

Savannah, the same ultrasound tech who's done all of my scans at the OB clinic in Edinburgh, is doing my sonogram today. "Where's Mr. Breckenridge?"

"Away on business." He's busy transporting illegal firearms so he can stay in good relations with an Irish criminal organization. And they're probably planning the demise of a third criminal organization that is our nemesis.

"What kind of work does your husband do?"

"Defense attorney."

"I'm so excited to see them, I can hardly stand it. I may pee my pants," Ellison says. She's fidgeting, her knees pumping her legs up and down.

Savannah moves the wand over my belly and zooms in on the two little lives growing inside me. "Felt any movement yet?"

"No." But I'm dying to. I'm disappointed I haven't felt any flutters at all. I thought for sure I would this week.

"You should soon. Probably within the next fourteen days."

I know this routine well. Savannah always does the things she must document first and then we get to do the fun stuff—spying on my wee ones. "They're active today. Are we checking to see if they're boys or girls?"

"Yes!" Ellison squeals.

"No. My husband and I have decided to be surprised."

Ellison huffs. "I'm going to die if you don't find out."

She can be so dramatic. "Dying now would be a tragedy since you won't be around to find out what they are when they're born."

"You and Sin don't have to know. Just let me find out. I swear I won't let it slip."

That's such bullshit. "You have the biggest mouth of anyone I know. There's no way you'd be able to keep it a secret."

"I can. I swear."

"No. We want everyone to be surprised with us."

She groans. "I can't believe you're doing this to me."

"Believe it or not, this is about what my husband and I want. Not you."

"I know but I'm an excited aunt. I want to buy them stuff."

Why does everyone think they must go out and get everything now? "You can still buy them stuff, just nothing gender specific until after they get here."

"You have the patience of a saint. Always have." While Ellison chomps at the bit.

"All right. Done with the measurements. It's fun time."

"Yes!" Ellison claps, reminding me of a two-year-old about to get a cookie. "Auntie Elli finally gets to see her babies."

She gets up and goes around to the monitor of the machine. "Oh my God. They look like they're butting heads."

"I hear siblings do that from time to time."

"They're starting awful early."

She studies the screen intently, never taking her eyes away from the babies. "Are you trying to see what they are?"

"Of course not."

"Yes you are." I don't know how familiar Ellison's ER experience makes her with OB sonograms, but it's possible she knows just enough to be able to read them. "Stop or I'm going to make you leave."

"Bleu. All I'm doing is looking at the babies, same as you."

She tries to look innocent but I can see the little devil sitting on her shoulder whispering in ear. "Get your ass over here and sit down. Now."

She takes her seat but she's wearing a shit grin. "You saw, didn't you?"

"Yes! But I could only make out one."

Now I'm pissed off. And maybe a little jealous. She shouldn't know what my babies are—or one of them—if I don't.

"If you change your mind about knowing, all you have to do is ask."

"No. And if you let it slip, I swear I'll never forgive you."

"I won't. Promise."

She's never been able to keep her mouth shut in her life. I suspect now won't be any different.

We leave my OB appointment and I'm feeling especially sulky. "I'm sorry, Bleu. I know you think I was trying to purposely see but I wasn't. It popped up when she moved the wand. And I could be wrong. I'm not even that familiar with reading them."

I can't tell if she's telling the truth or backpedaling. "Let's not talk about it anymore."

"How about lunch? Or maybe shopping?" she says.

Lunch sounds awesome. I know exactly what I want. Haggis.

I take Ellison to my favorite quick service restaurant. She isn't nearly as in love with the items on the menu as I am.

Our plates arrive and she stares at my food. "That is the nastiest-looking shit I've ever seen."

"I thought so too until I got pregnant. Now I crave it all the time." It's crazy.

"That's just wrong, whatever that is."

I hold out a bite on my fork in her direction. I know it disgusts her. That's sort of why I'm doing it. "It's good. Want a try?"

"Hell no," she snarls.

"All the more for me, then."

Ellison leans away and puts her fork down.

"What's wrong? Burger not good?"

"It's fine."

Something's up. "You aren't eating."

"I can't stop thinking about the babies and how I'll miss everything if I leave."

I wanted Ellison to be the one to bring this up when she was ready. I guess this means it's time. "You already know I want you here. Sin wants you to stay too." I sort of suspect Jamie wants her to stick around as well.

"I've been thinking about it a lot. I don't think I can leave."

"Is this your way of telling me you've decided to remain in Edinburgh?"

"I think so."

"Temporarily?"

"I want to stay long-term."

That means she must become a member. "As one of us?"

She shrugs. "There's a lot to work out where that's concerned so I guess that all depends."

Ellison will always be safe from harm by The Fellowship. She's my sister but our familial ties don't obligate the brotherhood to protect her from harm by anyone else. That's a precarious situation to be in since her affiliation with us places her in danger.

She knows there's no bigger advocate for women's equality than me, but the truth is that she's going to need a Fellowship member to step forward and take responsibility for her. "I wish I could've taken you to Sin's swearing-in ceremony. It would've been the perfect opportunity to meet every bachelor within The Fellowship."

"It feels weird knowing I'll be looking for a man to volunteer to be beaten nearly to death for me. I don't feel right about that."

"Endurance is normal practice for The Fellowship. It's a harsh way to weed out the weak, so know that only a strong man will come forward to claim you."

"I definitely want someone strong if I'm going to do this."

I'm not really sure there are weaklings in The Fellowship. "No worries. Sin will make sure he finds you a great match."

"My brother-in-law finding a husband for me doesn't sound the least bit romantic. Or hot."

I guess not unless you look at whom she could end up with. "Even if he's somebody like Jamie?"

"I can't say I'd mind being with someone like him."

"What if you were matched with him?" Jamie isn't in a relationship. He's available as far as I know.

"You already know I find him drool-worthy but I don't think he's attracted to me."

Ellison is beautiful. And so funny. I'm actually sort of surprised Jamie hasn't already made a move for her. "What makes you say that?"

"He's shown no interest."

Ellison doesn't understand the brotherhood. "The world of The Fellowship is a complicated one. No brother strays outside of it for a woman without chancing a harsh punishment."

"How will I find a potential mate if I'm not one of you but can't become part of The Fellowship until someone claims me?"

It's sort of a chicken-or-the-egg conundrum. "Valid question. I think we should have some sort of social event so you can meet the brotherhood bachelors."

"Brotherhood bachelors. Should be a reality show."

Umm … no. "I think not."

I sit back in my seat and tug on my tunic. "I can't avoid buying real maternity clothes any longer. I've outgrown all my loose-fitting, stretchy stuff."

"Ugh! The dreaded pregnancy wardrobe. Don't you dare buy those damn maternity overalls."

God, those things are fugly.

"If I can't buy anything for the babies, then maybe getting you some stuff will suffice. Let's shop before we go home. I'm sure Kyle and Blare would love nothing more than to accompany us to a mommy-and-me store."

"They'll hate me hard if I make them do that."

"They must have done something really bad to have been assigned to guarding you."

I'm sure it's the opposite. "I imagine they did something really right. My husband didn't choose them to watch over me and his children because they've proven themselves useless."

"They both look mean as hell. What do you think they've done?"

I look at my two protectors sitting three tables away. They remind me of military men. Short hair. Muscular. Stone-faced. Content to keep quiet. "They've killed. A lot."

"You think?"

"No doubt."

"Has Sin killed?"

I debate answering that question but decide she should know the truth if she's staying. "Yes. And if you join us, your husband will too. You'd better make damn sure you're prepared to handle that part of his life. There will be times when he needs to confide the things he's done. He may even cry like a baby on your shoulder because it's become too much to handle. And you'll let him. You'll be the light delivering him from the dark. The beauty of the ugliness is that it'll bring you closer."

"I'm guessing the first time would be the worst. How did you handle it?"

"Sin went after three men who'd beaten and raped Alanna, the girl from our self-defense class. Once he told me the horrid things they did to her, I knew he was doing the only thing he could—taking care of his own. I was glad to be with a man who would avenge a wrong committed against an innocent young girl. It made me wonder how different I might have turned out if someone like him had done something like that for me."

"I hate what happened to you, but it molded you into who you are today. I happen to like that person very much."

"I feel like I've hidden my true self from you my entire life. I'm happy you finally get to know the real me."

"I've always known the real you. All of this other stuff is just details."

ELLISON PLACES ONE OF MY NEW MATERNITY DRESSES ON A HANGER. IT'S THE black one embellished with metallic beading on the neckline. "This is so cute. I think you can wear it with leggings after the babies are born."

I'm pretty sure I'll be sick of wearing tents by the time they get here. "Or I can save it for you when you get pregnant."

"The dress will probably be out of style by the time I have a baby."

No. That would ruin my plan.

"I want our babies to be close in age, like us."

"You have high expectations if you plan on our children being that close in age. That means I'd have to find a husband and get pregnant within the next year. That would be completely putting my life on fast-forward."

It could happen. "I admit Sin and I are having babies way sooner than I would've planned, but fate and I didn't share the same schedule. I couldn't be more pleased about it now."

"I've literally never known you to be so happy."

It's not difficult with a husband like Breck.

"Sin changed everything. I realized the white knight wasn't for me. I prefer the alpha wolf. He never hesitates to devour me."

"Shit. That's hot."

She can't imagine how scorching it is.

"Is he alpha in all ways?"

"All the ways that count."

There's a tap on the door. I'm in the middle of changing into my new maternity comfies so I dart for the bathroom. "I'm sure that's Kyle or Blare. Will you see what they want?"

I'm pulling my hair into a ponytail when Ellison comes into the bathroom. "It was Kyle. He asked me to tell you that Mr. Breckenridge has come to see you and is giving him and Blare the rest of the evening off. Kyle said they'd report back for duty in the morning.

Thane went to Dublin with Sin. My heart immediately begins pounding. "Oh God. Something has happened."

I dash to the living room.

"Oh my. I believe that is excitement to see me."

Abram. Not the Mr. Breckenridge I was expecting but I won't complain. At least it's not Thane here to deliver bad news. "Why are you here?"

"We've not had the opportunity to talk since your husband gave me sixty lashes. I thought we might catch up while he's away on Fellowship business." Sin delivered sixty lashes to Abram? He didn't tell me that.

Abram's back is turned so he can't see Ellison when she comes to the doorway. He briefly looks away when he places his hand in his jacket so I motion with a quick nod for her to go. She promptly retreats.

"What do you want?"

"Things were pretty perfect in my world until you came along."

I can't believe he's going to be whiny about this. I expected better from him. "I'm sorry you had to join the rest of us in an imperfect world."

"I was on top, and now I have nothing."

I wonder if Abram was the same person he is today when they decided to appoint him. If so, that was a bad call. "You were on top because Thane and Sin temporarily placed you there. It was never truly yours."

"I took on Sinclair's responsibilities for years while he had fun and fucked around with any woman he chose. Believe me, there were plenty of them. I ruled with an iron fist. Did a fucking good job and have gotten little gratitude for my sacrifice."

Total psychopath. "I think sacrifice is a poor word choice to describe your role as second in leadership."

"Regardless of the name we use, it all came to an end because of you."

It's just like Abram to place blame. "It was agreed Sin would take his place after he finished his traineeship. It would've happened even if I had not entered the picture."

"He would've been content to continue the way things were for years, but you put ideas into his head. Marriage. Babies. Coming together to rule The Fellowship as a dual powerhouse while you push me out the door."

The longer we talk, the closer he eases toward me, putting me on high alert. "You need to back away before I have Kyle and Blare put you out."

He takes his gun from his pocket and waves it around as he speaks. "I sent them away. They needed a break so I'm your protector tonight."

Abram is my husband's uncle. Kyle and Blare don't know the troubles we've had. They wouldn't have a reason to think Abram would harm me. I'm certain they left without any concern for my safety.

An intelligent person can outwit one using a pistol in place of his brain. Isn't that what I've always said?

"What can you possibly think you'll gain by killing your nephew's wife and children? Surely you don't think that'll end well for you."

"Perhaps not, but it shall give me a great deal of satisfaction."

"Sin will never let you live if you do this. Killing me will be your death sentence."

"He won't know it was me. I'm going to make it look like The Order paid you a visit."

He has a plan. That means this didn't just occur to him but I must convince him he hasn't thought of everything. "You were the one to send Kyle and Blare away. Do you think they won't tell Sin?"

"They won't if they're dead." It may not be a foolproof plan, but he's clearly given that part thought. The lack of its ingenuity doesn't keep him from carrying it out.

He's delusional. He thinks he won't be caught because in his mind, he's too smart for that.

"Drop your weapon or I'll shoot." Ellison stands in the doorway pointing my Beretta directly at Abram.

I wasn't the only daughter Harry taught to use a handgun. This princess holds her own at a shooting range. On occasion, she outshoots me.

Abram takes his eyes from me but not his gun. "Ah. Sister Dearest is coming to the rescue?"

"I don't want to shoot you but I will to protect my sister. Lower your weapon now."

Abram turns from her and steadies his arm. He's aiming for my chest. My heart.

He smirks. Because he thinks he's won.

Ellison's first shot hits him in his right shoulder. The second in his right upper arm.

He staggers toward the wall and holds it for support. He drops the gun, sending a discharged shot into the wall, before falling to the floor. I move quickly to kick the gun from his reach.

"Oh my God. What have I done?" Ellison screams. Her eyes are large as she cups her mouth with her hand.

She needs reassurance. "You had no choice. He was going to kill me."

Abram is unmoving. Eyes closed. Bleeding on my wood flooring.

She assesses him. "He's breathing and has a heartbeat."

A heartbeat is a tough one to pull off when you're heartless.

"We have to call 911 or whatever it's called here."

She's out of her mind. I'm not phoning anybody to help him. "The only person I'm calling is Sin."

I fetch my phone and dial my husband.

Ellison sits on the floor beside Abram. "Who is this man?"

"Abram Breckenridge. Sin's uncle. Jamie and Westlyn's father."

"Shit! Shit! Shit! I just shot Jamie and Westlyn's dad?"

Sin answers. "Hello, my sweet Bonny. Missing me?"

"We have a problem."

I recount the events for Sin. He's relieved to know I'm all right but I'm not positive he won't be on the next plane home so he can finish Abram off. He's livid.

"He's lying in the middle of our living room floor unconscious and bleeding. I don't know what to do."

"This mess isn't for you to fix. I'll call Jamie to come for him. I'll catch the next flight home so I can deal with this quickly."

"What will you do to him?"

"I have no choice. Allowing him to live is giving him another opportunity to try this again. He could be successful next time. I can't let that happen."

CHAPTER FOURTEEN

SINCLAIR BRECKENRIDGE

It's early morning, still pitch-black, when I arrive home from Dublin. Bleu stirs when I come into our bedroom and turns on the lamp. "Hey."

I go to her side of the bed and pull her into my arms. "Did he hurt you at all?"

She puts her arms around me and squeezes. "We're fine."

I hold her for a moment, breathing in her aroma. Peaches and cherry blossoms.

"I knew he hated you but I never suspected he was capable of this." Had I known, I would have already killed him myself.

"No one really knows the things a psychopath is capable of until they act."

"How was Jamie when he came for Abram?" I ask.

"A fucking mess. And Ellison is as bad." I'm sure she is. This isn't the life Bleu's sister is accustomed to. I'm certain she's never shot anyone before.

"Ellison saved you and our babies. I'll need to find a way to thank her for that."

Bleu tugs on my tie. "Take all of this off and get into bed with me."

I remove my suit and toss it over the chair in the corner before climbing in next to her. "Better?"

She turns off the lamp and scoots close. She puts her head on my chest and tosses her leg over mine. "Much."

I rub my hand up and down her arm. "The only reason I'm not at his place putting another bullet in him is because I wanted to come home to you first. I needed to see for myself that you were fine."

I move my hand to her belly. She's hit a growth spurt this month. Her bump feels like a cantaloupe under her skin. "How are the wee ones?"

"Both looked perfect today."

Not being with Bleu for the ultrasound was painful. It means I've missed another milestone. "Tell me about them. Have they grown much since the last scan?"

"I couldn't believe how much. They were so funny—butting heads already."

Sounds very much like Mitch and me. "Starting early."

"That's what Ellison said."

I have a gut feeling. "I think both are boys."

"What makes you say that?"

"Just a hunch. You aren't getting a feeling about it yet?" I thought mothers had some sort of special intuition.

"Nothing. Nada."

Savannah said she could tell us their genders on this scan. "You didn't sneak behind my back and find out?"

"Absolutely not."

I feel so guilty about not being with her. "I'm sorry I missed it. I really wanted to be there. I swear I'll try my damnedest to not let that happen again."

Her hands are on my shoulders, massaging tense muscle. "It's okay. I understand you have to be away on business. It's disappointing because I always want you with me but I'm not angry."

Bleu never gives me shit about anything. I don't deserve her. "I'm damn lucky to have such an understanding wife."

I rise and push her on to her back. I kiss the side of her neck as my hand roams the side of her body. "I don't like being away from you. I want to be close. Is that okay?"

"Always."

I move to untuck the covers from beneath the mattress at the foot of the bed and crawl up her body, kissing her legs as I move upward. I suck the skin of her inner thigh into my mouth. It makes a smacking sound when I release it. "Did you miss me?"

Her fingers are laced through my hair, her nails lightly scraping my scalp. "Terribly."

I move up so we're face to face and push her legs apart. They're soft and smooth. "Freshly shaved. I like."

I try to kiss her but she moves her mouth away, shaking her head. "I need to brush."

I grasp her chin, holding her face in place. "Don't care."

I press my lips to hers but she's obstinate, refusing to open. "Stubborn arse."

"Hard ass." She palms my cheeks, digging her fingertips into them.

I chuckle as I move my mouth over her jaw to her neck. I grasp the backs of her thighs to pull them up and apart. She locks her ankles behind my back and I'm completely encompassed by her legs. "I love feeling you wrapped around me."

I glide my fingers through her slit. Not as wet as I like but I can fix that.

"Do you think it's safe to use the small vibrator?"

"Don't know why not as long as you don't put it inside."

I want three things: to make her forget the night's event, get her drenching wet, and give her a magnificent orgasm. "Let's play with it."

I fetch her bullet from the top drawer of my nightstand. I turn on the switch and use the orb to tease her outer lips. I can't see her because we're in the dark but I hear slow, deep breaths—the first sign I'm successfully warming her up.

I press the vibrator to her entrance. Her breath becomes louder. I slowly drag it up and down her slit. In no time at all, she's slick and prepared to have me slide inside her.

I position my tip at her entrance. I glide it through the moisture there, getting it slick, before thrusting into her. Once I'm inside, I press the orb against her clit above our union. She spreads her legs wide and pumps her hips upward meeting me stroke for stroke.

This little vibrator is powerful stuff. It's stimulating as hell, even for me.

"Ohh … shit."

I love hearing her say that. "That good, huh?"

"Oh … yeah. It's that good."

I thrust in and out while holding the bullet against her clit. "I missed you so much while I was gone."

She reaches for my face and pulls me down for a kiss. Still no tongue. "I missed you too. I hate being in our bed alone."

I move slowly, mindful of the hard bulge of her belly pressing against my abdomen. The vibration of the bullet intensifies as I allow more of my body weight to press against her. She squeezes her legs around me hard. "Shit. I'm already coming."

She tenses, holding me hard against her. She comes around me. An internal force grips my cock, milking it for everything it has. It's my undoing every time.

When I'm completely emptied and satiated, I roll next to her. I find her hand and bring it to my mouth for a kiss. "That was great. Quick, but still great."

"I can't help it. Everything down there is so sensitive right now. It's like dynamite ready to detonate with one touch."

"I'm not complaining."

We get quiet. I'm relaxed, my eyes shut. It feels like only a frayed thread connects me and consciousness.

Great sex is the best kind of sleeping pill.

I'm in that realm just before you drift into sleep when my phone rings. I'd love to ignore it, but such is not a luxury I'm blessed with.

It's Dad.

"I'm with Abram. He's asking for you and Bleu."

That gets my attention.

He comes to my house to kill my wife and then asks that we visit him? He's out of his mind. "You have to be fucking kidding me."

"Not at all."

I want to see him too. I'm anxious to tell him he's going to die. And not quickly. "We're on our way."

Bleu isn't keen about going to see Abram. I tell her she doesn't have to, but she's like me. She's curious to learn what the devil wants from us.

When we enter Abram's bedroom. He's lying in a massive four-poster bed covered in luxurious linens worthy of a king. He's surrounded by those who love him—Torrie, Jamie, Evanna, and

Westlyn.

It's difficult for me to believe I once loved him as well. But no more. I have nothing but hatred for him.

"Leave us," he tells his immediate family. "I have things to discuss with Thane, Sinclair, and Bleu."

His first words are for Bleu. "You could've killed me while I was lying on your living room floor. But you didn't. I think that's because you're Fellowship loyal."

Bleu smirks. "You're highly overestimating my character."

"You may have gone against your better judgment but you still called Jamie to help me. That means I owe you my life."

He's trying to smooth this over. "A life you won't be clinging to for much longer because you've given me no choice. Yours is the ultimate betrayal and there will be no other. You are a threat to my family and I have every right to end your life according to Fellowship code."

"I understand your feelings, Sin, but I called you here to atone for what I did. To make a barter. My life in exchange for what your wife wants most."

Of course he wants to barter so he can live. "No. I'm not leaving you alive so you can make another attempt against my wife."

"She didn't end my life but she had the opportunity. I'll never try to kill her again. You can trust my word."

I can't give him the chance to make me regret letting him live. The cost is too high. "You say that until you take the next stab at her. I can never put faith in you again."

Bleu puts her hand on my arm. "He said he could give me what I want most. I'd like to hear what he's offering."

A smug expression crosses his face. He's captured her attention and he knows it. "I've uncovered the truth about Amanda Lawrence's murder."

He's going to use my wife's torment as a way to save himself. "You've no honor. You're a disgrace to The Fellowship and I'll be happy to rid the world of you."

"Then you'll need to ask yourself which you want more: to kill me or end your wife's search, which will make her very happy."

"You'd deny me of the truth?" my father asks.

"I will, as long as I can use this information as a bargaining chip."

"I want to hear what he has to say." Bleu doesn't hesitate, taking no time to consider the consequences of his proposal.

"You want to know so badly, you'd choose to let him live after all he's done to you?"

I already know the answer. "Yes."

Abram will get to keep his life but he won't live it within The Fellowship. That's one thing I will not bend on. "I'll agree to this because it's what Bleu wants, but there are conditions. From this point on, you are exiled from The Fellowship. You'll never have contact with any of us, including your immediate family. You'll never see Torrie, Jamie, Evanna, or Westlyn again."

He replies without delay, void of any reaction to being told he'll never again have contact with his wife and children. "Done."

I want this over as soon as possible. "Get on with it."

"The Fellowship built its first US casino on the Mississippi coast in the early nineties. Amanda Lawrence came to work for us as a blackjack dealer."

"I never knew that," Dad says.

"You were unaware we once employed her because her position with us ended before you took Father's place. She also had no idea she had worked at a facility owned by The Fellowship. That's why it didn't come up when you met her years later. The coastal casino had two million US dollars to go missing after the doors were open for about a year. So did Amanda Lawrence."

Bleu puts her hand up. "You can stop right now if you're about to say that my mother stole from The Fellowship."

"There's no evidence leading us to believe your mother was the thief. She was a dealer without access to that kind of money. But I strongly think she stumbled upon the thievery and made a run for it. A man named Quinn Stroud was fingered for the crime, but he was likely framed."

I look at my father for validation. "That much is true. Money did go missing and Stroud was accused."

"You believe the thief is my mother's killer, so who is he?" Bleu asks.

"When we built that casino, Father sent many of our brothers there to work. We obviously needed someone with expertise in casino management to run it. Todd Cockburn was his choice," Abram says.

Todd Cockburn, our Edinburgh casino's current pit boss, was one of Bleu's suspects but she dismissed him early in her investigation.

"Years later we bought an existing casino in Tunica, Mississippi. We moved Todd to that location to manage. Amanda was employed at a different casino but Tunica is a tiny town. It stands to reason that their paths probably crossed at some point."

Bleu is rocking back and forth from one foot to another, chewing her lip. Thinking. It's the same thing she does when standing in front of her wall of suspects. "My mother was involved with Thane. If Todd knew that, it's very possible that he would've been desperate to keep her from talking about the coastal casino incident."

The pieces fit. Abram may be on to something.

"Because I owe you my life, I have some bonus information for you, and it won't cost you a thing. Amanda and Todd were lovers for more than a year while working together. They were romantically involved when she became pregnant with you. There's no father listed on your original birth certificate. I'm inclined to believe Todd Cockburn is your father. But whether he is or isn't, I can assure you that your likeness to your mother hasn't escaped his attention. Like me, he isn't going to accept that as coincidence. You're a threat to him and that's a potentially hazardous situation to be in with a man who's feeling the walls close in around him."

"Todd Cockburn cannot be my father. If that's true, then it means my own father murdered my mother and attempted to kill his own daughter."

"I can lead you to the truth, but I can't make you believe it. You're the agent. Figure it out."

We go into the living room where Torrie, Jamie, Evanna, and Westlyn are gathered. I'm certain they're anxious to hear the verdict.

"What will penance be?" Torrie asks.

They know The Fellowship creed. No member shall bring harm to another member or his family. I have every right to execute Abram. No need to remind them of that. "We bartered. He had information Bleu wanted. He discovered her mother's killer so he negotiated that knowledge in exchange for exile instead of death."

Torrie stands. Her lips are rigid as she speaks. "You're banishing him after all he's done for the brotherhood?"

I'm certain there will be no love lost between Abram and his wife. I suspect she's more upset about what his leaving will do to her status within the brotherhood.

Torrie's concern for herself sends me into a rage. My body shakes from anger. "Do you so quickly forget he attempted to kill my wife and children?" I growl.

Jamie goes to his mother and places a hand on her shoulder. "Our family thanks you for your lenient decision."

"I'm giving him three days to recover and then he must go."

I love Jamie and Westlyn. It saddens me to see them hurt, but my wife and children come first. Always.

CHAPTER FIFTEEN

BLEU BRECKENRIDGE

THE DRIVE HOME WITH STERLING ISN'T THE PLACE TO DISCUSS THE NEW information provided by Abram. Sin and I wait until we're in the privacy of our home to bring it up, although it never leaves my mind for a second.

"Would you like some tea?"

I prefer whisky—and I'd probably have some despite the time—if I weren't pregnant. "Please. Mint, if we have it."

I go to Ellison's bedroom and ease the door open to ensure she's sleeping. She's like the dead.

I return to the living room and sit on the sofa as unmoving as a statue while I wait for Sin to brew the tea. A million things clutter my mind at once so no single thought has the space it needs.

Sin places a cup and saucer on the table. "Two cubes and a dash of milk, just the way you like it."

"Thank you."

I lift the cup and hold it, not bringing it to my lips. "My mother told me my father's name was Bryan Fletcher and he was killed in a drunk driving accident before they were able to marry. She had a picture of them together."

"Is he named as your father on your birth certificate?"

"It's blank." Abram had that much right, but it could be coincidental.

"How did your mother explain that?"

"She didn't. I was a young child so the only thing I ever asked was why I didn't have a daddy like the other kids."

Is it possible that everything she told me was a lie? "Do you believe Abram was telling what he believes to be the truth, or was all of that fictitious—him grasping at straws to hold on to his life?"

I'm asking Sin a question he can't possibly have the answer to.

"This is what I know. Abram was obsessed with learning what brought you into our lives. I'm confident he's telling the truth about continuing to dig into your past. He gained leverage by having information, but as far as truth versus fabrication, I don't know."

I think of all the times I spoke with Todd while gambling at the casino over the last several months. To think he could possibly be my father is bizarre. "I'm trying to remember every little detail about Todd Cockburn. I want to compare myself to him for similarities, but I'm having a hard time envisioning his face for some reason."

"I've known him my entire life, and I see no resemblance between you."

I agree. Todd has nearly black hair, brown eyes. He's on the short side for a man. I'm not incredibly tall but I look down on him when I'm wearing heels.

Physical appearance isn't a tool for determining paternity. "I'm my mother's clone. There wouldn't be much room for anyone else's features to come through. We can easily prove or disprove what Abram is claiming. Do a paternity test to see if he's my father and examine his leg to see if he's my mother's killer. Those things will tell us everything we need to know."

Concrete evidence. Finally.

This is happening. I could actually be confirming my mother's killer—with the help of my worst enemy. That's unexpected, to say the least.

We need a paternity test without him knowing we're on to him. "I can go into his apartment and collect the DNA sample while he's gone," I say.

"Hell no, you're not. I'll do it." I should've known he would put a block on that.

"Do you even know how to collect DNA?"

"No, but I'm sure my highly intelligent former FBI agent wife can give me proper instructions. I'll do a search of his place while I'm there. If he's not your mother's killer, we still need to know if he's a thief."

Definitely. There's no room for thieves within The Fellowship. "When do you think you'll do it?"

"The next time he works so I'm guaranteed the time I need to perform a full sweep."

Good idea. "I want you to take someone with you just in case. If Abram is right, Todd might respond like a cornered animal." That could make him very dangerous.

"Sweeps aren't Leith's strong suit. And I can't ask Jamie. Not after this."

There's potential for a bad outcome. "Are you afraid of what this might do to our relationships with Jamie and Westlyn?"

Sin looks at the ceiling and runs his hands through his hair. "Aye. They aren't blind to his ways, but he's still their father."

Sin's phone rings. A confused expression materializes. "It's Dad."

We just left Thane at Abram's house so I instantly imagine the worst. Please don't let him be calling to nullify the exile.

Thane knows Abram for the man he is but still has a soft spot for him. They're brothers. I'm sure he doesn't want to see him leave forever. But Abram made his bed. Now he must lie in it.

The call with Thane is over almost before it begins. "Dad wants us to come to his house."

We just got home. "Right now?"

"Aye. He says it's important."

Oh God. This is going to be bad.

I'm thinking of every possible scenario on the drive over but there's one front runner. "I'm afraid your father wants Abram to stay."

Sin is already holding my hand but he gives it a supportive squeeze. "We don't know that."

My father-in-law loves his brother despite his evil nature. "Thane always lets Abram off the hook. I don't have to tell you that."

"You're right, but I'm not letting Dad overturn my decision."

I love Sin for wanting to stand up for me, but Thane is still head of The Fellowship. His word overrides anything Sin decides. If Thane says Abram stays, then he does. End of story.

He'll come for me again. I'm sure of it.

I'm going to face the same scenario again and again. Kill or be killed. My choice will be the same every time.

Kill instead of be killed.

We go into my in-law's home and find them waiting for us in the living room. "We apologize for dragging you out into the cold again, but it's with good reason."

Sin wastes no time jumping straight into why we're here. "I assume something happened after we left Abram's."

"Aye. He demanded to be pardoned and allowed to return to The Fellowship. He threatened to join The Order and become their new leader if I don't agree."

Oh God. Here we go. Abram manipulates Thane and gets his way again.

Isobel places a supportive hand on Thane's leg. It's odd. I've never seen them within touching distance. "Their organization is in complete mayhem right now. I think they're desperate enough to accept his offer regardless of him being raised Fellowship. His reputation precedes him. They'd be happy to have him for a leader," Thane says.

Motherfucker. I hate his guts.

"I told him there would be no pardon and asked him to not join The Order because it would make us sworn enemies. In fact, I forbid it as his leader. His response was that your twins would be the first to die under his rule if he wasn't allowed to return to The Fellowship."

My stomach flips. I may literally be sick.

Sin reaches for my hand and looks at his father. "I let him keep his life by exiling him and now he threatens to kill my children if he's not allowed back in? Surely you know I can't let this go on any further. He's giving me no choice. I have to kill him."

I sit on pins and needles awaiting Thane's response to his son's declaration. My heart will break if he rules against Sin in Abram's favor.

"He's ruthless. Can't be controlled," Thane says.

I see the pain in his eyes and know what's coming next.

"Even from an early age, there was something wrong with Abram. A disconnect somewhere in his head. He enjoyed hurting people. I couldn't fix him, but I did my best to control him. But now he has threatened to go to The Order. Become our enemy. The only choice we have is who will be the one to kill him."

"I'll do it," Sin says. "You can't kill your only brother. It will haunt you the rest of his life."

I'm relieved, yet sad for Thane. He will not soon stop grieving the loss of his brother.

It was inevitable. Abram had to die so it wasn't one of us, particularly my children. I'm not sorry he'll soon be dead.

CHAPTER SIXTEEN

SINCLAIR BRECKENRIDGE

NO DOUBT. THIS IS GOING TO BE THE HARDEST THING I EVER DO IN MY LIFE. NOT because of any love I have for my uncle. It's the pain I'll cause his family. Especially Jamie and Westlyn.

How do you tell two people you love that you're going to kill their father?

The family is in the living room when I return to the house. They immediately know why I've come when they see Sangster at my side.

"No. You negotiated for exile!" Evanna shouts.

I tell them of Abram's demands and threats. "He sealed his fate when he vowed to kill my children. I can't give him another chance to be successful. There'll be no more bartering."

My word is final and no one tries to convince me otherwise.

I go into Abram's bedroom. I'm hopeful he'll come with us peacefully. It would be awful to kill him in their home but I will, should the need arise.

"Thane must have discussed my new terms with you." He appears so self-assured, as though he's untouchable. Wrong.

"He informed me of your threats. But there was no discussion since neither of us are bending to your demands."

Abram's eyes narrow, his jaw stiff. "Then I can promise you that your twins will never see their first birthday!" he shouts.

"I can promise you they will. You're the one who won't be here to see it."

I call out for Sangster to come into the room. "You can exhibit honor and come with us peacefully, or we can kill you with your family in the next room."

I'm not oblivious to his arm easing beneath the covers. "I'm not going anywhere with you."

He's a coward without honor. I know this so I'm prepared when he pulls a gun from beneath the bedding.

But I'm the faster shooter. One shot to the center of his forehead and it's done.

A woman's screams carry into the bedroom. Torrie's.

Only one thing to do. I phone Oscar Lennox, resident cremator for bodies we need to dispose of. "Come to Abram's for a pickup."

I'm sitting on a cold concrete bench in Torrie's extravagant garden when Jamie and Westlyn find me.

"Oscar has taken him away," Jamie says.

Killing Abram wasn't the difficult part. This is. "I didn't want to hurt you, but he gave me no choice. He was going to offer to lead The Order. First on his agenda was killing my children."

"I came to Dad's bedroom. I wanted to talk to you. To see if we could work something out. But then I heard him tell you that your twins would never see their first birthday. And it was over for me after that. You did what a husband and father does to protect his family. Westlyn and I understand. We don't bear a grudge against you."

Westlyn puts her arms around me and squeezes. "We understand."

Relief washes over me. "I was so afraid both of you would hate me."

Westlyn continues, "We will grieve the loss because he's our father. But he wasn't the same man we knew when we were children. He wasn't well and hadn't been for some time. He gave you no choice."

IT'S BEEN FIVE DAYS SINCE ABRAM'S DEATH. MY FATHER WON'T SOON STOP mourning the loss of his only brother. But I think it's important for him to do something to get his mind off it. That's why I've asked him to accompany me on the sweep of Todd Cockburn's flat.

I remove Bleu's lock-picking kit from my pocket and choose the tools I need. "This may take a minute. I'm rusty."

I insert the tension wrench into the lower portion of the keyhole. I put the pick into the upper section and rake the pins. Though I learned this when I was eight, I haven't had to use these skills in a long time.

I continue unsuccessfully raking the pins with the pick. "I should have brought Bleu for this. She's damn good at it. She can pop a lock in a snap."

I pass the pick a final time and hear the magical click. "Got it."

I push the door open and look inside before entering. A thief stealing large sums of cash will be looking to hold on to it, so I inspect the entrance and foyer before entering. "Looks clear."

I've never visited Todd Cockburn's home. It's clean—no, immaculate is a better word. Most bachelors aren't this organized, even if they have housekeepers. I know I wasn't before I married Bleu.

We need to get what we came for first in case we have to leave. "I'll collect the sample now and then we'll do a search front to back."

I go into Todd's bathroom and retrieve his toothbrush from its holder. I swab the bristles just as Bleu directed.

I rejoin Dad at the front of the house. We comb through one room at a time, not moving on until each space has nothing left to search.

Nothing.

"If he's a thief, he's a thorough one," Dad says.

My gut says we're missing the evidence. "I wouldn't expect anyone in The Fellowship to be less than methodical. It's here. We just have to find it."

"There's nothing else to check unless you want to start ripping open furniture and mattresses."

I look at all the potential hiding places. I don't think we can call this an extensive search if we don't take it all the way. "Let's do it."

I take my knife from my back pocket and stab it into the center of a sofa cushion, dragging it downward in one motion like gutting a fish. I find zilch.

Foam and feathers litter the floor after each piece of furniture has been dissected.

"He isn't smarter than we are, so let's think about this for a minute."

I sit on the living room floor so I can get a look at my surroundings from a different angle. It's several minutes before I notice multiple dents and scrapes on the ceiling above the top of the built-in bookcase. Definitely looks as though something has been going on there.

I stand on a dining room chair and run my hand over the top that's hidden by the wide decorative dentil molding. "Got something."

"He's hiding something good up here," my dad says.

Stacks of money is not what we discover. "Looks like a coin presentation box. And it's locked."

"People hide things they want to protect from others. Rare coins can be worth a ton. It would be a good way of ensuring there was no money trail if he traded with the right people." My dad is right. There's no telling how many millions this little wooden container could hold.

I inspect the bolt on the box. "This is going to require a tiny pick."

I open Bleu's paraphernalia collection for a second time and choose the smallest tool.

"Bleu's little kit is coming in handy tonight. I'm glad she had the foresight to send it with you."

"Aye. My wife's a clever one."

I push the tip of the tool into the lock's hole and pop my second lock of the night. "Got it."

I open the box but rare coins worth millions aren't what we find. A pair of women's diamond stud earrings. A child's ring with a green stone in the center. A small golden locket. There's at least a dozen more items that have absolutely no value.

Why would he lock these worthless things in a box and hide them? Only the diamond earrings can possibly be of value.

My eyes are drawn to the necklace so I take it from the box. I hold it by the chain, the golden locket dangling back and forth. I recognize it.

"CEB." Cara Elizabeth Breckenridge.

Dad takes the necklace with his trembling hand. "My sweet Cara."

This is my sister's. She never took it off but it was missing from her neck when we found her smothered body. Only her killer would have this.

Dad closes his fist around it and brings it to his chest. "My own Fellowship brother killed my daughter."

The epiphany of what this collection of items is nearly knocks the breath from my chest. "These are his trophies. Taken from people he's killed."

Which would make him a serial killer living among people who taught him how to kill and get away with it." It couldn't be more perfect for him.

I look at the tiny ring with the green stone. "Emerald is Bleu's birthstone. I think this could be hers."

My father inspects the diamond earrings. "I gave these to Amanda."

There's no doubt in my mind. Todd Cockburn murdered my sister, Bleu's mother, and attempted to kill Bleu when she was seven. They aren't his only victims judging by the contents of this box.

Todd Cockburn is the worst kind of monster. He kills for sport. Not necessity.

It's after midnight when I arrive home. Bleu's already asleep. She said she'd wait up for me but it looks as though her body had other plans.

I turn on the lamp and lower myself so I'm squatting beside Bleu. I nudge her shoulder gently. "Wake up, Bonny." I kiss her temple. "Wake up for me."

She finally stirs. "Sorry I fell asleep. I stayed up as long as I could."

"It's okay. I hate to wake you but I need you to take a look at something."

"Now?"

"Aye. It's important."

She rises to sit and stretches. "What is it?"

"That's what I need you to tell me."

She swings her legs to the side of the bed and slides off the edge. She presses her hand to her lower back as she walks to the bathroom. She has developed the pregnant sway. "I gotta pee first."

Of course she does.

"Dad's here so put on your robe."

Bleu has brushed her hair and pulled it into a ponytail when she comes into the living room. Her robe barely meets over her pregnant abdomen but she's growing fast these days. Give it a few weeks and it won't.

"Sorry to get you out of bed at this hour, Bleu."

I place the wooden box on the cocktail table in front of her. "We have a suspicion about what this is but you're more experienced in this department."

She cocks her head. "Sounds intriguing. I'm going to assume there aren't coins inside."

"We found this in Todd Cockburn's house. It was hidden and locked." I open the box. "Do you recognize any of these contents?"

She immediately reaches for the emerald ring. She takes a close look and holds out her hand. She slips it onto her middle finger but it stops at her second knuckle. "This is my birthstone ring. My mother gave it to me for my seventh birthday."

She stares at the ring for a moment before looking at the rest of the collection. She removes the diamond stud earrings next and studies them intently. "My mother's ears were pierced twice. She wore diamonds like these in the second hole. She never took them out but there was no mention of them in her autopsy report. I assumed they'd been stolen by someone who handled her body."

I take the child's necklace from the box. "This is my sister's locket, engraved with her initials. It went missing the night she was murdered."

"These are probably trophies from kills."

"What does he do with them?"

"Killers typically take them as a show of accomplishment. For him, it's a souvenir to extend the fantasy. He needs something to get him through his downtime until he can kill again. He's using these as a way to relive the murders over and over." That means he takes these items out often to look at them. That would explain all the marks and dents on the ceiling. He was excited and careless when removing and replacing the box.

"Would it be a fair assumption to say that Todd Cockburn is a serial killer?"

"It's very likely. There must be three separate murders with a period of time between to be classified as serial. The circumstances should indicate that he felt a sense of dominance over the victim."

"Such as smothering a child with a pillow or stuffed animal."

"Exactly."

I hold up the specimen I took from Todd's toothbrush. "Are you sure you want to know?"

In light of this new information, I'm not sure Bleu needs to hear that he's her biological father. "You don't have to find out."

"Yes I do."

"Harry raised you. He was your father."

"I want the truth." But at what price? Can she handle learning that she's his daughter?

"You've believed all these years that your biological father was dead. What will you accomplish by finding out Todd fathered you?"

"Nothing but the truth. Clear and simple," she says.

I can't leave him unleashed. He's too dangerous. "We'll need to contain him immediately so he can't kill again."

"I want to know the paternity results before we do anything with him." *We* aren't doing anything with him. I am.

"Why do that to yourself?"

"Because I want to know if I'm killing my biological father."

This is the part I've been dreading since swearing that oath to my father-in-law. I promised Harry that I wouldn't allow Bonny to kill. I gave him my word because I believed it was the right decision, and I still do. My sweet Bonny Bleu will never know the darkness that accompanies cold-blooded murder.

CHAPTER SEVENTEEN

BLEU BRECKENRIDGE

SIN KISSES THE SIDE OF MY FACE AND NUZZLES HIS SCRUFF AGAINST MY NECK. "Wake up, sleepyhead."

"Mmm ... no. I don't want to."

"Yes. We have an appointment with Ani at ten o'clock to look at houses. We'll be late if you don't get up now."

"What are you talking about? We didn't have an appointment when we went to bed last night."

"I called her to set up something for next week and she told me her client for today had canceled."

How convenient. I wonder if Sin had anything to do with that. "I know what you're doing, and I love you for it, but I'm not sure I have the right mindset for looking at houses today."

"You aren't sitting around for the next three days fixating on the results of that paternity test."

I'm not planning to be fixated but I'm not sure I can help being distracted by it. "House shopping probably isn't the wisest thing to do during these three days."

"You're a week away from the halfway point of the pregnancy. If you deliver early like the doctor expects, then you're already beyond midway. We can't keep waiting so get your arse up. We're doing this today."

I groan loudly as I swing my legs over the side of the bed. "You're such a bully sometimes."

"Dear wife, I'm no such thing. I would be far too afraid to bully you."

Has he forgotten he has a job? "What are you doing about work?"

"I have several cases going to court next week but none the next few days."

I'm not going to have the energy for this. But Sin is right. We need a house. "How many are we looking at?"

"Your top three choices from the options Ani is sending over plus the Hameldon estate by my parents."

I already know which is my favorite. "I want to see the Hameldon estate first."

"Anything you want, Bonny."

Two hours later Sterling parks in the drive of my favorite property. Ani takes her folder from her briefcase. "This home is an elegant and spacious six bedroom with an attached garage. As you can see, the property has been well maintained by the current owners."

We've driven by this house often on the way to Thane and Isobel's. I've always admired it from the road. "I love the mixture of modern architecture with the round corner castle thingy."

"It's called a turret. You'll see a lot of those paired with modern architecture on newer houses."

We get out of the car and Sin reaches for my hand. He brings it to his lips for a kiss and mouths, "I love you." We stand in the front yard looking at the exterior. "What do you think?"

"The house is beautiful and the landscaping is lovely but it's a lot of yard to maintain. You're going to be tied up with work and I'm going to be busy with babies. Who's going to keep it up to par?"

"We'll hire a lawn service." Of course we would.

"I like growing my own tomatoes. Can I do that in this climate?"

"You can when you have a greenhouse, which you will have if this is your final choice. It's small but the current owner successfully grows a variety of vegetables."

I like the idea of growing my own vegetables. "I'm going to introduce you to fried green tomatoes. And you will love them."

We go inside and Ani stops in the foyer. "Total square footage comes in at a little more than forty-five hundred square feet. The first thing I want to point out is the ornate cornice work throughout. All of it is original to the house along with the wood flooring and fireplaces."

I'm only in the foyer and I already love it, just as I knew I would. "It's very beautiful. Elegant."

We complete the walk through of the house with our final stop in the master bedroom. "That concludes our tour of the inside. I'll give you a little time to look around on your own and we'll finish up in the backyard when you're ready," Ani says.

Sin comes up to me from behind and wraps his arms around my expanding waist. "What do you really think?"

"Of course I love it, but it's so big. We'll never fill six bedrooms."

"But we'll have them just in case." He kisses the side of my neck and chills erupt down my body. "Can you see us going to bed in this room every night?"

"Not in this peachy beige color, I can't."

"Imagine the walls in a different color. Something more suited to our style."

When I picture this as our bedroom, I envision cream and pale blue posh linens. "I can definitely see it."

He twists me so we're facing the bed. "Now imagine waking up right there to our wee ones climbing all over us."

It isn't a hard image to conjure. "I can see us being happy here."

"And my parents are just down the road. Mum can come at a moment's notice when you need her."

"Which will please her to no end." I'm certain Isobel is pulling for this house.

He takes my hand and leads me to the bedroom across the hall. "Imagine this bed gone and two cribs in its place."

"With what color walls?" I'm curious to know if he has an opinion.

"Your choice."

I already know how I'm going to decorate the nursery, regardless of gender. "Gray and yellow is what I want for boys or girls."

"You can have any and everything you want for this house, Bonny."

He's being very accommodating. "You're trying to sell me on this one harder than Ani."

"Because I can see us here as a happy family."

He wants this one. I can tell. "Do you even want to look at the others?"

His lone dimple makes an appearance. "Would you be terribly angry if I told you I already had?"

I'm not sure if I should be pissed off because he went without me, or relieved that I don't have to traipse through more houses today.

"They aren't nearly as wonderful as this one but I'm more than happy to look again with you."

I'm leaning toward being peeved now that I'm thinking about it. "I can't believe you went house shopping without me."

"Think of it as a preliminary to narrow down the choices."

A single house doesn't qualify as choices. "Seems you've narrowed it down to one."

"But you do love it, don't you?"

What's not to love? "I do. Very much."

"Would you be terribly angry if I told you I'd already made an earnest payment on it? There was another couple looking at it. I didn't want them to buy it out from under us before we had a chance to look."

I would've been heartbroken if someone else bought this house. "I'm not mad."

"Thank God."

I laugh aloud. "We have a house."

"We have *this* house."

"I love it. I really do."

Sin puts his arms around me. He scoops me from the floor and spins me full circle before returning my feet to the floor.

I cradle his face with my hands and plant a kiss on his mouth. "I love you so much."

He pulls me close and kisses me like crazy in the room where our babies will one day sleep.

"I want to bring Ellison out to see it as soon as possible. And Isobel. I want her help with decorating."

"Don't let my mum fool you. She has someone to do all her decorating."

I don't care. This is my first real house. And I'm the wife of a leader. Fellowship events will be held here. I want it to look great.

"Then I want to hire your mom's decorator."

"I told you, Bonny. Anything you want is fine with me. Always."

"When do we get to move in?"

"Should be ours first of next month." Much sooner than I thought.

I place my hand over my growing tummy. "Another chapter in our story."

"The happily ever after part."

SIN WAS SUCCESSFUL AT DISTRACTING ME YESTERDAY WITH THE HOUSE. NOW IT'S day two. He wouldn't tell me his plans but he says he has another full day planned for us. I'm glad. Otherwise I'd be preoccupied by Todd Cockburn.

"Wakey wakey, Mrs. Breckenridge."

"No! Go away. It's too early."

He tickles the tip of my nose. It's annoying so I slap at him. "Stop."

He tickles the inside of my nostril this time. Feels like he's picking it. Ugh!

"Wake up, Bonny."

"I'm awake!" I yawn and groan loudly while stretching. I feel a sudden, sharp pain in my lower abdomen. "Oh!"

My reflex is to turn on my side, bend my legs, and bring them to my belly. The change of position instantly relieves the discomfort.

"What's wrong?"

I massage the area above the bend of my leg. "Sharp pain in my groin."

"Are you all right?"

"Yeah. I stretched and it felt like I pulled something. The pain stopped when I brought my legs up."

"Aye. I remember reading about that. It said it's worse with twins because your womb is growing so rapidly."

Bound for him to have read about it. He's a know-it-all when it comes to pregnancy. "I can believe that."

"If you don't feel like doing anything, we can cancel our plans."

Yesterday was pretty perfect. I can't wait to see what he has in store for today. "Absolutely not. What's on the agenda?"

"We're going on a day tour to Stirling Castle, Loch Lomond, and for my pleasure, a stop at a whisky distillery for a tasting."

"Well, that seems a little unfair."

"Perhaps, but we're doing it anyway. It's part of the tour package."

I don't think he's kidding. "We're going on one of those bus tours?"

"Yes, ma'am. You're married to a Scotsman. You'll soon bear two Scottish children and you're almost clueless about Scotland. I mean to remedy that."

Sin's right. I know very little about his homeland. I have to play catch-up. "I look forward to being enlightened."

I move to get out of bed but he catches me by the waist and pulls me close. "Not so fast, Mrs. Breckenridge. We have about twenty minutes to spare."

"Your pregnant wife could have slept longer but instead you woke her up early for a morning shag?"

"Maybe something like that."

He pushes me on to my back and tries to kiss me. "You know I don't do that in the morning until teeth are brushed."

"I've brushed."

He makes several attempts to kiss my mouth but I dodge him each time. "But I haven't."

"Don't care." He growls against my neck and my skin breaks into goosebumps. "You really irritate me sometimes."

"You really irritate me a lot of times," I say.

"I believe I shall make you pay for that." I can tell by his naughty grin that I'm in trouble.

He pokes me in my ribs with his finger. I hate being tickled. Despise it. And he knows it.

I just woke up so I haven't been to the bathroom yet. "Don't, Breck."

"Or what?"

I press my legs together. "I'm going to pee the bed if you don't stop."

His finger instantly abandons my side. "You just foiled my evil plan."

"Sorry. Tell your kiddos to get off my bladder."

He slides downward and taps my tummy before pressing his mouth against it. "Hey, you two in there. You heard your mum. Stop jumping on that big balloon."

He places his ear against my stomach. "They say no, so you better go to the toilet."

Don't have to tell me twice. "Be right back."

I return and climb back into bed. "We're down to fifteen minutes now."

"Because you were slow," Sin says.

"That's going to get progressively worse." He should probably prepare himself for that now.

"Fifteen minutes isn't as long as I'd like but still plenty of time to do what I have in mind."

He crawls over me and kneels between my legs, pushing my gown up. "Let's take this off first."

I lift my bottom and then sit up so he can peel me out of my sleepwear. He rubs his hands over my tummy. "I didn't know pregnancy could be so sensual. Knowing you have my babies inside you is sexy."

He lowers his mouth to my abdomen and kisses the skin above the waist of my panties. His mouth is hot enough to melt them right off me. "You're my passion. You consume me."

He moves down and kisses me through the fabric of my undies. His teasing makes a million and one tingles rush straight to my groin. I'm dying to feel his tongue on me. I have no shame about it so I take the initiative. I lift my hips and push my own panties down. "I really want you to make me come. Hard."

He laughs. "Using what?"

"Your tongue. Now."

"I think I can manage that."

He nudges my legs further apart and lowers his face. He licks me a single time and then nothing else.

I lift my head and look down. "Why are you stopping?"

"I want you to watch me eat you."

Oh. My. That's a terribly nasty thing to say. And I love it. I'm even more turned on.

I wedge several pillows under my back and prop on my elbows to watch the performance happening below my tummy—his head bobbing between my legs. I can't—and don't want to—stop the instinctive rocking motion of my pelvis. Together, my hips and his tongue are working against each other. And it's a glorious thing. "You know how to make me feel so good."

I'm not sure what's happening here. I think this could be classified as me fucking his mouth. But I don't care. It's too damn good to stop. "Oh. Here it comes."

I grip the sheets beneath me and fall back against my pillow. "Suck my clit, Breck. Hard."

He does and the stimulation makes me come apart, shattering into a million shards. "Ohh … ohh … ohh."

My toes are curled tight. My heart beats a million times a minute. My face pulsates, as well as my hands. Warm euphoria spreads down my arms and legs.

"Damn. That was mind-blowing."

"Perfect. Now turn over. We're running out of time and I really want to take you from behind."

My body has turned to mush but I manage to get face down. He puts a knee between my thighs and pushes them apart. His finger glides down my cleft. "You make me want to fuck you so hard. I can barely stand it."

He is in a nasty-talk mood this morning. And it is turning me on all over again. "I wish so much that you could."

I put my head down so my bottom is where he wants it. He presses his tip against my entrance. I push backwards, forcing him to enter me a little. He pulls away and slaps my cheek. "I'm in control. Always."

"Keep telling yourself that." He glides his cock up and down my slit, teasing me. I want to push back against him again so badly. "You're killing me."

"Tell me what you want."

"You inside of me right now." He continues teasing me so I say the magic word. "Please."

"Since you said please." He enters me in one fluid movement and goes motionless. "Oh! Bonny, that feels so good. Being inside you is pure heaven. Every time."

He rocks against me, thrusting in and out. I can't help but move in counteraction. It's carnal instinct.

He pops me on my ass again. "Stop. I'm in charge."

The spat doesn't hurt. It's intended to gain my attention—and obedience—but it only manages to make me want to move faster. So that's what I do.

"Bonny!"

I'm not doing anything that's going to cause harm. "You can keep spatting me if you like but I'm not stopping. You'll have to tie me down if you want me to be still."

He holds my hips firmly. "That can be arranged."

I hear his "prelude to an orgasm" sound. He's going to come any minute.

He pushes inside me one last time. "Ahh … oh."

His body is hovering over mine, his mouth pressed against my ear. "I fucking love you."

He finishes and pulls out. His hand rubs my ass before bringing it down hard.

"Ow! That one hurt."

"I meant for it to. Have I gained your attention?"

"You always have my attention."

"Perhaps, but that doesn't mean you always heed what I say."

That's the truth. "No, it doesn't."

"I know you think I worry too much and maybe I do, but it's because I want to keep you and our bairns safe. I don't do it as hard as I'd like because I'm afraid of the consequences. I'd never forgive myself if something happened to them because I gave in to selfishness for a moment of pleasure."

"I don't want anything bad to happen, either, but please trust that I know my body and what it can tolerate."

"We're keeping it tame until they're born."

"Fine, but after that, I'm getting everything I want. The day they turn six weeks old, I want you to fuck me like a beast."

"Deal."

SIN AND I FILE ON TO THE BUS WITH THE OTHER TOURISTS AND CHOOSE SEATS AT the back. It's where we belong. That's where the bad kids sit.

The bus is warm but the window is still cold. The glass is fogged so I write in the condensation: *Bleu loves Sin.*

I draw a fat heart around our names.

"That's a work of art," Sin says.

I take out my camera and snap several close-ups, making the words the focal point. "That one is definitely going in a frame."

Sin smiles and leans over to kiss me. "Sin loves Bleu too."

I peek over the tops of the seats to see if anyone is paying us any attention. Nope. They're all too busy looking at their brochures.

"You don't even come close to looking like you belong on this bus surrounded by normal folk."

Sin laughs. "I'm not so sure you do, either, but what makes me look so different from what you refer to as *normal folk*?"

"First of all, you're in a ridiculously expensive tailored suit. That's a weird thing to wear for a day of sightseeing. Secondly, you have a gun on you. You'd better hope we don't go through a metal detector at any of our stops."

I'm wearing leggings and boots with a long tunic, not a suit that probably cost what most of these people earn in two weeks. "You say I don't look like I fit in, either, but I think I look pretty normal."

"Your face is flushed and glowing. You look freshly fucked."

"Pregnant women glow. It's common knowledge."

"There are two different kinds of glow, and you have the orgasmic sort."

"That's ridiculous."

"Men can take one look at a woman and know if she's recently had great sex."

No way. "Shut up. You're screwing with me."

"Aye, I am. But I wasn't kidding about the way you radiate." Sin leans over and kisses the side of my face. "Pregnancy looks good on you."

"Thank you. That's a very sweet thing to say."

"Just the truth."

Eight o'clock arrives and we pull away from our departure point. "The bus is less than half full. I thought there'd be more people."

"Scotland doesn't get as many tourists in the winter. I'm sure this bus is crowded in the summer months."

"I'm glad we're not packed in like sardines. We can stretch out and get comfortable."

It's an hour drive to Stirling Castle. You can lean against me and nap if you'd like."

"I'm good."

Well … I thought I was. I wake nearly an hour later to Sin nudging me. "Bonny. We're here."

We unload from the bus and I walk to the edge of the property. I take out my camera and focus on the snowcapped Highlands in the distance. What a beautiful view. It's no wonder they built Stirling Castle in this location with uplands like these as the backdrop. "Absolutely gorgeous. I'm really excited about the photos I'm going to get today."

We hang toward the back and let our group go ahead since we want to explore on our own. "How old is this place?"

"The oldest sections were built in the early twelfth century. A lot of kings and queens were crowned here, including Mary, Queen of Scots."

The inside isn't at all what I'd imagined. It's like a small collection of buildings to form a small kingdom. It's amazing that this place was built so long ago and still safely stands for us to tour today. "I should probably consider taking a course in Scottish history for the sake of our children."

"You'd better do it soon because I highly doubt you'll have much time for such after August gets here."

I look over the pamphlet I was given with our admission as we approach the entrance to the castle called The Forework. I feel the need to stop and take in the magnitude of what I'm seeing. "This is what Americans think of when they envision Scottish castles. Or at least it's what I always imagined."

This place was constructed for kings and queens. Countless royals have been delivered through this processional entrance by horse-drawn carriages. They've walked these same paths we're on right now. Perhaps even stepped upon the same cobblestones beneath my feet.

We stand at the highest location of the castle and Sin points in the distance. "That's the Wallace Monument for Sir William Wallace. Not *Braveheart*."

I laugh. "I understand William Wallace was a real man who died for a real cause."

It's pretty far so I change my lens out for the one made for long distances. "Will you bring me back one day so we can visit the monument?"

"Sure."

We don't get to explore near as long as I'd like. We're due back at the bus so we can move on to our next stop. "We're coming back on our own. I don't feel like I saw half of this place."

We're walking hand and hand as a light drizzle begins. My foot slips on a cobblestone. Thank God Sin catches me before I go down. "Careful, Bonny. This pregnancy has shifted your center of balance."

"I'm sure that's going to get even worse as I grow."

I stop and grind my sole against the stone. "Not all my fault. The heels of these boots are slick. Bad choice of footwear for today."

Sin loops his arm through mine and uses his other to grip my bicep. "I can walk without assistance."

"I'm just protecting you and the babies."

I slow because we're walking downhill and I'm not confident in the grip my soles have against the ground. "Have you stopped to think about the way our lives are going to change, beyond the dream of having two cute little chubby-cheeked babies? They're going to require a ton of care. It's going to dominate all our time. Or at least mine."

"You aren't going to do this alone. We'll get through it together. Promise."

"We'll know each other a year and a half when we become parents to two children. That's scary as hell."

My boot slips a second time and Sin saves me from tumbling down the cobblestone incline. "I'll never let you fall."

I straighten and look at him. "Let me rephrase what I just said. Becoming parents is scary as hell but I can't think of anyone I'd rather be terrified with."

Our next stop on the tour is a charming village. I've seen them from the road but I've not stopped to visit. "It's lunchtime. Want to get a bite now or shop?"

As if he has to ask. "Food."

The dining hall is housed in the general market where you shop for clothes and souvenirs. Goats are fenced in around the exterior of the building.

"You don't see that back home." Not even in the rural south where I'm from.

"No billies living outside of your shopping center?"

"Definitely not."

I grow to love this way of life more every day. I could see myself being happy in a village.

We walk down to the restaurant, which is really just counter service with a few tables and chairs within the general store. We choose to sit next to a window so we can look out over the tree-covered uplands and watch the kids come to the fence to play with the goats.

A pair of young boys is poking their fingers through the wire to pet the animals. They're wearing matching Peruvian-style monkey hats with the tassels hanging on each side. Adorable. A woman, their mother, I presume, photographs them.

That could be me soon. Snapping pictures of two little boys. Except I always imagine us with a little girl. Maybe one with red hair like Isobel.

Day two of distractions is a success. I had a wonderful time with Sin. I visited my first castle. Explored a loch and walked on its beach while holding my husband's hand. Ate fish and chips for lunch in a charming Scottish village and shopped in the market. Sin enjoyed the distillery and tasting. Perhaps a little too much. The bus is pulling away and he already appears to be asleep.

We spent the day hanging with normal folk. It was nice while it lasted. Now we return to Fellowship life.

And wait to learn if I'm the daughter of a monster.

SHIT. IT'S ALREADY MORNING. I SLEPT TEN HOURS AND I'M STILL EXHAUSTED. Yesterday's tour involved a lot of walking so it robbed me of the small amount of energy the anemia leaves me.

My mouth waters when I smell food. Maybe waffles. Possibly pancakes. Definitely bacon. Except what the Scots refer to as bacon is what I'd call ham. Whatever the name, it's delish.

I roll on to my side and I feel something. A bubble? A flutter?

The realization of what it is hits me and I squeal. "Sin! Come here. Quick."

He rushes into the room with wide eyes. "What's wrong?"

"I just felt the babies move!"

"You scared the fuck out of me."

I did shout pretty loudly. "Sorry. I got really excited. It was only a tiny little flutter but I know that's what it was. It was exactly as the book describes it."

I knew it was fine that I had not yet felt them at nineteen weeks but the anticipation has been killing me.

Sin comes to me and puts his hand on my tummy. "Not feeling it now?"

"No. It lasted two or three seconds and was gone."

"I'm pretty sure they'll have to be much bigger for me to be able to feel their movement," he says.

I would think so as well. "Sorry to call you in here for nothing."

"It wasn't nothing. You felt our babies move for the first time. That's very exciting."

"I smell pancakes or waffles and bacon."

"Waffles. I was going to bring you breakfast in bed but would you prefer to come to the table?"

No way. I want to be catered to. "Let's have breakfast in bed together."

"As you wish."

I get up and perform my morning routine before springing back into bed to await my food.

Sin comes into our bedroom carrying a tray. There's even a vase with a fresh rose. "Where did you get that?"

"The market."

"You've already been out this morning?"

"I had to pick up the things I needed for breakfast." He places the tray over my lap. "You look fresh. Does that mean you brushed your teeth and won't dodge me if I try to steal a kiss?"

"Yes."

He leans down and kisses me. "Mmm ... minty good."

He goes around and climbs in on his side of the bed.

I'm excited to hear what today's distraction will be. "What are we doing after breakfast?"

"I made an appointment with my mother's decorator. We're meeting her and Mum at our new house in two hours."

"I can't believe she was available on such short notice."

Sin laughs. "It helps when your mum is her most important client. She's willing to bend her schedule to accommodate when Isobel Breckenridge calls."

Isobel made the arrangements. That's so sweet.

"Is it all right if Ellison comes?"

"Of course."

"Was she up when you brought breakfast?"

"No. That lass can sleep like the dead. I bet she didn't budge when you squealed earlier."

"She worked nights for years. Her internal clock is still out of kilter." I put my fork down. I've eaten as much as I can. "This was very good but I'm stuffed."

"I'm glad you enjoyed it." Sin takes my tray from my lap.

I couldn't ask for a better husband. "I'm still awed by how good you are to me."

"I promised you I would do everything I could to make you happy. I meant that."

"And you do. Every single day."

CHAPTER EIGHTEEN

SINCLAIR BRECKENRIDGE

HOUSE BUYING. CASTLE TOUR. VILLAGE SHOPPING. INTERIOR DESIGN. IT WAS FUN while it lasted but my game of distractions has come to an end. Three days of waiting have come and gone. Time for the truth.

Bleu and I go into our bedroom since it's the only place we have complete privacy. We sit side by side on our bed. She clutches the manila envelope containing her paternity results but makes no move to open it.

"You aren't obligated to read the results. If you don't feel ready, you can put it away until a later time. If you never feel ready, that's fine too. Understand that reading it right now isn't your only choice."

"I don't think I can deprive myself of the relief I'll feel if it proves I'm not his daughter."

She's assuming Todd isn't her father. "That might not be what it says. What then?"

"You know me. I can handle anything as long as it's the truth." That's proven true so far but this is a completely different circumstance. I'm afraid for Bleu but I must support her decision. That's my job as her husband.

She takes a deep breath and opens the flap, pulling out the test results. She passes it to me without a glance. "Please read it for me. I can't do it."

One doesn't simply glance at paternity test results for a quick answer. There isn't a yes or no box. It's complicated but after a moment, I decipher the verdict. Conclusion: cannot be excluded.

Paternity probability is ninety-nine point ninety-nine percent. Todd Cockburn is her father.

"You aren't saying anything. That can't be good."

I fold the results and place it on the bed. "He's your biological father."

Bleu nods and stares straight ahead at the wall. "Okay. The only thing this changes is what I'll say before I kill him."

We've had this argument before so here's the same song, second verse. "We've talked about this, Bonny."

"You said you didn't want me putting myself in danger. Todd's contained. He won't be a threat to me. Firing a weapon doesn't put me or the babies in danger." That's her opinion.

"Physically, no. But you don't fully understand the impact a premeditated murder can have on your mental status. Now it's further complicated by the fact that he's your biological father." There's no way that won't wreak havoc on her emotionally.

"It's not a complication. It's an unfortunate detail."

"One you've not yet had time to process."

"What is there to process? He knocked my mom up. She ran from him and gave birth to me. He killed her and tried to kill me. I think I've processed it all quite well." I wish it were that simple.

What I'm about to tell her is going to cause problems. "I can't let you do it."

"You won't *let* me? What does that mean?"

"Exactly what I said."

"Who do you intend to have do it, then?"

"Me."

"You know what this means to me. It's my one last sin. I've spent eighteen years searching for this man. I've devoted my life to it. It's all I've lived and breathed since I was seven years old. Seven! My entire childhood and adult life has revolved around this and now you tell me you're going to take it from me."

"Please try to understand where I'm coming from."

She shakes her head.

"Bonny."

I move toward her but she puts her hands up. "No."

She's furious. She needs to cool down before we discuss this further.

I gather my laptop and case files from the corner chair, putting them into my briefcase. "I'll be at the office if you need anything."

No reply.

"Love you, Bonny."

She responds by going into the bathroom and slamming the door.

"See you tonight."

THIS SITUATION IS ALREADY TURNING MY WIFE INTO SOMEONE SHE'S NOT. BLEU IS always mature and rational, more so than any other woman I've known. The person I just argued with was not.

I arrive at BI but it's not my office I go to first; it's my father's. I tap on his door. "Do you have a minute?"

"Sure."

"I need to update you about some new findings."

He places his pen on his desk. "Sounds serious."

"Bleu is Todd Cockburn's daughter."

My dad motions for me to shut the door. "I assume she isn't taking that well."

"Her only reaction is that she wants to be the one to kill him."

"She'll need to take a number because she's not the only one. I'm not sure how I've kept from going over to the black site and blowing his head off his shoulders."

My father did not take well to finding out that Todd had killed Amanda Lawrence, but learning about Cara is what broke him and Mum. They immediately blamed themselves because Todd is part of our circle. They felt as though they didn't protect her from him.

"I appreciate you not doing that while we waited for the paternity results."

"Bleu's in no condition to be assassinating anyone." He doesn't have to convince me.

"Do I need to step in as her leader to solve the problem?"

"No. She's very aware that the possibility is off the table if I say so."

"You're her leader, yet she's fighting you on this." Bleu doesn't have a submissive bone in her body.

"She feels she can because she's my wife. And she's a hard-ass. It complicates things."

I'm about to ask the impossible of my father. "I understand how much you want to kill Todd. He took your daughter and the woman you loved. But Cara and Amanda are gone. Bleu lives and won't be whole until her mother's murder is avenged. I fear carrying it out herself will bring her more damage than healing. As her husband, I need to do this for her. With due respect, I'm asking you to pass this duty on to me."

"This is a lot to ask."

"I know, Dad. My father and my wife want the same thing. I know what it means to both of you, so it's with a heavy heart that I make this request."

"I can't bring back Cara or Amanda. If you believe this will help heal Bleu, I won't deny you of that possibility."

My mind is at ease. "Thank you."

"When will you do it?"

"I suppose that depends on how well things go with Bleu."

"I wish you the best of luck, son."

My day is long. I'm distracted. I can only think of Bleu and how she'll react to what I'm going to do.

I've texted her three times without any kind of response. I'm not at all pleased about that. I would be worried about her safety if Kyle and Blare weren't with her.

The workday ends and I'm not ready to go home to another fight, so I make a detour to Duncan's. Jamie has agreed to meet me for a whisky or two. Maybe ten.

I'm pleased he accepted my invitation. The last few days have been devoted to Bleu so Jamie and I have only spoken briefly over the phone. He's told me several times that he's fine, but saying the words and them actually being true are two different things. I need to see for myself.

He's waiting at our table when I arrive, two whiskies already in front of him. He's usually a Guinness man. "Starting without me, I see."

He pushes one of the whiskies in my direction. "Only on my first. But definitely not my last."

I gulp the Johnnie Walker down. Damn smooth stuff. Every time.

"How are Westlyn and Evanna?" I ask.

"Westlyn's grieving but she's all right. Evanna's not handling it as well." I'm not surprised; Evanna was Abram's favorite.

"And Torrie?"

"Mad as hell. She isn't receiving the treatment of a leader's widow." Predictable. She's yet to realize how lucky she is I don't have her thrown out of that ostentatious house she calls home.

"What's going on?" Jamie asks.

"Argument with my wife. A big one."

Jamie laughs. "I'm glad you married a lass with a backbone. Watching her go head to head with you is entertaining. No one else could get away with that."

I have news for him. My wife has more than a backbone. She has balls. Big ones.

"I'm not looking forward to part two when I get home."

"I'm guessing a former FBI agent can hold her own in an argument," Jamie says.

She damn sure can.

"It's going to get ugly fast. And I'm pretty certain Ellison will be home. I don't want her to hear us."

"Would you like me to come by and take her for a walk or a drive so she's not in the middle of it?"

"Oh fuck! That would be awesome. Sure you don't mind?"

"No problem."

I'm careful to not have too many whiskies since I don't need to be steamin' when I have this conversation with Bleu.

It's late when I get home but Ellison is still up. I hear music coming from her room. "Do I Want to Know?" by the Arctic Monkeys. I recognize the song because Bleu listens to it all the time.

I tap on her bedroom door. "Elli. It's Sinclair."

"You can come in."

I open the door and find her painting her toenails. "I hate to bother you but I have a huge favor to ask. Bleu is really pissed off at me."

Ellison giggles. "Yes, she is. Your name is shit." I figured as much.

"I need to talk to her. I expect it to get loud and unpleasant. Is it all right if Jamie comes by to take you out for a walk or a drive?"

She bugs her eyes at me. "I haven't seen him since the night I shot his dad. That's going to be uncomfortable as hell."

"He volunteered. I don't think he would've done that if he thought it would be awkward."

Ellison rubs her face and sighs as she leans over to look in the mirror. "I look like shit but I don't guess it matters. If there's going to be a screaming match between you and my sister, I'm out of here."

I wait for Ellison and Jamie to leave before I go into the bedroom. Bleu's already in bed but stirs when I come in, so she's not asleep. I suspect she's too troubled for slumber to find her easily.

She rises to sit, adjusting her pillow at her back. I go to her, kneeling beside the bed. I take her hand, kissing the top. "I love you. That's what's most important so that's where I'd like to begin."

"I love you too."

Her response gives me hope this will go better than it did earlier.

"I didn't do a great job of explaining myself earlier but it's important you understand why I feel the way I do. You believe being Todd's executioner will heal you. I fear it will cause more harm than good. The repercussions of bridging the gap between good and evil are real."

"I'm conditioned for that to not happen. I've killed before and I was fine afterwards."

What she's planning is different. I have to make her understand that.

"You've killed but never by choice. Each time, it was forced upon you. I've made the decision time and time again for myself. What follows isn't easy and I don't want that for you."

"I have to see this through to the end." She can, just not the way she wants.

"I understand that turning away from this must seem like the hardest thing in the world, but I promise you, it's profoundly easier than what you're contemplating."

"You're asking me to give up the one thing I've wanted most in the world for nearly all of my life."

"It's time for you to want me and these babies more than you want to kill Todd Cockburn."

She places her palm to my face. "Never think for a single moment that you and our children don't come first."

"You're good, Bonny. I don't want you tainted by what this will do to you."

"You keep saying I'm good but I'm not. And it's because of him."

"You're wrong. You couldn't love me or these babies if you weren't. I'm asking you to love us enough to let go and allow me to do this for you."

She doesn't reply. At least it's not an argument.

"You're filled by a darkness that isn't your fault. I'm asking you to pass it on to me. Let me carry it for you."

"I don't know how to let go."

"Refuse to be a slave to your demons. Be proactive. Make the decision to let me kill Todd Cockburn for you. Do it because you love our children enough to reject anything that could potentially destroy the person you are."

She's struggling. I see it. "I'm already filthy, but you don't have to be."

She closes her eyes and nods before the words come. "Okay. Do what you gotta do."

CONCRETE FLOOR . CINDER BLOCK WALLS. SINGLE LIGHT HANGING OVERHEAD. Nothing in this room would be what I'd want to see as I took my last breath.

Todd Cockburn has known four walls of iron bars as his home for four days. A cage for an animal. Very fitting.

He's been freed from his enclosure. He now sits with his wrists and ankles securely buckled to the arms and legs of an execution chair in a corner of the black site.

My parents, Bleu, and I approach him. He looks relieved but he shouldn't be. "Thank God you've come, Thane. These fools have kept me in a steel cage for days. I'm not even sure how long I've been here."

I motion to two brothers. "Find chairs for my wife and mother so they may sit."

"I don't understand. What is this about?"

I'm not sure if Todd has yet to realize he's caught or if he's figured it out and is planning to lie. "You'll find out what this is about when I'm good and ready for you to know."

Bleu takes a seat and stares daggers at her mother's killer.

"Todd Cockburn. You are accused of the murder of Cara Breckenridge, Amanda Lawrence, eleven victims who are unaccounted for, and the attempted murder of my wife, Stella Bleu Lawrence MacAllister Breckenridge."

He feigns surprise. "I have no idea what you're talking about."

"Then allow me to refresh your memory." I place the opened box of trophies on the table in front of him. He fails to react.

My father steps forward. "You attended a casino staff meeting in my home sixteen years ago to discuss changes we'd be making at our Edinburgh location. Sometime during the meeting, you slipped away unnoticed and went into my daughter's room. You used her favorite stuffed animal to smother the life out of her."

My father takes Cara's necklace from the contents of the box. "When you were done, you took this locket from her neck and positioned her body as though she was sleeping so we wouldn't discover her death until the morning."

"You murdered my only daughter." My mother gets up from her chair and stands before Todd. "My God, how I loved that child. She was the only one Thane didn't take from me."

"Isobel. Please believe me when I tell you that I did not kill your daughter."

"Cara was the most beautiful child I'd ever seen. Dark curls all over her head from the day she was born. So sweet. So kind. I only got to have her for five short years because you took her from me."

"I didn't kill that precious girl."

My mother slaps Todd hard across his face. "Shut yer lying gob!"

I go to my mother and guide her away.

My father continues, "Eighteen years ago, you went to the home of Amanda Lawrence, the woman I loved, and you shot her to death. She was wearing the diamond earrings I had given her."

My father displays the diamond studs in his palm. "These. You took them from her body and when you finished, you went into her daughter's room. You shot their dog, but not before being attacked by him. Next you plucked her daughter from her hiding place beneath her bed and put a pillow over her face to smother her."

Dad takes the ring from the collection. "You took this birthstone ring from that little girl's body and left her for dead. But something happened that you couldn't possibly have anticipated."

Dad points at Bleu. "She was saved and there she sits. My son's wife is the little girl you thought you murdered eighteen years ago. But I'm guessing you already have that figured out since I strongly suspect it was you who phoned the authorities the night we were making a trade with The Order for Bleu's return."

"I didn't do any of these horrible things. Someone is framing me."

"Let's entertain the idea of you being innocent. Amanda's killer was bitten by their German shepherd on his right leg. If you didn't kill her, you won't bear the scar of a dog bite."

One of our men steps forward and takes a knife from his pocket to slice open the fabric of Todd's trousers from the hem to the knee. My father motions for Bleu to come closer for inspection. "Is the scar on Todd's leg consistent with the one you'd expect from the attack you witnessed?"

Bleu goes closer to examine his leg. "That's exactly what I'd expect to see from Max's bite."

She stands before Todd, studying his face. "Do you know who I am?"

"You're Bleu Breckenridge, wife of my leader."

"Before I was Bleu Breckenridge, I was Stella Lawrence. Amanda Lawrence's daughter. I'm your daughter as well. Did you know I was yours when you put that pillow over my face and smothered me?"

"You aren't my daughter. You can't be. I had a vasectomy thirty years ago so that would never happen."

"As much as I hate being genetically tied to you, I am your flesh and blood." Bleu takes the paternity results from her pocket. "We obtained a sample of your DNA and ran it against mine. I'm yours and here's the proof."

Todd says nothing.

Bleu's trembling, her face pained. "Why did you kill my mother? She ran from you. She wasn't a threat."

No reply.

"Answer my wife."

Still, nothing.

Bleu has waited eighteen years for this moment. I'm going to make certain Todd gives her the satisfaction she deserves.

I can see that he'll need some persuading. "Oh … Todd. There are so many things that are much worse than death."

Sangster has been standing in the corner silently waiting to have his chance at Cockburn. He's going to get it.

I motion for The Fellowship's master of torture to come forward. "Take a finger off and see if that convinces him he should respond to my wife's questions."

Sangster grins and moves toward Todd.

"No!" Todd yells as he uselessly fights to get away from him. "I'll answer any questions your wife has."

Sangster stops, waiting for me. "Take it off anyway for good measure."

Sangster displays the cutting pliers for Todd and snaps them closed several times. You can hear the friction of metal on metal.

Todd fights to pull his hand away but it's useless.

His screams fill the room when Sangster closes the blades. Blood drips to the floor while he twists the pliers back and forth to force Todd's finger free of his hand. Crunch.

Sangster finishes and tosses his finger on to the table. He returns the pliers and holds up the saw for Todd to see. "Ignore my wife again and you'll lose your hand next."

"Why did you kill my mother?"

"I was skimming off the top at the Biloxi casino. She found out and didn't want to be tied to it. She left without a word. I ran into her eight years later and she was with Thane. I knew he'd kill me if she told him I was stealing from The Fellowship so I had to keep her quiet. I had no idea she was pregnant with you when she left me. I didn't know she even had a daughter until that night. And I certainly didn't know you were mine."

"I wouldn't have been able to identify you. You could've left me unharmed but you chose to kill an innocent seven-year-old. Why?"

Todd closes his eyes and lifts his face to the ceiling. "I couldn't help myself. I don't know why I do the things I do. It's something I don't understand and can't explain."

Bleu paces back and forth in front of him as she speaks. "It starts as an itch and spreads until you have no choice but to scratch it. If you don't, you'll explode. You fantasize about the ways you'll make it happen. Because it isn't always possible to do it when the desire presents itself, you use these items to get you by until you're able. Each represents the respective victim, and each helps you relive the murders. That temporarily satisfies the drive you have. Until it becomes too much to handle and you have to do it again. And again. And again."

A grin spreads on Todd's face, quite possibly the most sinister I've ever encountered. Pure evil. "You understand because you are my daughter. You're like me."

Bleu shakes her head. "Don't mistake my knowledge for understanding."

"You thirst for the knowledge because it's inside you too."

Bleu walks toward him and leans down so she can spit in his face. "My only thirst was to hunt you down so I could kill you."

"Your craving is displaced. You can't see it but you're just like me. You're my daughter. A part of me is inside you. And in those babies you carry."

"Don't you dare speak of my children. Ever!" Bleu shouts.

"Your babies have two parents who kill. Their potential is endless."

I've heard enough of Todd's insanity. Bleu has her answers. It's time to end this for good. "You're plagued by a sickness that can only be cured one way."

"Let my daughter do it. She knows she wants to."

"I've spent my life dreaming of the way I'd kill you. I was so obsessed, I allowed it to ruin me. And then I met Sin. He sees the damage you've done to me and wants to take all the ugliness away. And I'm letting him."

"Killing me isn't going to fix what's inside you."

"I'm certain it won't, but it's a damn good start."

Bleu comes to me. "I can't listen to him anymore and I don't want to be here another minute."

Todd's taunting can be heard loud and clear as we walk out of the building.

She stops by the car and puts her arms around my midsection. "Knowing you're going to do this for me is enough. You were right all along. Killing him won't bring me the closure I need. Only more torment. It would be the worst mistake of my life because I'd always wonder if on some level, he's right."

"He's not."

"I know, and I'm proving it by walking away. Being the one to kill him isn't what is going to heal me. It's you and these babies. It's the life we're going to have together. Our happiness."

I pull Bleu into my arms. "I'll take care of everything."

I kiss the top of her head. "Mum doesn't need to stay for this. I'm going to send her out so Sterling can take her home."

"I probably shouldn't expect you home soon."

"No. I'm going to make him tell me who the other victims are so I can give their families closure."

She cradles my face in her hands. "I love you, Breck."

I press my forehead to hers. "Love you too."

She kisses me quickly and gets into the car.

I wait until Mum is gone to pick up where I left off. "Now, let's talk about who these items belong to."

"I don't remember."

"Sangster. What do you say about refreshing his memory?"

He chooses the saw. "As you wish."

CHAPTER NINETEEN

BLEU BRECKENRIDGE

I WAKE TO THE SOUND OF WATER RUNNING IN THE SHOWER. IT'S BRECK'S ROUTINE after a kill. He's never admitted it but I strongly suspect it's his way of washing away the filth he feels after taking someone's life—even if they deserve it.

I need to go to him. This is the time he needs my support more than ever.

I slip out of my gown and panties. "I'm coming in with you."

He needs fair warning so I don't startle him. "No, Bonny. Go back to bed."

"You need me to be with you."

He's standing with his hands pressed against the tile wall, water cascading down his back, head lowered. He won't look in my direction. "I don't want you to see me like this."

"I'm not leaving you." I wrap my arms around him from behind and squeeze, placing my face against his wet back. "You aren't alone. You never are."

Sin shivers. "He admitted to horrible acts. Things that will haunt me until the day I die. Had you not left on your own, I would've sent you away."

"I'm sorry you had to endure that."

"All females. Mostly adolescents from the States. The ones he killed here are from The Order. Their deaths and disappearances were blamed on us anyway."

"The whole thing is horrible regardless of who they are or where they came from."

"He'd been toying with the idea of murder for years before he killed your mother and attacked you. Since it was his first slaughter, he'd not yet honed his skills. It's likely the only reason you survived."

I was his first taste of blood, so to speak. "His initial involvement in the death of a child was with his own daughter. The irony is extraordinary. You can't make that kind of stuff up."

I squeeze body wash into my palms and work it over his back. I want to help him wash away the night's events. "Todd Cockburn's death had to happen. We both know that. Don't suffer a single minute of guilt over an act that was completely unavoidable. Despite what you're feeling right now, you righted a wrong within the world. You have saved innocent children from whatever he had in store for them. He wasn't afraid to kill Fellowship children. For all we know, our babies could have become his victims."

"Don't say such things."

"I'm trying to make you see that you shouldn't regard what you've done as bad or evil. It's good. Serial killers are creatures of habit. He would've done it over and over again but you've stopped him. You're a hero because you've saved the victims who would have fallen into his snare. But you're my hero as well. You've saved me."

Sin looks at me for the first time since I came into the shower. "Saved you from what?"

"Myself. I don't feel that dark place inside anymore. You've taken it from me and its vacancy is filled with hope and love."

He turns in my arms and holds my face. "Say it with me, Bonny."

We look into one another's eyes and together speak the words that express the deep intimacy we share. "Into me … you see."

I'M IN FRONT OF THE BATHROOM MIRROR WEARING ONLY A BATH TOWEL. MY teeth are brushed and I'm twisting my wet hair into a pile on top of my head when Sin calls out for me from our bedroom.

"Be right there."

I find him standing by the bed holding an envelope. "Harry wrote a letter to me before he died. He gave it to me the day he passed away. There were three additional letters inside the envelope with mine. One is addressed to you and labeled with instructions to give it to you after it was all over. The second is for Ellison, and the third is for the man she marries. Theirs are to be given to them on their wedding day. He entrusted me with delivering them."

Sin holds out my dad's last words for me. "Per Harry's instructions, it's time for you to read this."

I hold the letter in my trembling hand. Butterflies have invaded my insides.

Writing four letters would've been a lot of work for Dad. "He could barely breathe. How was he able to do this?"

"I'm not sure. Perhaps he had help?"

I open the letter and immediately recognize the chicken scratch he called penmanship. "He wrote this. It's his handwriting."

Girlie girl,

You're reading this letter so that means that after more than eighteen years (hopefully not too much longer), you have exposed your mother's murderer and brought him to justice. He's dead and gone. Good for you. Now is the time for real life to begin, the one you're building with your husband. Sin loves you dearly and will do anything to protect you. Never doubt that.

What you were doing the last few years doesn't qualify as living. But that chapter of your life is closed. A new one has begun. I wish I were there to see where the journey takes you, Sin, and the babies you'll one day have. Wherever it is, I'll be watching from afar. I'm always with you. I love you.

— DAD

I can't stop the tears rolling down my face. And I don't want to. I was already happy but this letter pushes me beyond ecstatic.

I fold my Dad's last words and clench them to my chest. "Thank you for this. And for giving me the gift of freedom. I can't tell you what it means that you would shoulder an undertaking of this magnitude for me."

"I would do anything for you."

I place my father's letter on my nightstand and go to Sin. I move my hands to the tucked corner of his towel at his waist and tug. "Today was rough. You're in a bad place right now but the worst thing we can do is allow today's events to distance us. I want to be close to you. I think it's what we need."

I kiss his shoulder where be bears the gunshot scar that sent him into sepsis, nearly taking his life. "Tell me you want to feel that connection with me."

His hands glide down my sides and cup my bottom, pulling me against him. "What I want is for us to fade into each other until we can't tell where one begins and the other ends."

He has the power to make me swoon. "Such pretty words."

I drop his towel to the floor and place my hands on his hips, using them to pull him with me toward the bed. "I don't need any of the fancy stuff tonight. I just want to feel your skin pressed against mine and have you inside me."

We turn so he can sit to take off his prosthesis. Thud! It drops to the floor and he grabs me around my expanding waist. "Get yourself up here, Bonny Bleu."

I open my towel and drop it to the floor next to his. I climb knees-first so I'm straddling him. Our skin, still damp from our hot shower, sticks together.

Sin presses his face between my breasts and turns his head from side to side. His scruff scrapes my skin. There's little I love more than the feel of that.

He palms by breast from the bottom, pushing them up and together. He opens wide and sucks my areola and nipple into his mouth, using the tip of his tongue to circle the hardened bud. They're incredibly sensitive. I almost think he could make me come doing that.

When he finishes giving both breasts equal attention, he grasps the sides of my face and brings me closer. His lips touch mine and he kisses me hard, as though he's trying to possess the soul within me.

I reach between us and position his erection at my entrance. I sink down until he's fully inside. I rotate my hips a few times before rising and lowering myself down on to him again. I wrap my arms around his shoulders and press our bodies harder. My baby bump rubs his abdomen as I move up and down.

His hands find mine. We lace our fingers together.

I know when he's close because he releases my hands and hugs me tightly, pulling me down harder while thrusting with his hips. His face is pressed between my breasts. "Uh! I love you."

"I love you too."

He groans when he spasms inside me. Once. Twice. I lose count of how many times I feel it.

I don't come but I don't need to. This wasn't about sexual gratification. It was about getting as close as possible.

I hug tightly, so I can feel his skin against mine. I'm wrapped around him like a tangled mess I never want to be freed from.

"I'll always do what I must to protect you and our babies. Lie. Steal. Cheat. Kill. Whatever it takes. You never have to question the lengths I'm willing to go to for you or our children."

"I know."

This isn't The Fellowship way. It's the Sinclair Breckenridge way. When he loves, it is without limits. There is no boundary he won't cross for our children and me.

IT'S THE FIRST OF THE MONTH. THE HOUSE IS OFFICIALLY OURS. IT LOOKS LIKE A tornado visited and dropped hundreds of moving boxes throughout the place but we don't care. We're spending our first night here anyway, mess or not.

"I want to have everyone over for dinner after we get things together."

"Who is everyone?"

"Your parents. My sister. Our best friends."

Sin looks skeptical. "I'm not filled with high hopes for getting Leith and Lorna in the same house."

Those two are giving me fits. "I know. There might need to be some trickery involved."

I'm carrying the box containing my toiletries to the bathroom. "What the hell do you think you're doing?"

"I'm taking the things I'll need at bedtime to the bathroom for later."

He reaches for the box in my hands. "No, you're not. Hand it over."

He's completely overreacting. "It's light."

"You're almost six months pregnant with twins. You have no business carrying anything."

Granted, my bump is no longer a bump. My tummy is probably the size of a regular pregnancy about a month further along. But it's not yet a decent prop for a carton of ice cream.

"Good grief. It probably doesn't come close to weighing ten pounds."

"I don't care how light it is. You could trip. You know your balance isn't its best right now. Let me or one of the brothers know if you need something moved." He's referring to me falling at Stirling Castle, which had nothing to do with the pregnancy. It was totally footwear and weather related. He would have slipped too had he been in those boots on that wet cobblestone.

"Fine. I need my lightweight box of toiletries taken into the bathroom."

"Happy to." I follow Sin, feeling useless. "Want it on the counter?"

"Yes, please."

"I'd like your input on something. I'm thinking of keeping the flat. We're thirty minutes from Edinburgh here, which is great since we wanted to get out of the city but there could be times when I need to stay in town. I thought it might be a good idea to hang on to it since the location is prime."

Makes total sense. Thane keeps an apartment in the city as well. "I don't see why not."

"I've also been thinking of something else. I don't mind Ellison living here with us but she might enjoy having a place to herself. If she wants, she can live in our flat."

It's a very nice idea. And generous offer. "I'm sure she would enjoy living in her own place."

"If she decides to stay at the flat, she can still come out and stay with us whenever she wants."

"I'm betting we won't be able to beat her off with a stick after the twins arrive." Her excitement is beyond ridiculous. She couldn't be more excited if she were the one about to give birth.

"If we're here and Ellison's there, I might have to call on Jamie to play a more active role in her life."

I'm not opposed to that, and I suspect she wouldn't be, either, but I don't have a lot of confidence in my husband's matchmaking skills with his best mates.

"Maybe you should let me handle that. You didn't do such a great job encouraging a match between Leith and Lorna."

"Leith is the one who fucked that up. I had Lorna on board. She would've married him right then and there if we would have had an officiate on hand."

Leith was never going to accept Sin being the one to suggest he take Lorna as a wife. I can see it clearly now since everything is out in the open.

"Is Lorna still planning to go to work at the gentlemen's club when it opens?" Sin asks.

I'm not a fool. Topless dancing isn't the only thing that'll be going on in that club. I won't allow her to work in an environment where it would be so easy to fall back into her old ways. "She says she is but it's not going to happen if I have anything to do with it."

"Lorna does what Lorna wants to do. No one stops her."

The whole thing is so transparent. "She's doing this as a reaction to what Leith said. He called her a whore so she's going to behave like one. How soon does the club open?"

"Maybe a month or so, depending upon construction."

"Then we have time to talk her out of it."

"Good luck with that. Lorna can be a real hard-ass." Good thing I'm a bigger one.

"Westlyn and I can talk some sense into her." We have to.

"Speaking of jobs, I've been thinking about mine lately. I'm kicking around the idea of sending someone else to law school to replace me as solicitor," Sin says.

I like this idea a lot. "I'm all for it."

"I'm juggling three positions. Husband. Leader. Lawyer. Father to two newborns will soon be added to that list. It's a lot. My position as leader is growing by leaps and bounds every day. It's interfering with my role as solicitor for The Fellowship and that's not beneficial to the brotherhood. But it's interfering more with my time at home. I think it's best to head it off now rather than later."

I know the perfect person to take his place. "I think it's a wonderful idea. You should offer the position to Linsey. She's already familiar with the job and she's driven. She would be great at it."

"You think?"

Without a doubt. "She'd be an asset to The Fellowship."

It would be beneficial for the other women to see a female in an important role such as solicitor. It might inspire them to shoot for higher goals.

It doesn't escape me that all decisions being made now are in preparation for Sin to take over. I'm not ready for that. I don't want to sour this happy time by thinking about this right now.

I take his hand and pull him toward the door. "I couldn't choose which color paint I liked best for the nursery so they rolled on samples of my two favorites. We have to choose the one we like best so they can paint tomorrow."

We examine the samples on the walls of the room our babies will soon occupy. I went with gray, just as I planned. "The one on the right looks too lavender."

Sin laughs. "They look the same to me. Both gray."

"One's more on the purple side while the other is more green."

He stands behind me and puts his arms around my tummy. Won't be long until they're completely stretched to encompass my roundness. "Whatever you say, Bonny."

My doctor said he wanted me to make it to thirty-seven weeks. That's thirteen weeks away. Not long. "We're going to have babies soon."

"That's what they keep telling us."

"Two little people are going to be sleeping in this room in just a few months. They're going to depend on us for food and shelter and safety. And love. Lots of it."

"You're the one they're going to depend on for food." Sin pats his chest. "They'll get nothing from me."

The thought overwhelms me. "Two babies needing to nurse at the same time. How do you even do that?"

"Two babies. Two breasts. I bet we can figure out something."

I hear a ringtone in the sea of boxes. "That's my phone but I have no idea where it is in this mess."

Sin finds it and passes it to me. I don't recognize the number. "Hello?"

"Hi, Bleu. It's Brooke." The widow of Callum Drummond, one of the brothers killed during a raid on The Order several months ago. "I bet you can guess why I'm calling."

"Your baby must be coming."

"Aye. My water broke about an hour ago and I'm already dilated four centimeters."

I look at Sin with wide eyes. "That's wonderful. Everything is going well, then?"

"They say it is, but I'm scared and alone. I know it's a lot to ask—and I'll completely understand if you can't—but I'd love for you to come to the hospital to be with me."

I've spoken with Brooke on several occasions since Sin's swearing-in but I was not expecting to be asked to attend her baby's delivery.

Sin vowed to personally take responsibility for Callum's family. He died by Sin's side. As Sin's wife, the duty falls to me if Callum's widow needs someone to be with her while she gives birth. I can't tell her no.

"Of course I'll come. I'll be there within the hour."

I end the call and look at Sin. "Brooke is alone. She asked me to come be with her."

He looks as surprised as I feel. "Is that a good idea? It might make you want to back out of having these two."

"Ha-ha. Very funny."

I'm not sure I need to see all of that so close to my own delivery. "There must be dozens of women she could've asked. Why me?"

"The women of The Fellowship adore you. I'm sure she considers it an honor to have the wife of her leader attend the birth of her child."

Maybe, but it still feels weird. "She has no immediate family?"

"No. She and Callum were both orphaned when they were children."

And now she doesn't even have her husband. It must be horrible for her. "She has no one."

"Not true. She has her Fellowship family. We'll always be here for her."

There's one very honorable thing about The Fellowship. They take care of their own.

I need to change. I can't go to the hospital wearing a T-shirt and yogas. "Will you call Sterling while I get dressed?"

"You can't go to the hospital alone. I'm going with you."

"What will you do while I'm with her? I'm sure it'll be hours."

"I'll sit in the waiting room. I can catch up on reading since I haven't had as much time for that lately." He waggles his brows at me.

"Her water is broken and she's four centimeters so maybe it won't be a long time."

"The pregnancy book says normal progress is a centimeter an hour for a first-time mother. We should be looking at a delivery about three in the morning."

I guess he would know. I swear he's a walking, talking pregnancy encyclopedia. And I think it could possibly make him even hotter.

"THANK YOU FOR COMING , BLEU. YE'LL NEVER KNOW WHAT IT MEANS TO ME that ye'll be here for the birth of my daughter."

My heart melts. "Ah! A baby girl! Have you chosen a name yet?"

"I still don't know. I decided it would come to me when I look at her face."

"I'm sure it will." Maybe that's what Sin and I should do since we can't seem to agree on anything.

"Do ye have names for yer babies yet?"

"We have a few we're thinking about but nothing definite."

"Still haven't found out what they are?"

"It's a mystery."

"I don't know how ye can stand not knowing, especially with two of them."

It's really not been that difficult. "I was forced to learn patience at an early age."

Brooke grabs her abdomen and begins breathing deeply. "Another one already. They're coming much closer."

She's hurting so I think it's safe to assume she doesn't have an epidural. "Nothing for pain?"

"Don't need it. Women have been having babies forever without anesthesia. I can too."

Baby number one was breech on the last sonogram. Of course there's time for him or her to turn but as it currently stands, it looks like the only anesthesia choice I'll get is spinal versus going to sleep for a C-section.

"Have they checked you for dilation since you called?"

"Aye. Up to six."

That's two centimeters in an hour. "You're making great progress."

"I know. The nurses are a little concerned about how much bleeding I'm having."

She needs reassurance. "I'm sure they'll keep a close watch on it."

"Where's Sinclair?"

"In the waiting room."

She's beaming. "I'm so grateful ye came to be with me. Thank ye."

"You're family. We want to take care of you."

Four hours after my arrival, the doctor places a screaming baby girl on Brooke's chest. She's wrinkly and bloody, looking around through squinted eyes. Simply beautiful.

"Oh, look at her, Bleu. I can't believe she's finally here. I think she's the most beautiful baby I've ever seen."

"She is lovely."

Brooke strokes the top of her head. "She has Callum's dark hair. I was so sure she'd take after me and have bright red."

"Think of it as a nice reminder of your husband when you look at her."

"I hope she looks like him."

Five minutes pass. Ten. Thirty and Brooke's placenta hasn't delivered. I'm not sure that's normal.

"We've given it plenty of time," her doctor says. "It should have released on its own so I'm going to remove it by hand. The nurses are going to take yer baby to the nursery now."

No way that's going to feel good without an epidural and after having a seven-pound baby pass through. "You can hold my hand if you'd like."

She shakes her head. "I don't want to hurt ye."

I remember the way Harry would talk to me when a nurse would poke me with an IV. "Just breathe. In deep and out slow. Try to not tense up. It'll be over in a minute."

But it's not. The extraction is becoming more aggressive. And bloodier. I've never seen so much blood in all my life.

Brooke's yelling. She's no longer tolerating the pain. It's too much for her.

The doctor sighs. "Even manually, I can't get it to deliver. The only option we have is to take ye into surgery to remove it."

Her eyes grow large. "I've never had surgery before."

I move out of the way so the nurses can prepare Brooke. She's frightened. It's my job to calm her. "It'll be fine. They do this every day."

"Ye have to promise ye'll take care of my baby if I die." This is fear talking.

"You aren't going to die. All they're going to do is put you to sleep and take the placenta out. It's not a life-threatening procedure. The doctor is going to take wonderful care of you."

"My baby has no one if I don't make it. I need ye to promise ye'll take care of her for me."

Another thing I can't say no to. "Of course I will, if the need arises. But it won't. You're going to be fine."

The staff comes in to take her to the OR. "Dream up a great name for her while you're snoozing. She'll need one soon."

Brooke grins. "I'll do that."

I go to the waiting room to sit with Sin while Brooke is in surgery. "That was intense."

"Then the baby's here?"

"Yes. A girl. Seven pounds, eight ounces. Nineteen inches long."

"Mom and baby are both well?"

"Baby's fine, but Brooke had to go to the OR for the doctor to remove the afterbirth. She's never had surgery so the poor thing was scared to death. Made me promise I'd take care of the baby if she died."

"Damn. That is some serious fear when you start saying things like that."

"I know." I feel so sorry for her.

I lean over and place my head on Sin's shoulder. Between the move into the new house and being here five hours past my bedtime, I'm exhausted. "You predicted three o'clock. She delivered at 2:12. Not bad."

He wraps his arms round me and pulls me close. "I should have made some kind of bet with you."

"I wouldn't have bet against you. You've done too much research on this pregnancy stuff for me to ever think I know more." I yawn. "Sorry."

"Close your eyes. Take a nap if you're able. I'll wake you when Brooke's out of surgery."

He doesn't have to tell me twice.

CHAPTER TWENTY

SINCLAIR BRECKENRIDGE

"YOU'RE WITH MRS. DRUMMOND?"

"Aye."

I nudge Bleu's shoulder. "Wake up, Bonny. Doctor's here."

Bleu straightens in her seat. She pushes her hair from her face. "Everything went all right with Brooke?"

The doctor sighs before beginning. Uh-oh. That typically isn't a good precursor. "There were some unforeseen complications."

"But she's okay?"

"Mrs. Drummond had an undiagnosed placenta percreta. That's a condition where the baby's placenta grows deeply into the muscle of the uterus. The degree was extensive. The placenta had grown into her organs. Her bladder was nearly taken over by it. I've never seen a worse case."

He said undiagnosed. Shouldn't they have seen something like that on her ultrasound?

"How do you treat that?"

"Hysterectomy and corrective surgery for the involved organs. I called a general surgeon to assist but Mrs. Drummond had excessive bleeding in the meantime. That blood loss led her body to develop a condition where the blood clots abnormally. The disorder resulted in the formation of a life-threatening clot. I'm very sorry. She didn't survive."

"No." Bleu dissolves into a sobbing mess in my arms.

"I'm so sorry. Do you know if Mrs. Drummond has family we

should notify?"

"No. She was a widow and her parents and in-laws have been dead for years. We are her only family."

"Our social worker won't be in until the morning, but she'll need to speak to you in regards to the baby and the handling of the body."

"Of course."

The doctor leaves and Bleu sits upright. "That poor woman. She was terrified and I told her not to be because they did procedures like this every day. I convinced her everything would be fine. And she believed me."

"Then you did your job well."

"I didn't. I think she knew she was going to die. She made me promise I'd raise her baby if she didn't make it through the surgery."

"Bonny. We can't take her baby."

"I promised her I would."

"Surely you don't think the hospital is going to hand her over to us. We have no claim on her. The legal system isn't going to recognize her as a child of The Fellowship and allow us to have her."

"You're a lawyer. A damn good one at finding ways to bend the law. Even if it's not us who takes her, I'm certain you can find a way to keep her within The Fellowship."

"I don't know family law."

"Then learn it fast. Because we aren't allowing that baby to go to anyone outside of The Fellowship. She's one of us, so she stays within the circle. It's what Brooke would want. Otherwise she wouldn't have asked me to take her."

MY WIFE IS VERY GOOD AT GETTING WHAT SHE WANTS. PROBABLY BETTER AT IT than I am.

Bleu stands over the bassinet intended for our children, rocking Brooke and Callum's baby. "I never imagined we'd become foster parents before we became parents to our own children."

When we bought this house, I pictured us bringing our babies home to it. Not someone else's. But Bleu was adamant. No strangers in the foster care system were taking this baby.

We had to jump through a lot of legal hoops but we managed to be granted temporary custody of the baby until the case goes to family court. That means we have to find a family to adopt her before the proceedings are heard by a judge.

Bleu's eyes are a little too dreamy so I feel the need to remind her again that she shouldn't develop too much of a fondness for this child. "Don't get attached."

"I'm not. I understand this is temporary until we can choose a family for her."

We have to work on that immediately. It isn't wise to let Bleu spend too much time with Brooke's daughter. "I'm going to set up interviews for Friday with all couples who are interested." Bleu isn't listening to me. "Did you hear what I said?"

"I'm sorry. What?"

"I said I'm going to have all the interested couples come so we can interview them. We'll stagger the appointments on Friday."

"How many do you suppose there will be?"

Infertility isn't something every husband and wife would choose to make public within The Fellowship. "I'm not sure. There are a few couples who've been married for several years and have not had children. That could be by choice, so I have no idea how much interest there will be."

"We have to call her something. It, her, the baby, she—not working anymore. She needs a proper name."

Choosing a name for her probably isn't the best idea. It'll only deepen what Bleu feels for her, but she's right. We can't continue calling her "the baby." "Do you have a suggestion?"

"Brooke was going to choose her name when she looked at her. She said it would come to her based on her looks. To me, she looks like a Lourdes."

I like it very much. "Very pretty."

"But it's not Scottish."

"Doesn't have to be. And it probably won't be her permanent name anyway. Whoever adopts her will want to give her a name of their choosing."

"I know. So I guess for now, Lourdes it is."

"Is it a name you had chosen for us to use if one of the twins is a girl?"

"I had considered it."

"Are you sure you want to use it for her? That means we can't give it to our daughter."

"We don't know that we're getting a girl." Bleu caresses the baby's cheek with the back of her hand. "I want her to have it. It suits her."

We have to find a family for this baby soon. I can't let Bleu become too attached. It'll cause her too much pain when she has to let her go.

THE THIRD COUPLE WE INTERVIEW IS BARELY OUT THE FRONT DOOR WHEN BLEU rejects them too. "I don't think they're right for Lourdes."

Finding parents for this baby isn't going well. "You don't think anyone is right for her."

"They seemed cold and unfeeling. She needs parents who are warm and welcoming."

I see no foundation behind the things Bleu is finding wrong with these couples. "You say these people were cold and the first husband and wife were too young. Which, by the way, they happen to be older than we are. You got an overall bad feeling about the second couple because you claim they didn't smile enough. You're going to find something wrong with anyone who wants her."

"Choosing a family for Lourdes is an enormous responsibility that I accepted. Getting it wrong means we sentence her to an unhappy life. Nothing is wrong with being picky on her behalf. Think of it as me trying to make a good match for her, only with parents."

"None of these couples are going to mistreat her. They're all very well aware they'll have me to answer to if they do."

"They'll have to answer to me as well because I can't let anyone have her without watching their every move."

I'm not sure when Bleu thinks she'll have time to be a social worker since she'll soon have her own babies keeping her busy.

"Let's hope this last couple is the right family for her."

Agnes appears at my office door. "The last couple is here."

"Thank you. You can show them back."

Bringing Agnes out to help Bleu with the house was one of the better decisions I've made. She has been more assistance than we could've imagined with caring for Lourdes.

Our last couple of the day arrives. Like the others we've interviewed today, I've known Josh and Rachel Glenn my entire life. They're good people and would love Lourdes as their own. I'm sure of it.

"You've met my wife Bleu?"

"Yes. We met at the initiation ceremony," Josh says.

"And I'm in your women's self-defense class on Tuesdays." Good. Maybe that means Bleu has some kind of relationship with Rachel.

"Of course I remember you. You signed up for the beginner Muay Thai class as well."

"I did, and I am very excited about it. Have you found an instructor yet?"

"I'm interviewing with a master next week. I'm hoping he'll be a good fit for our group. I want a male instructor with a larger build so the women can gain hands-on experience with fighting against a larger assailant."

"That's smart. You make it sound like so much fun. I'm eager to get started."

The meeting with Josh and Rachel goes perfectly. Far better than the first three so I'm wondering what in the world Bleu can find wrong with them. "I think that's all the questions we have. Can you think of anything else?"

Bleu shakes her head, saying nothing.

"We'll be in touch after we make a decision."

Bleu trails behind to see them out. "Thank you for coming. I'll see you on Tuesday night."

I wait until they're gone to say anything. "That was unquestionably a better interview than the others, don't you agree?"

"It was, but I'm still not sure they'd be right."

"What could you have possibly found wrong with them?"

She shrugs, saying nothing.

"They're perfect, Bleu. Mature. Stable. They clearly want a child."

"I can't argue that. They are all of those things."

"They would love Lourdes, so what is wrong?"

"They aren't us."

I knew this would happen. "I understand that you care deeply for Lourdes but we can't keep her. We have two more that will be here soon. Three is too many."

"You aren't saying anything I'm not already aware of but I don't know how to let her go."

"You do it because you love her and want the best for her."

"I do. But what if I think we're best for her?"

Bleu has no idea what she'd be setting herself up for. "You can't take on raising a third baby when you don't yet know what it is to mother two."

Her jaw is set. She's ready to argue. "I've been taking care of her all week. I know it won't be easy to split myself three ways, but I'm not afraid of the challenge. I'm much more fearful of what letting her go will feel like."

"You're letting your heart dictate your actions. You have to use your head on this."

"I am listening to what my heart is telling me. I'm not ignorant to what keeping Lourdes means. It'll be difficult but not impossible. I'm certain giving her away will be much harder."

Bleu acts as though we're throwing her away. We're not. We'd be entrusting her to a family who will love and cherish her. "She'll be adopted by a good family within our circle who will raise her with love. She'll remain within our family. You'll be able to watch over her."

"I don't want to watch over her from afar. I want to be her mother."

"You're going to be a mother to our two babies. Let a woman without a chance have this opportunity." It's the only right thing to do.

"I'm very aware of how selfish I'm being. Keeping her means I'm taking another woman's chance at being her mother. I should be ashamed of that, but I'm not."

Keeping her will have an impact on our children. Our marriage. She'll be another person I have to share Bleu with. I'm not sure I can do it.

"We don't have to make this decision right now. Our day before the judge isn't scheduled until October."

The twins will be here by then and she'll have a full taste of what it'll be like to care for three newborns at once. This situation will likely fix itself.

She comes to me and puts her arms around my neck. She rises on tiptoes and presses a kiss to my lips. "I understand you aren't saying yes, but thank you for not saying no."

"I always want to give you everything you want but I don't know if I can give in on this."

"A week isn't long enough to make this kind of commitment. Let's give it time. I'm confident that the right answer will come to us."

"You are going to be a wonderful mother." It's so apparent in the way she cares for Lourdes.

"I love you." She rises again, this time kissing the side of my neck. "She's asleep. We should have at least thirty minutes before she wakes for her next feeding."

She tugs on my hands. "Come to the bedroom with me."

I'd better take her up on her offer at every opportunity. I'm not sure there will be many of them after the babies get here. "How could I possibly decline such an attractive invitation?"

FOUR MORE WEEKS UNDER THE PREGNANCY BELT. JUDGING BY THE SIZE OF BLEU'S belly, the babies have grown a ton this month. She looks like she might pop any minute.

The complications associated with twins are rearing their ugly heads. Borderline blood sugars. Rising blood pressure. Lots of Braxton Hicks whenever she's active. Luckily, the contractions aren't enough to send her into preterm labor but who knows when that could change? All of these things combined were enough to convince Dr. Kerr that Bleu needs to be on modified bed rest for the remainder of the pregnancy.

A one-month-old does not understand the concept of bed rest.

The majority of Lourdes's care should have fallen to my shoulders when Bleu was put to bed but I'm not here all the time. Hell, I'm not even here half the time. Changes are happening within The Fellowship and our alliance with The Guild. I'm expected to oversee that.

We've been forced to hire Agnes as a nanny in addition to housekeeping. It's working out, but she can't be here twenty-four/seven. Lourdes requires care around the clock so my mum comes to help Bleu when Agnes is off.

I don't have a fucking clue how we're managing to make this work, but we are. For now.

I meet my mother in the living room when I come into the house.

"Thank God you're back."

I was only gone two days. "Something wrong?"

"Everything's fine. I just can't help myself from worrying about you more now that you have a family. All went well this trip to Dublin?"

"Aye. We negotiated the takeover for October."

Three months and The Order will cease to exist. It won't come a moment too soon. "The Guild understood that I couldn't agree to anything earlier since the babies are due in September."

"You and I both know she'll never make it that long."

I'm hopeful she'll last another six weeks so the babies won't have to be admitted to the neonatal intensive care unit. But I can't lie. The blood sugars. The blood pressure. The Braxton Hicks contractions. All of it worries me.

"How is she?"

"Fine. She had me put Lourdes in bed with her about twenty minutes ago. They're both sleeping."

My mum and I haven't had a chance to discuss the newest addition to our household. "Bleu is utterly in love with Lourdes."

I say her name and even my mum lights up. "I can't say I blame her. She's pretty easy to love."

"Bleu wants to adopt her. That's crazy, right? Taking on a baby who doesn't belong to us when we have two of our own on the way?"

"I think Bleu feels complete for the first time in her life. She finally has the ability to nurture. That's what she wants to do."

"But we have two babies on the way who she can nurture."

"You're failing to see what's happening here. Lourdes has been orphaned. Bleu sees herself in that child. She wants to save that sweet baby the same way she was saved by Harold MacAllister."

"I might feel the same if there were no one to take her. But we have a good family who wants to adopt her."

"That window is closed, Sinclair. Bleu's in too deep. She's fallen head over heels in love with that baby."

"You don't think that will change when our twins get here?"

"No. She's a mama bear and she considers Lourdes her cub. You couldn't pry her from Bleu's arms if you tried. And you don't really want to do that. You love that little girl too."

"I'm fearful of how our lives will change with three bairns."

"I can promise you it will be crazy. But you'll get by. And you'll look back on it one day and wonder why you were so scared."

Speaking to my mum changes my perspective. I feel like I'm able to see things from Bleu's point of view for the first time. "I appreciate the talk."

"Anytime, son. Can I do anything for you before I go?"

"Are there plenty of bottles?"

"Aye. I sterilized and mixed six just before you came home. They're in the fridge. That should be more than enough to get you through to morning. You can probably expect her to wake up hungry in about thirty minutes. You should take one out now so you don't have to heat it."

"I'll do that."

"Call if you need anything. I can be back in five minutes." Buying a house so near was the best decision we ever made.

"I will. Thanks, Mum."

I grab a bottle from the fridge and go into our bedroom to see my sweet Bonny Bleu. I was only gone two days but I missed her terribly.

She's napping in the middle of the bed, her upper body propped by two pillows since she can't tolerate lying flat. Lourdes's sleeping soundly on her chest only inches above Bleu's swollen abdomen.

It's in this moment that I realize these might not be the three most important people in my life—they could be the four most important. I'm not sure I can ask Bleu to let Lourdes go because I'm not sure I want to give her up, either.

I don't wake Bleu. Instead, I sit in the corner chair and take in the beauty of my family. My wife. My children. I don't deserve any of them but by some miracle, they are mine.

Just as Mum predicted, Lourdes fusses for her feeding at the thirty-minute mark. Bleu wakes and rubs her back. "Hey. It's okay, sweet girl."

I catch Bleu's attention when I get up from the chair. "You're home! How long have you been here?"

"I got in about forty-five minutes ago."

"Why didn't you wake me?"

"I couldn't. You and Lourdes looked so peaceful."

Lourdes begins fussing louder. "I think our moment of peace just ended."

Bleu reaches for the bottle but I hold on to it. I haven't seen her in two days, either. "I'd like to feed her, if that's okay."

"Of course."

I climb into bed next to Bleu and take Lourdes from her chest. She opens her mouth and searches for the nipple with her tongue. "She's a greedy little thing."

"Yes. Her appetite has really increased this week. She's taking up to four ounces a feeding now."

"How did her appointment with the pediatrician go? Has she gained weight?"

"Her appointment isn't until tomorrow. Of course I'm not going to be able to take her since I have a long-standing engagement with this bed. Your mom is carrying her for me."

I don't have anything scheduled at the office tomorrow. "I think I would like to take her. That is, if my mother will go with me. I don't feel confident doing it alone."

"Isobel was going to do it anyway, so I'm certain she won't mind going with you."

I'm guessing Bleu sees pediatrician visits as her job but I want to have an active role in my children's lives.

"Did you see Lainie while you were in Dublin?"

"I did. She's quite well. Seems to be fitting in perfectly with The Guild."

"I'm happy she's all right, but I wish she were here instead. I'd really like her to come back to Edinburgh once this mess with The Order is over. Perhaps join us." I like Lainie as well but that will open a whole other can of worms considering she's Order and was once married to its leader. Even I might not be able to convince the brotherhood a change like that would be okay.

"She sent a gift for the babies. I put it on the dresser."

Bleu gets up to snatch the package. I laugh because her waddling has worsened.

"What?"

I'd be crazy to tell her. "Nothing."

She climbs back into bed and tears into the present before I can blink twice. She lifts the top of the box. Inside are three silver coins engraved with a B.

"What are these?"

"Some Scots believe it's good luck to place silver in an infant's hand. I guess each baby is getting their own personal piece as a keepsake."

I told Lainie we had taken in an orphan but I never mentioned keeping her. I guess she assumed.

"I love these. They're very thoughtful."

Lourdes has sucked down half of her bottle so it's time for burping. I lean her tiny little body over my hand and pat her back just the way Bleu showed me. "We're going to figure all of this out, aren't we?"

Bleu leans over and kisses the top of her head. She places her finger inside Lourdes's tiny palm. She instinctively grasps it. "I think we already have."

CHAPTER TWENTY-ONE

BLEU BRECKENRIDGE

IT'S OFFICIAL. I'M THIRTY-SEVEN WEEKS PREGNANT WITH TWINS. FULL TERM. MY pregnancy lasted longer than we ever thought it would. Weight gain. Stretch marks. Pelvic pressure. Insomnia. That's just the shortlist. I've achieved a level of misery I never dreamed possible.

My belly is getting sliced open tomorrow. That's okay because it means we're getting babies. We will finally meet our children. I can hardly wait to know what we're getting. Boys, girls, or a combo package.

I'm showered and shaved. Everywhere. Can't lie. That wasn't an easy thing to accomplish. But I did it for Sin. I want to give him one good night before his six-week dry spell.

I'm wearing the only piece of sexy lingerie I have that still fits over my tummy. Sort of. A baby-doll top with matching G-string. My breasts are spilling out of the top but I don't think he'll mind.

I'm standing next to the bed when he comes into our room. He doesn't notice me. I guess he thinks I'm still in the bathroom since he calls out. "I think Lourdes is finally down for the night."

"Is she?"

He stops dead in his tracks. "What do we have here?"

"You, Mr. Breckenridge, have a wife who'd like to show you a good time before our six-week vacation from knowing one another."

"I do enjoy getting to know you better."

"I thought you might."

He comes to me. I go up onto my tiptoes and lace my fingers

through the back of his hair as I kiss him.

His hands are at my lower back. He pulls me closer but it's mostly my belly pressing against his.

We move toward the bed, kissing en route, before we stop next to it. His hands are exploring my breasts through my baby-doll top. They've gotten bigger the last couple of weeks, so they're really jacked high.

"These are fantastic." He caresses each one before pulling my top up and over my head. He thumbs my nipples, watching them harden. I fist the back of his hair when he takes one into his mouth.

I should probably warn him. "They've been leaking. A lot."

"Maybe that's why they taste so damn sweet."

When he finishes, he pushes my panties down my legs. I'm left standing completely naked before him. He steps back, looking me over from head to toe, and I suddenly feel self-conscious about my body like never before. I clasp my hands in front of my large belly because I'm afraid my stretch marks will turn him off.

He comes to me and caresses my bump. "Please don't cover yourself. I love looking at your pregnant body. The only thing I see is the beauty of my children growing inside you."

He pulls me close and my abdomen presses against his again. He holds my hips as he drags his lips over my shoulder. "What position is going to work best for you?"

It used to work best with me on top before this last round of bed rest. But my belly is much bigger now. I'm not sure I can ride him like I did five weeks ago.

It's going to be a long time before we get to do this again. I want it to be good for him. "I can get on my stomach—sort of. I mean I can get on my hands and knees. Maybe." That may not work, either, if the weight of the babies is too heavy in that position.

"I think I know a better way."

We sit on the bed and slide to the middle. "Lie on your side."

Once I'm situated, he positions himself as though he's going to spoon me from behind. He bends my top leg at the knee and pulls backwards so it's resting over his legs. "You came across this during your research, didn't you?"

"Maybe. I've been wanting to try it for a while. It's supposed to be very pleasurable during pregnancy. Seems this is my last chance since you won't be pregnant after tomorrow."

He positions himself at my entrance but doesn't enter me.

"Something wrong?"

"It's been a month since the last time we did it so I'm giving my cock a pep talk, trying to convince him he doesn't have to come after three strokes."

"If he doesn't obey, you can always do it again."

"You know I'm always the hardest on round one, so I'd rather make it last a while if possible."

He kisses my shoulder in the bend where it meets my neck. He eases into me slowly and groans. "Fuck, that's good stuff!" He pulls back and thrusts slowly again. "I can't believe how tight you feel." He moves inside me a few more times. "Is this good for you?"

I move my hips to deepen the penetration. "Mmm-hmm."

He bends my knee and puts the sole of my foot flat against his top leg so my leg is hiked out. He reaches between my legs and strokes the sensitive spot above our union. "Is it okay to make you come?"

"Yes. Please. And thank you."

He circles my clit fast and hard and then slow and soft. He's stroking me on the outside with his fingers while his cock does the same job against my G-spot on the inside. It's fucking fantastic.

It's been too long. I'm the one who's going to come in three strokes. "Shit. It's already building."

He's moving faster now. "Come all over me. I want to feel your body quiver and contract because you're orgasming so hard."

I move my hips, meeting Sin stroke for stroke. Then the first wave arrives. "Ohh … that's it. It's starting."

"I'm there with you, Bonny."

Very little sets him off faster than hearing me say that he's making me come. I think it's because he loves knowing he's the only man in this world holding the power to shatter me into a million magnificent pieces.

My orgasm feels different, like quivers radiating throughout my vagina. It's tingly and weird. I assume it's because my womb is so full and pushing my cervix lower.

When he's finished, he kisses my bare shoulder. "That was

fantastic."

I still and the babies suddenly become very active. I put my hand to my belly and it gets kicked. "I do believe they've been provoked."

"I want to feel."

Sin places his hand on my abdomen. I grab his wrist and move his palm to where most of the action is happening. "My God. They never cease to amaze me. Won't you miss this? Feeling them move inside you?"

"Maybe a little." But I won't miss all the other discomforts that accompany a twin pregnancy.

"I can't believe we get to meet them in fourteen hours. Still no premonition?" Sin asks.

"Two babies. That's all I'm certain about." I wish I did have some sort of mother's intuition.

"Don't you think we should have their names since they're arriving tomorrow?"

The boy names are half chosen. "Well, we know one will be Liam something. And the other will be Harrison something if we get two boys."

"Aye. The something part is what we have to work on."

It's such a hard decision. "Have you thought of anything new?"

"How about we combine the boy names if we get one. Liam Harrison?"

I like it and the combination makes sense. "That would work."

"We have Harrison after Harry but what about MacAllister for a girl? We could call her Alli."

Alli. It's sort of like Elli. "Yes. I like it. And I've been thinking about Avalyn."

"Aye. Alli and Avalyn go together well. At least we have one name per child. That's progress."

I'M TOO EXCITED TO SLEEP SO I'M VERY AWARE WHEN THE CONTRACTIONS BEGIN. I'm accustomed to having mild ones but these are closer and stronger. The ones I've had over the last hour are downright painful.

I get up to walk hoping it might relieve the discomfort in my back. It doesn't. I try a warm shower. The pain only becomes worse. I give up on any relief after an hour. I have to wake Sin so we can go to the hospital. I'm going into labor.

I turn on the lamp by his bedside and say his name. I nudge his shoulder when he doesn't stir. "Wake up, Breck."

After a third attempt, he finally awakens. His eyes widen. "What's wrong?"

"We have to go to the hospital. I think I'm going into labor."

"Okay. We need to call Agnes to come stay with Lourdes."

"Already done it. She's on the way."

He sits on the edge of the bed and reaches for his prosthesis. "Do you want to call the family now or wait until we get there and find out what's happening?"

"I think your mom would never forgive us if we didn't call but let me get dressed first so she doesn't beat us to the hospital. We can call her and Ellison when we're on our way out the door."

"At least we're already prepared to do this today."

Sin goes to my set of drawers. "What do you want to wear?"

I'm all about comfort right now. "Yoga pants and a T-shirt. Second drawer."

"Black or gray?"

Another contraction is starting. I can already tell it's going to be a bad one. "Don't care."

"Which shirt?"

I breathe deeply and slowly. "Again, don't care."

Once I'm dressed, I pull my hair into a ponytail and brush my teeth. "All ready. We can leave as soon as Agnes arrives."

Sin's impatient. He calls Isobel to let her know what's happening. "Mum says she can come stay with Lourdes until Agnes arrives so we don't have to wait."

Agnes lives thirty minutes away. And she's older, so she's slower about getting here. "The pain is getting much worse. That might not be a bad idea. Tell Isobel I would very much like her to come. And thank her for me."

Sin relays my message and promptly ends the call. "You must be in a lot of pain since you agreed to let my mom come now."

I can't lie. "It's getting bad, Breck."

I've known since I was early pregnant that I would likely have a

C-section. That's where my mindset has been for months. I'm not prepared for labor. I thought I would get to bypass this part.

"No worries. Mum will be here in a minute."

I'm leaning over the sofa, holding it for support. "My lower back is killing me."

Sin comes to me so he can rub it. "Up? Down?"

"Lower. Both sides."

I have a couple of really bad pains before we hear the sound of a car in the drive. "Thank God she's here."

"See? Good thing we bought this house instead of one thirty minutes away."

Isobel comes in with a change of clothes and her cosmetic bag. I've never seen her without makeup. For the first time, I see more than a little resemblance between her and Sin.

"Thanks for coming so quickly."

"Happy to."

"Agnes shouldn't be long."

She holds up her change of clothing. "I'll be ready to go as soon as she arrives."

"I have to kiss Lourdes before we go."

I go into the nursery and stand over the crib to look at my sleeping angel. I love her so much, it hurts.

I try to bend down to kiss her but my belly gets in the way. Instead of waking her, I kiss my fingertips and transfer it to her cheek. "I love you, girlie girl. I'm going to miss you."

I'll be back in a few days with your brothers or sisters. I don't say it aloud but it's what I'm thinking.

I feel like crying.

"We'll be back before you know it."

"I can't imagine three days without her. It's going to break my heart." If I can barely manage a few days, how will I manage forever? Sin probably thinks the twins will fill the space in my heart reserved for her. But that's not true.

I can't think about this now.

The drive to the hospital is almost unbearable. The pain is worsening by the minute. "This could get crazy fast. The baby coming first is breech. If I'm dilated a lot, I think they're going to have to do an emergency C-section."

This is one of those times when living thirty minutes away from Edinburgh is a problem.

Shit. I just remembered I forgot to call Ellison. "Guess … what." I drag the words out like only a true southerner can do.

"You went into labor on your own." She squeals so I take the phone from my ear until she's finished. "I'm getting up now but I'll have to wait on a taxi. Don't you dare give birth before I get there."

I'm starting another contraction so I'm done talking. "I'm hanging up now because I'm in too much pain to talk. I'll see you in a few."

I'm immediately taken into the observation area of labor and delivery. Sin helps me change into a hospital gown and get into the bed. It's a slow process since my contractions are so close.

The nurse takes a quick assessment and does an exam. "You've dilated five centimeters and thinned almost all the way."

"I was pretty sure these pains had to be the real thing."

"The baby coming first feels vertex. Head down. We'll need to do an ultrasound to be sure. If that's the case, Dr. Kerr would probably let you attempt a vaginal birth if you wanted to try."

Baby number one has been breech for months. He or she has been stubborn without a single sign of turning. I've mentally prepared myself for a surgical birth so I've not given a vaginal one any thought.

I think Sin is as thrown off by this new information as I am. "Is a natural delivery something you'd want to try with twins? It seems like it would be easier to have the C-section and be done."

I know I'll have pain with the cesarean. It's surgery. My belly will be cut open. It would probably be easier to recover from a natural delivery. That's something for me to consider since I'll have three babies to care for when I get home. "We should talk to Dr. Kerr and see what he recommends."

Dr. Kerr comes in and scans my abdomen with the ultrasound. "She was right. Baby number one is presenting head first so this changes things. It's perfectly safe for you to attempt a vaginal birth. If you want to proceed with the C-section, we can do that as well. There's no right or wrong decision."

A thought occurs to me. It would be horrible to deliver the first one vaginally and then be rushed to surgery for a C-section with the second one. I could potentially have pain in my butt and abdomen. That would make it very difficult to recover. I don't think I want to risk it since there's no guarantee things will go well.

"I prefer to deliver both babies the same way. The only way I guarantee that is to opt for the C-section. I don't want to attempt the vaginal delivery. Is that okay with you?"

"It's your body, Bonny. Your decision. I'm fine with whatever you decide."

"Then my mind is made up. Let's do the cesarean."

I'm moved over to a surgical table. The room is freezing cold, the lights bright. A nurse helps me to sit on the edge of the OR table and I'm told to curl my spine like a C. I'm shaking. Jerking. I can't control it. It's impossible to be motionless despite the warning it's what is expected of me.

"Just getting started. This part feels like a bee sting."

"Oh!" Shit. It does. A huge-ass bumblebee.

"Hold very still for me." Easier said than done.

The worst part of being told to hold still is when a contraction comes and all you want to do is move. "Here comes another contraction."

"Got it. It's in."

"We can't wait on your contraction to finish. We have to get you on your back now. The medicine spreads by gravity so your level of anesthesia won't be high enough for surgery if you're not lying down. It'll all go to your legs." The nurses assist me into a lying position and shove something under my left hip so I'm tilted. My arms are spread to my side, stabilized with Velcro. An oxygen mask is placed over my face.

I'm scared. I need Sin with me. "Where is my husband?"

"Don't worry. A nurse will bring him in just a moment."

I'm strapped to this OR table without the use of my arms. The mask presses on my face and I can't move it. Doesn't matter that it's blowing oxygen into my mouth and nose. I feel trapped. Helpless. The onset of a panic attack is dancing across my chest. "I can't breathe."

"Your oxygen saturation is at one hundred percent. I assure you that you are breathing just fine."

The anesthetist doesn't know my history. Doesn't understand that my body may be breathing fine but my mind tells me it isn't. "I'm having a panic attack. I feel like I'm smothering. I need to sit up."

My doctor calls out, "Tilt her to her left side a little more and see if that helps."

I feel the surgery bed beneath me move. "Try to calm down, Mrs. Breckenridge. Your surgery has started so we can't allow you to sit up."

Dammit. I haven't had an attack in two months. Everything has been going so well. Why now? "Where's my husband? I need my husband. Right now!"

"Hey. I'm here, Bonny."

I hear his voice but I can't see him yet. "Where are you? I can't breathe, Breck."

I lift my chin to look in the direction where I think I heard his voice. I'm relieved when I see him coming to me.

Sin notices the restraints around my wrists. "She has issues with her mobility being restricted. Is there any way we can take those off?"

"We can if it's contributing to her problem."

The Velcro wraps around my arms are removed and I immediately feel better.

"Inhale slowly and deeply. Blow it out gradually. Concentrate only on your breathing. Think about moving air in and out of your lungs." He strokes my forehead with the back of his hand. "Own it, Bonny. You're not a slave to it."

"I can put you to sleep if it becomes too much for you, Mrs. Breckenridge."

Going to sleep means I don't get to see my babies when they are born. I don't want that.

I reach out to touch Sin's face. "I'll be fine as long as my husband continues to talk to me." Only he can soothe me.

"Close your eyes and visualize yourself breathing. In. Out. The mask you're wearing is giving you more oxygen than you need. Breathe it in."

My hysteria spirals downward. Sin's voice always does that for me. "It's getting better."

"Good."

Sin sits on a stool next to my head so I'm looking at him upside down. "You look weird."

"Says the woman who is wearing a plastic mask over her face."

"Right," I laugh. "I'm sorry I freaked out."

"Perfectly understandable."

Dr. Kerr calls out, "Just made an incision into your uterus, Bleu. Won't be long now."

Sin kisses my forehead. "Only a few more minutes and we finally get to meet them."

I'm trembling, almost violently.

"Nervous?" Sin asks.

Nervous doesn't even begin to cover it. "Extremely."

"Just broke the bag of waters on the first baby." The room immediately fills with the sound of suctioning very similar to what you hear during dental work.

Oh my God. This is it. Our first child is about to make his or her entrance into this world.

Sin leans down to kiss the top of my head. "Boy or girl? Last chance to make a guess."

I've been taking care of Lourdes so now it's hard to imagine myself with a boy. "I think this one is a girl. What's your guess?"

"Boy."

A high-pitched cry fills the room. The most beautiful sound I've ever heard.

Sin and I look at one another, grinning and waiting for the verdict. "Number one is a boy."

Sin leans down to kiss my forehead. "I can't believe it, Bonny. We have a son."

A moment later our newborn is placed upon my chest. I stroke my hand over the top of his head. "Hello, Liam. We've been waiting for you for a long time."

The nurses wipe him off and cover his head with a beanie before tucking him inside my hospital gown so we're skin to skin.

I don't get to admire him for long before a second cry pierces the room. I look at Sin. "Quick. Boy or girl?"

"I'm going with another boy. It's what I've been saying for two months."

"I'm sticking with girl."

"I hear some guessing going on down there," Dr. Kerr says.

"My husband says boy. I'm going with a girl."

"Mr. Breckenridge has it right again. Another boy."

Liam is scooted aside to make room for Harrison so both of my sons are lying against me, skin to skin. "Oh my God. I can't believe how much hair they have. They must get that from you because I was almost bald until I was two."

"I had a head full of dark hair, just like them."

"I thought one might inherit Isobel's hair." When I imagined what our children would look like, I always saw one being a little red-haired girl.

It's difficult to see their faces the way we're positioned. "Do they look anything alike? I can't tell from here."

Sin gets up and looks back and forth between their two faces. "I think they do."

"I'm going to send the placenta to pathology to confirm that they're identical."

Identical isn't a possibility. "They're in vitro babies. They have to be fraternal."

"It's possible only one embryo implanted and then split. That would result in identical twins. It's unlikely, but not impossible. I should have an answer for you in a few weeks."

Sin leans forward to study them. "Thank you for giving me not one, but two healthy sons. Two grandsons for my parents." He leans close to my ear. "Two future leaders for The Fellowship. And two brothers for Lourdes."

My heart pounds. "What are you saying?"

"What do you want me to be saying?"

"That we're keeping her."

"Then that's exactly what I'm saying."

I want to throw my arms around him but I can't. They're full of babies. "You are amazing. I love you so much. Thank you."

I may be looking at him upside down but I recognize his expression. He presses his forehead to mine and together we whisper so softly that only we know and hear what we're saying.

"Into me … you see."

EPILOGUE

BLEU BRECKENRIDGE

"THIS WAS BOUND TO HAPPEN . THREE BABIES. THREE NAPPIES. I KNEW AT LEAST one of them would shite and need a changing before the ceremony."

"Language, Sin." We've had this conversation. They're babies but they won't always be. We must learn to control our tongues now so we don't teach them to be cursing toddlers.

Sin holds Liam out to me. "Here, Mummy. Take your son. He stinks."

I don't even glance in Sin's direction. He isn't going to charm me into diaper duty with his dashing smile and lone dimple. "Then change him."

Sin uses his baby voice and wags Liam as though he's the one talking. "But, Mummy. You do it so much better than Dad."

Cute. But not convincing. "Because I have far more practice. You always manage to sweet talk me into doing it so you don't have to."

"Can I sweet talk you into it this time?"

He's still holding my sweet boy out for me but I'm not taking the bait. "No. I have to finish getting dressed."

"I thought you had already gotten ready."

This is rinse and repeat. "I did, but Harrison spit up all over me and my dress. I smelled like soured baby puke so I had to shower again."

Raising three babies is so much more work than we could have imagined. But it brings us a joy we've never known. We couldn't be happier.

"Then I guess I have no choice." He sounds defeated.

"Good luck with that," I call out as Sin leaves with Liam.

I know my husband. He's going to find his mum. "Don't even think about asking your mother to do it. She's busy making sure everything is perfect for the ceremony."

I'm entertained by what just played out. Finally, I get to laugh at Sin for a change.

Hell may have just frozen over. My entire family is ready on time. I'm glad because today is a very special event for my children. Consecration day.

All Fellowship children are formally dedicated to the brotherhood, but our children's ceremony will be much different since they were born to a leader. Sin and I must vow to nurture them in all ways Fellowship. We will pledge to teach them how to one day lead our people. It's a huge undertaking, the same one Sin's parents took and his grandparents before them.

Isobel and her event planner have struck again. Our home looks worthy of any king's coronation. Our backyard is overrun with dozens of tables, each covered by a cream tablecloth and enormous floral arrangements in varying shades of salmon and lime. Elegant chic baby is the theme. That's what the event planner calls it. It's gorgeous.

Parents gather their children when we take our place on the rostrum with Thane. "Today is very special for The Fellowship. It's been twenty-one years since an infant was consecrated into our brotherhood." He's referring to Cara's ceremony.

"Sinclair and Bleu have been ardent in their duties to produce future leaders for our brotherhood since they are bringing forth three children." That earns a laugh from the crowd.

Thane motions for us to come forward before taking Liam from me. "What name is given this child?"

"Liam Thane Breckenridge," Sin says.

"Liam Thane Breckenridge is Sinclair and Bleu's child. But today he becomes our child as well. This covenant reflects a solemn, symbolic act on the part of his parents to rear him in the nurture and admonition of The Fellowship. Do you accept this responsibility?"

Sin and I say the words together. "We do."

We pledge the same vows for Harrison MacAllister and Lourdes Elizabeth.

It's done. All three of our children have officially been dedicated to The Fellowship.

With the formalities behind us, Westlyn, Lorna, and Ellison take over temporary care of my wee ones. My hands are empty. It's a rare moment so I'm not sure what I should do with myself.

Sin comes up behind me and slips his hands around my waist. I'm still a little self-conscious about the stubborn bulge that hasn't gone away. "Dance with me, Mrs. Breckenridge."

He leads me on to the dance floor and pulls me against him. The band is playing their rendition of "Blessed" by Elton John.

The songs were chosen by the event planner with the idea of maintaining consistency with the ceremony's baby theme.

Sin brings our clasped hands to his mouth so he can kiss the top of my hand. It never gets old. "I'm blessed with everything I didn't know I wanted or needed. I have it all—a beautiful wife I love. A precious daughter who already wraps me around her tiny finger. Two sons who will one day make me proud by taking my place as leaders to our people. What else could I possibly ask for?"

I can hardly recall the person I was before Sin and our babies. I was dead inside, filled only with hate and thirst for revenge. But then hate met love. My desire for vengeance became a longing to love. And be loved.

Sunshine meets rain and makes a beautiful thing. The same can be said about me meeting Sin. I was in the dark. Our love illuminated my world with its light. And together we have made beautiful things.

The End

ABOUT THE AUTHOR

GEORGIA CATES

Georgia resides in rural Mississippi with her wonderful husband, Jeff, and their two beautiful daughters. She spent fourteen years as a labor and delivery nurse before she decided to pursue her dream of becoming an author and hasn't looked back yet.

Sign-up here to join the monthly newsletter for Georgia Cates. You will get the latest news, first-look teasers, and giveaways just for subscribers.

For the latest updates from Georgia Cates, stay connected with her at:

@georgiacates

georgia.cates.9

www.georgiacates.com

authorgeorgiacates@gmail.com

THE
Beauty
SERIES

Beauty
FROM PAIN
THEY AGREED ON THREE MONTHS...
BUT THEIR LOVE KNEW NO BOUNDARIES.
NEW YORK TIMES AND USA TODAY BEST-SELLING AUTHOR
GEORGIA CATES

Beauty
FROM SURRENDER
HOW DO YOU MOVE ON ...
WHEN HE'S EVERY SONG YOU SING?
NEW YORK TIMES AND USA TODAY BEST-SELLING AUTHOR
GEORGIA CATES

Beauty
FROM LOVE
HAPPINESS IN FOREVER ...
IS IT POSSIBLE WITH A PAST LIKE HIS?
NEW YORK TIMES AND USA TODAY BEST-SELLING AUTHOR
GEORGIA CATES

INDULGE

INDULGE
NEW YORK TIMES AND USA TODAY BEST-SELLING AUTHOR
GEORGIA CATES

VAMPIRE AGAPE SERIES

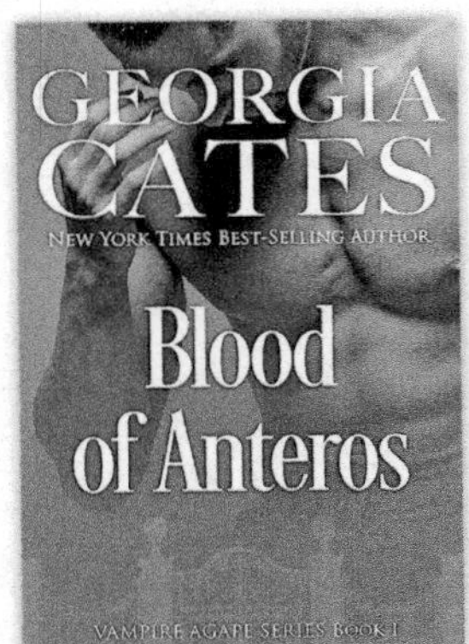

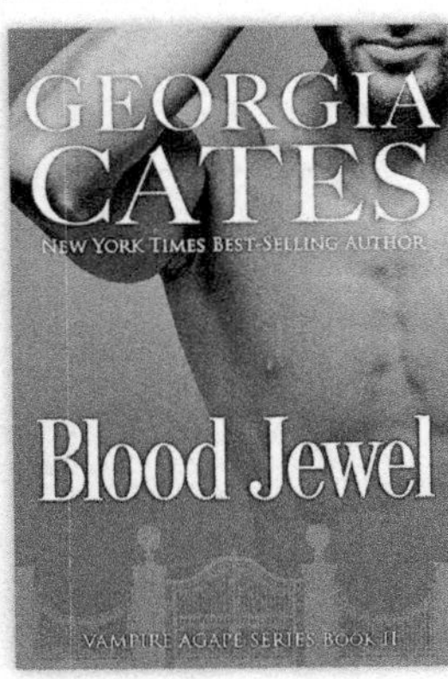

Made in the USA
Las Vegas, NV
10 May 2022